KILL
EVA

Also by Alex Blackmore

Lethal Profit

KILLING
EVA

ALEX BLACKMORE

An Eva Scott Thriller

NO EXIT PRESS

First published in 2015 by No Exit Press,
an imprint of Oldcastle Books Ltd, PO Box 394,
Harpenden, Herts, AL5 1XJ, UK
noexit.co.uk

Editor: Steven Mair

ISBN
978-1-84344-657-6 (print)
978-1-84344-658-3 (epub)
978-1-84344-659-0 (kindle)
978-1-84344-660-6 (pdf)

2 4 6 8 10 9 7 5 3 1

Typeset by Avocet Typeset, Somerton, Somerset
in 11.5pt Ehrhardt MT
Printed and bound in Denmark by Nørhaven, Viborg

For more information about Crime Fiction go to @crimetimeuk

For John, Vicky, Pippa and B.

With special thanks to my family who have listened, supported and been there on repeat. Thanks also to the late Henning Mankell for taking the time to get to know Eva and providing feedback on my writing, as well as being an inspiration. To everyone at No Exit for bringing the book into being, especially Ion, Claire and CQ, and Jem for the digital skills. Thanks to Annette for tireless support and enthusiasm and Steven for perceptive and intelligent editing. To Jill for showing me a Ceret sunrise and Anna for the therapeutic phone calls and generally being an awesome woman. Thanks also to some of the finest human beings in existence: Jacinta, Emily, JP, Christophe, Katie, Bea, Helen, Adam and Leora who have, at various points, provided exactly what I needed to take a next step, sometimes without even knowing they're doing it. And finally, the pup, who cannot read or write, but who has kept me sane and down to earth, mostly by eating my favourite shoes.

ONE

EVA DREW BACK from the dying man. His breath was hot on her face, the grip he had on her wrist was tight, but she knew that he had just moments left.

Her heart was beating fast – too fast – and the adrenaline pumping through her body made her muscles burn.

There was now a large crowd of onlookers – it was Waterloo Station at rush hour – but no one else had stepped forward. People just stood and watched, texting or tweeting what was unfolding before their eyes, one eye on the departure boards. Don't miss that train.

The man had collapsed only moments before. Almost in front of Eva as she ran from a tube train to a bus that would take her to the pub after an unforgiving day. For a split second she had almost swerved round him but the look in the man's eyes – the terror – stopped her in her tracks.

'Are you ok?' she had said, breathlessly, as she tried not to stumble under the man's weight. His eyes had rolled up towards the ceiling before settling on her once again as he tried to speak. His breath smelled of stale alcohol and he had the unmistakable odour of someone who had not been under a shower for weeks. But he was still alive. Just.

'Are you ok?' she had said, again, lowering the man to the cold, hard floor, requiring all her strength to prop up at least 180 pounds of bodyweight. Her muscles shook from the effort. No one helped. It was easy to see why the flock of commuters around her kept their distance. The man had string tied around his waist where the belt to his stained raincoat should be. His hat, now on the floor, was full of holes, and frayed at the brim.

Eva could see a sock through the toe of one of his shoes.

Finally, she managed to gently lay him on the floor, took off her scarf and folded it, trying to make him a pillow. She heard mutterings in the crowd – 'should we call the police?' 'tramps, I'm so sick of them' 'this problem is getting worse' – and she saw a flicker of what looked like shame cross the man's face. He looked at her, eyes suddenly lucid and clear.

'Kolychak,' he whispered firmly.

What was that – Russian? Czech?

'I'm sorry I don't understand.'

'*Kolychak*,' he said again. And then louder, but still whispered, 'KOLYCHAK.'

He made a sudden grab for the front of Eva's coat and pulled her face next to his.

'*Ko-ly-chak*,' he said fervently and tears started to fall from his eyes.

Somewhere in Eva's mind, recognition flared. But she couldn't reach it.

'I don't understand. Can you tell me who you are, what's happened to you? We need to get you some help.'

Suddenly, the man let out an ear-piercing shriek that echoed around the station hall. Every person in the enormous space stopped; most turned to face the direction from which the unearthly sound had come.

Eva pulled herself away, stumbled, fell and then sat and stared at him in horror. The noise made her blood run completely cold.

Then the man began to buck and writhe, as if someone was extracting his insides with a toasting fork. No one else moved. Liquid began to bubble and froth at his mouth. It had a bluish tinge. Abruptly, he stopped choking. His body became completely rigid, his eyes wide. Finally, he was still.

Eva heard her heartbeat thumping in her ears. She stared at the man on the floor. Reaching out a shaking hand, she felt his wrist for a pulse. Nothing.

'Shit, is he ok?' asked one of her fellow commuters. She looked at him for several seconds.

'He's dead.'

When she reached the pub – a 'historic' site just off High Holborn – she walked up to the ground floor bar and ordered a straight shot of brandy. She had barely reacted to the dying man at the time – the desire for flight had been too strong – but now she felt shaky and unsettled. Her friends, she knew, were in the bar upstairs in an area reserved for some birthday or other but she needed five minutes alone. Not that she would have it here. Even though it was only a Tuesday night, seething crowds had descended on the City and the man to her left appeared to be planning an imminent introduction. She turned away from him, looked out at the room around her and finished her drink.

'Do you have a cigarette machine?' she asked the barman.

'No, love. There's a supermarket round the corner though.'

By the time Eva returned to the pub, she was 20 minutes late for the party but still she didn't go upstairs. She bought herself another brandy from the bar and leaned against the wall outside the building. She smoked three cigarettes in a row. After that, she felt pretty awful.

'There you are! We thought you weren't coming!'

Three of Eva's friends tumbled out of the pub door, rosy cheeked from booze and laughing. Behind them came Sam, the man who had most recently shared Eva's bed. She looked at him and he smiled. She smiled back but there was no stomach flip.

She made her excuses for being late but when she tried to tell the story of the man on the floor at Waterloo words failed her. She tried again when Sam went to the bar but she couldn't. Ok, she reasoned eventually, why ruin their night with something she wanted to forget anyway. Sam returned with the drinks and then was at her side. He took her hand. She freed it to light a cigarette.

'You're smoking?' He raised his light eyebrows towards a shock of blond hair.

She nodded and smiled. 'Bad day.'

He gave her a hug. 'Go on, give me one too then,' he whispered in her ear.

She pulled back and then handed over the slim white cigarette and watched him try not to smoke it like a non-smoker.

Conversations in the group continued as one, and then two, more cigarettes were smoked to avoid a return to the cold for an hour at least. Then, the others drifted back inside. Sam pulled at her hand but she remained planted against the wall.

'Are you ok?'

He came and stood opposite her, put his arms around her waist and stepped forward so that their faces were close.

'I'm fine.' She could feel that she was rigid in his arms. You're still adjusting to being in a relationship, she told herself. It's not him, it's you.

He kissed her. 'See you upstairs,' he said and walked back into the pub smiling at her over his shoulder, attracting admiring glances as he went.

Eva turned the other way and leaned sideways against the wall. Her head hurt.

The word the man at the station had uttered was circling round and round her mind: *kolychak-kolychak-kolychak*. It was maddening.

She didn't understand, she had never even seen him before. But she couldn't forget what he had said – the incident had shaken her more deeply than it should.

She felt her phone vibrate in her bag and, grateful for the distraction from her thoughts, dug it out.

The display showed two words, starkly white against the blood red background she had chosen as a screensaver:

'Jackson Calling.'

When she arrived at her flat that night, Eva double locked her front door and drew the chain across – something she never really did, despite living in one of the more 'up and coming' neighbourhoods of London.

Once inside, she stood with her back to the door and took several deep breaths.

As soon as she had seen that name on the display of her phone, Eva had started to run. She wasn't sure where the instinct came from but she hadn't even picked up the call. In fact, she had dropped her phone and had to rush after it as it skittered towards the edge of the kurb. A bus pulling up at a stop she hadn't noticed was forced to skid to a halt, the driver sounding the horn angrily. She had been shocked, unaware of the peril so close, and had snatched her phone from the gutter and continued to run.

After that, a bus opposite Holborn station transported her to Camden, where she decided to walk home. On the way, a supermarket stop: a bottle of wine, another packet of cigarettes – a tin of tomato soup as an afterthought.

She'd made the journey home on autopilot. In her head the words 'kolychak' and 'Jackson' revolved mercilessly.

Jackson was her brother – her dead brother.

She had last seen that caller ID 13 months ago before she had journeyed to Paris and then Paraguay to try to find out what had happened to him. It had been a reckless, dangerous trip – and one that had nearly cost her her life – but she was still none the wiser about the circumstances of his death. Or who it was who had called her from his phone the last time, and why.

For 13 months she hadn't had to think about it.

Eva moved away from the door and dropped her purchases on the sofa. She noticed she was shaking.

She walked quickly into the bedroom and stripped off her clothes, shivering in the cold air of the spacious flat. She should learn how to set the timer on the heating. She pulled on a pair of running leggings, sports bra and a fluorescent lightweight running top. She tied her long, dark hair back into a ponytail and secured it loosely with a tattered elastic band. It swished from side to side as she walked back through the flat, collected her phone, headphones and keys, slammed the front door behind her and made for the street.

Outside, it was dark and the street was quieter than when she arrived home several minutes earlier. She lived in an area where 'people like her' had chosen to put down roots because it was well connected, up and coming but the rent wasn't yet eye-wateringly expensive. It suited her – it was a cheapish taxi fare home and there were great local pubs. She had been unable to stay in her old flat in Camden as the memories there were too overwhelming.

Outside, she walked for several minutes as she connected her headphones, selected a playlist on her iPhone and then began to run. Her feet pounded the pavements and, gradually, as she settled into a rhythm, she began to relax.

She could think clearly for the first time that day.

Jackson. Jackson was dead. Even before she had gone to Paris 13 months ago to try and follow in his footsteps, she and her father had been told Jackson was dead – a fatal gunshot wound to the head, apparently by his own hand.

By the time Eva returned from Paris, she knew her brother had been working for the government and that he may or may not have been tortured to death. Ultimately, no one – not Irene Hunt, Jackson's handler, or even Daniel – could confirm or deny whether her brother was still alive. As she thought of Daniel, she felt her fists clench. He had been a friend of Jackson's at school – a privileged and manipulative boy who had grown into a violent and cruel man. She had encountered him on her first few nights in Paris. He had casually assaulted her when she needed his help. But that was not the only part he had played.

With the calculated cool of a sociopath, Daniel had driven development of a virus that he had planned to release to create a market for a new drug. In the end, his 'people' – the Association for the Control of Regenerative Networking – had found his greed made him dispensable. He became a liability and so he was killed. Even now, Eva could remember the look on Daniel's face in the moment that the shot exploded his skull; she could still smell the metallic odour of his blood on her skin.

Jackson.

She stopped running as she realised she had said the name aloud. She quickly picked up her pace again and continued moving almost soundlessly through the dark streets, her wraith-like figure flitting in and out of lamplights at a steady pace.

She had received several similar calls from her already dead brother in Paris but had never been able to figure out who had made them. Since his death, Jackson had existed only as a caller ID on a smartphone screen – not the Jackson she knew, or even a tangible pretender. Then for 13 months he had been silent. But now someone somewhere wanted her to believe that he was still alive.

'How do you invade a country without an army?'

'You don't.'

'But you just said…'

'An invasion does not have to involve movements of troops.'

'Then I'm not sure I understand.'

The conversation was taking place in the hushed environs of a thickly carpeted Geneva hotel lobby. It was casual, the two participants apparently uninvested. But the first was better informed about the second than the second man would be comfortable with – if he knew.

'England is a nation of shopkeepers.'

'Bonaparte.'

'He was a wise man.'

'He died a prisoner.'

'Nevertheless…'

Two tiny white coffee cups with shimmering gold rims were deposited onto the table between the two men by a crisp suited waitress, who departed in silence. Both cups were left untouched.

'Your intentions are unclear. I think you have obtained this meeting under false pretences.'

'My intentions are the same as yours.'

'No, what I mean is I do not understand why you have come to *me*.'

'Because I believe I have what you're looking for.' He had carefully rehearsed the line.

'And what might that be?'

'The key you need.'

'I do not need a key.'

The air around the two men was becoming hostile. That one could know anything about the other was inconceivable to him. And a threat. The particles bristled as the conversation continued.

'You have no idea who I am,' deflecting the threat.

'I know everything about you.'

'That… is not possible.'

One of the men – the younger by some decades – reached into the pocket of a cheap suit and pushed a blue memory stick across the gleaming walnut wood of the low coffee table.

The other man looked at it. He was middle aged but well kept. He had a ski tan and it was possible to see the outline of where his goggles had sat. He looked at the memory stick.

Then, he looked up at the younger man. An almost imperceptible flicker of fear passed momentarily in front of his eyes.

'You know I will not take it.'

'Take it. Read it. And then we will meet again. I believe that this is the final step for you.'

After some hesitation, the man across the table reached for the memory stick. He held it up in the air and waited. A second man rose from a chair at a table behind. Silently, he took the memory stick, sat down and reached under his chair for a slim laptop case. He opened the zip, flicked up the screen on the machine and inserted the stick into the side of the brushed metal.

'Unless you can back up your boldness you will not leave here alive.'

The younger man was surprised. He had not expected such an immediate test. Nevertheless, he refused to allow his face to betray him. He waited.

The associate with the laptop stood and deposited the machine in front of the older man, who spent several minutes scanning the information.

'What do you want in exchange for this?'

'I want to work with you. I want to be part of it. Use me where you can.'

'And that is all?'

'That is all.'

Suspicion in the eyes of the older man. 'That is never "all". What else is it you want.'

'I am ambitious. I want to progress. Nothing more.'

It was plausible. Just.

'You could not have a position of authority.'

'I understand.'

A second silence, deeper than the first, settled on the area around the two men. The air of hostility had faded but a deep distrust remained.

'I still do not understand how you came upon this.'

'You do not need to know.'

'I wonder whether that is the case.'

'It is genuine.'

'That's not something I can verify without knowing its origin.'

'Scott.'

The older man glanced up quickly at the younger man, who was about to play the trump card.

'Scott,' repeated the younger man, 'Jackson Scott.'

TWO

THE NEXT MORNING, Eva struggled even more than usual to push herself through the daily commute. Whether it was the cigarettes from the night before or the two hour run through a heavy rain shower, her cheeks were flushed and feverish and she felt uncharacteristically shaky. She left her flat, slamming the door and pulling up the collar of the thick blue oversize coat she had bought in a fit of fashion. An Investment Piece. The quality material was solid and warm and she felt comforted as she went to the mobile coffee cart under the glass canopy next to the station. As she stood in the queue, she watched the hordes of people flowing into the Underground, heads down, eyes glazed, the odd angry shove or curse when personal space was breached.

When she had bought the biggest, strongest coffee she could, Eva began to walk down the hill, through the busy high street, towards the nearest bus stop. It would take her along a circuitous route to work but she could not face Waterloo today. Besides, the bus offered better thinking time. After her experiences in Paris and Paraguay, she had tried to figure out her life and had concluded she needed to do something vaguely 'worthwhile'. The job at the environmental NGO had appeared from nowhere. She almost couldn't remember whether she had applied for it, or whether it had applied for her. It had seemed the perfect option – a worthy cause, a better salary, a role that sounded just about challenging enough. Whilst she may not have achieved some other 'adult' milestones – the husband, the house, the pension, the baby – she did at least have a 'grown up' job. Whether she herself was happy about that she hadn't yet worked out. She wasn't even sure how much the concept of 'adult' appealed.

And then there was Sam. Much like the job, he seemed to have appeared out of nowhere and, before she knew it, she was tentatively taking first steps towards something more than her accustomed-to flings. Or was she? Eva was unable to shift the feeling that, deep down, she had opened up nothing, that she remained as shut off from Sam emotionally as she had done from every other man she had met in the last ten years. What she struggled to understand was why.

'We have a new project for you – algae.'

Eva looked up, surprised, from her seat opposite her line manager. Janet had a nasal tone of voice that was coma-inducing and she had been half asleep.

'Algae?'

'Yes, an outbreak in an area around London.'

Eva's heart began to thud. The genetically engineered strain Daniel had developed to spread his virus had begun its release like this.

Eva realised she was sitting forward in her chair. 'Is it serious?'

Her line manager laughed, sneered a little. 'Relax Eva, it's just a little algae – all we need is someone to write a report on it.' She pushed a file across the desk.

Eva sat back. She was one of the few people in the country who knew how many people the PX3 algae could have killed in the name of commerce. Were it not for the fact that she couldn't prove any of it she wondered whether she would still be alive. Cleaning up that mess quietly had posed only a temporary inconvenience for the powers that be, more important to hide what had happened than show the vulnerability it revealed. Who really cared about algae anyway? A strain of bird flu that claimed a number of lives and coincidentally appeared at exactly the same time got much more coverage. It was expert media-manipulation, using one already established fear to cover something much worse.

Eva had once felt a passion for politics but now it seemed like a sham – behind it sat the real web of control: money. Global finance, profit motive and the sway of influence held by large corporates defined political policy, whether with respect to global warming emissions targets or food labelling. Most people would believe what they read in the news and never see the world they lived in for what it really was.

'Read this. Everything's in there. Any questions, just ask Sam.'

Her supervisor Janet smiled. It wasn't a pleasant smile. Eva knew Sam – who also worked at the NGO – had been Janet's favourite before Eva had arrived. As Janet was fond of jokingly stating herself, she was now 38, single and 'desperately looking (lol)'. Eva had endured several weeks of having doors slammed in her face and being cold shouldered in front of other staff after her and Sam's 'relationship' was revealed. Eva had heard the rumours about Janet and other men in the office but she knew that gossip in a place like this was rampant, thanks to the boring nature of the work, and a nearly-40 single woman always seemed to attract the same kind of slurs. Although she didn't understand why Janet willingly made herself such a caricature. Eva didn't like the woman but, for the sake of sisterhood, had stayed away from bitching about her.

She picked up the file. 'Thanks.' She stood up. She felt appraising eyes on her back – and lower – as she left the room.

Outside the door, Sam was there.

'What happened to you last night?'

'I didn't feel well, sorry.'

They started walking in the direction of the office kitchen that was only a few paces from her desk. Sam lowered his voice. 'I hope you're ok,' he said and then, very self-consciously, kissed her on the side of the head. She had the odd feeling he was looking at someone else when he did it.

In the kitchen, Eva made yet more coffee. Sam was silent until she sat down opposite at the table. He pulled something out of his pocket.

'I got you this.'

A small, colourfully wrapped chocolate biscuit in the shape of a heart. She smiled at him, but it was a mechanical response.

'You're sweet.'

He smiled as if she had declared her love for him. Which she hadn't. Even though he already had to her. After three months. A shaft of sunlight streamed in and illuminated his blond hair, as if it were a halo.

'I have to go,' he said, suddenly standing up. 'See you for lunch?'

She nodded and he bent down and kissed her again.

Eva pushed the little heart around the table with her finger. She watched it fall to the floor, sparkling in another shaft of sunlight. She realised she was thinking about Leon.

Eva took a long sip of her coffee and opened the file she had been given. She read the contents once, made herself another coffee and read it again. She sat back in her chair. The information was fluff. It was pointless and groundless. The algae outbreak was minimal, it wasn't even worth a report. She was being given something to write that was essentially a waste of everyone's time.

Eva picked up the biscuit heart Sam had given her from the floor, unwrapped the paper and shoved the whole thing in her mouth. Love tokens when you were not in love... awkward.

She turned the final page of the report and there at the back was a sheet of questions. She skimmed through them. Whether generated by the enormous amount of caffeine she had drunk or the sugar hit of the heart she had just consumed, anxiety plucked at her insides. The questions seemed personal – very personal – and apparently directed specifically at her – despite the 'hypothetical scenario', she was being asked to record her own experiences of dealing with an algae outbreak 'for the report' and to give details of everything from the type of algae involved to the eventual resolution of the situation. It wasn't exactly subtle.

She flicked the file shut. What was going on?

All through the expensive lunch with Sam at the local deli (he paid), Eva just couldn't stop thinking about the algae questions in the file. She had drunk far too much coffee that morning – that always made for spiralling paranoia – but, nevertheless, the task felt strange. She generally wasn't asked to produce content but to edit it and it was, on the whole, newsworthy content that the NGO would use to generate a media profile for itself. This algae information was pointless and would do nothing to attract the right kind of attention – it wasn't what they had hired her for.

Was it a coincidence it had ended up on her desk or was it intentional?

She looked at Sam and realised he was waiting for a response.

'Hmmm?'

'You're half asleep today, Eva.'

'I know, sorry, too much coffee this morning, I'm having a post caffeine slump.'

He laughed enthusiastically.

'Paris this weekend.'

'What?' Eva looked at him shocked. Paris was where Jackson had died.

'I-I-I I thought you'd be pleased. It's such a romantic city.'

Eva stared at him.

It began to get uncomfortable.

'I'm sorry, Sam, I'm really not feeling that well today, I think I might go home.'

'Want me to come over later?'
'I think I just want to go to sleep.'

Eva left work without bothering to make excuses. She had to get out and, besides, she knew that Sam would make them for her. Back in her flat, she changed out of her work attire and into her running clothes. She took to the streets for two hours and, by the time she returned, she had quelled what was probably caffeine-induced paranoia. More than once when she had tried to draw some conclusion in terms of what to do about Sam, her thoughts had turned to Leon. The ex-addict, her brother's friend and a self-admitted mercenary, he had both assisted and saved her life in Paris and then, at the end, tried to kill her. When she returned to London, she had no idea if he was still alive. It troubled her and it excited her. And the fact that it excited her troubled her even more.

When she had showered after her run and changed into comfortable clothes, Eva decided to make a phone call. She called Irene Hunt's office – if there was one person who could put an end to this gnawing paranoia, it was her. The phone was answered by her secretary.

'She's on indefinite leave.'

'But I spoke to her two weeks ago and she didn't mention anything about that – has something happened?' Irene and Eva stayed in regular contact. Eva was never sure whether it was motherly or monitoring.

There was a clicking sound on the other end of the phone. The secretary took too long to answer.

'Family affairs, I think.'

'Right, ok. Thanks.' Eva hung up.

Something wasn't right.

Perhaps he knew something was wrong when he left the research lab that night. But Stefano Cirza was simply too preoccupied with the intricate details of his research to be troubled by instinct. He was excited by the leaps forward he had made in recent months – the project he was working on was virtually complete. Two projects, interlinked, although one he preferred to talk about more than the other. The first (and the more citizen friendly) was an ingenious key that allowed an individual to use their own unique genetic code as a 'lock'. A simple blood sample could be used to create it and he had even come up with a way of ensuring that, when it came to using the blood key to open whatever it was required for, this could not be done under duress. The second project was still in trial but used a combination of drugs, cranial implants and face mapping technology to give one person the power to change their appearance in the eyes of another. It was not yet complete but, when it was, it would give the technology-user the ability to appear to be whoever they needed to be to convince a specific person to trust them. Trust – that most fragile of things – could be established artificially.

Stefano would not be feted for curing an incurable disease, or wiping out famine, but what he had done was still important. Not just important, but lucrative too.

His mentor had been a great man, a renowned scientist whose work had done much for the world. But he had died almost penniless, troubled by the heavy burden of debt until his very last day. And with nothing to leave his daughter or ex-wife, he had died with disappointment in his eyes.

Stefano was as yet unmarried and had no children, but he did not intend to go the same way. Which is why he had chosen an area of genetic science he knew was marketable.

But also pioneering.

There would be acclaim as well as money. When he was approached about developing the key he had hesitated but the Englishman who had later become his business partner was convincing. So convincing, in fact, that they had been friends. At least, until the man disappeared.

When Stefano had made the decision to work on the project, he comforted himself that at least he was not working on genetics that could cause loss of life – biological warfare, for example. Far worse causes existed to which he might have applied his very considerable skills for a significantly larger sum of cash. There was little chance that his coding could be used for anything 'bad'. It was important security technology. And it was inevitable progress.

In fact, neither project had been much of a leap from technology that already existed but there were few people in the world who really understood it – at least outside the scientific sphere – and it was in such technology that the money lay. If he had not produced this, someone else would have done it.

He had initially struggled with the idea of finance backing science, of monetising his research. Just like every other area of life, as soon as there was a profit motive, only those who could afford to pay would benefit. As a scientist and medical professional, Stefano knew there should be no barriers to anyone accessing medical innovation – especially if it related to life or death – but, as a person, he was not sure the future of the world would be positively influenced by such an approach. Everyone surviving everything. It was unsustainable. If we all survived every disease, the drain on resources would be too much. Some had to die. And perhaps the easiest solution was simply to offer survival to those who could pay – it was something people could work for, they could create their own opportunities to have the lives they wanted, to afford treatment they needed. As long as you didn't believe in luck, that is – or bad luck to be more precise.

Anyway, Stefano thought to himself as he began to shut down his equipment for the night, he was becoming distracted. For both projects there had been only one live test subject so far. That first test had been a bad decision, perhaps his only one recently – using someone so completely unknown who had offered himself up for the testing. And testing the two products together... Stefano had allowed his ego to get the better of him and accepted the volunteer because he claimed to be a fan.

The man had been older and, looking back, had seemed frightened, perhaps as if he was being coerced. Realistically, there was no reason anyone would put themselves through the process involved voluntarily unless they had their own agenda. The drugs, the implants, the mental effects of the unfinished product were harsh indeed.

The man had disappeared, taking the evidence of a substantial part of Stefano's work with him. But it was several months ago and he knew from personal experience that, if his work had fallen into the hands of another scientist, it would already be on the market – but it wasn't, so it couldn't have. Perhaps the procedure had killed the man, and Stefano's secrets had died with him. The only other key in the system belonged to a woman connected to Stefano's ex-business partner – but she had been set up remotely using a sample and the entire test system had not been run on her. Not yet. That was the next step for both projects, a new test subject, someone within Stefano's control – otherwise this woman remained the only person who could be used to activate Veritas. He often wondered whether she was aware of her importance, whoever she was.

Regardless, it looked as if Stefano's key was still going to be the first of its kind to make it onto the market. And without his English partner, the revenue would be his and his alone.

Feeling satisfied, Stefano finished shutting up his lab. The rest of the building was almost entirely dark, it was late. He was just about to input his code into the main door to the lab when he stopped. He felt someone was watching him.

Ridiculous, he thought but, nevertheless, he moved his body to block the keypad.

Then, he silently left through the back entrance. He was not in the mood for a conversation with the jolly security guard.

THREE

'HER NAME IS Eva Scott. She is resident in London. We found her yesterday.'

Two sharp-suited men in a darkened room gazed at a projection of Eva's face on the wall opposite.

'She's pretty.'

'Hmmmm.'

'Is there anything full length?'

A snap of the projector and the image changed again. This time, the shot captured all of Eva, straight backed, hair shining in the wintry morning sun as she waited at the mobile coffee stand under the glass canopy in her oversize coat.

'What would you suggest that we do?'

One of the men, who wore a slim-cut grey tweed, turned away from the image on the wall. He was not a young man anymore, he felt the effort of middle age underneath his fading Mediterranean tan. He reached for a thick cigar and rolled it between his fingers before cutting and lighting it. He could feel his younger colleague becoming frustrated, both by the smoking indoors and the time he was taking to respond. He sat down at an enormous walnut wood desk and took several long, luxurious puffs on the cigar. His colleague said nothing.

'What would you suggest we do, Paul?'

The younger man was a new addition to the team. He was an untested quantity and no one had taken kindly to such a late arrival, especially one so unexplained. Nobody intended to make things easy for him – he had an excess of ambition written all over his face.

This time, it was the younger man's turn to respond slowly.

He leaned against one of the antique bookshelves in the library, knowing full well that his disrespect of the priceless furniture would drive the older man mad.

'Well, I know less about this business than you,' he appeared to concede.

The older man nodded and continued to smoke.

'But it seems to me she is a loose end. Her presence at Waterloo Station – was it really a coincidence, given her history?'

The smoke in the room was thick now, hanging blue and fragrant in the warm morning air.

Neither of the men spoke for some time, as the effect of the younger man's words began to sink in.

Suddenly, the subject was changed. 'What have you planned for the man?' asked the elder, still working his way through the cigar.

A noticeable ripple of excitement travelled through the younger man and he moved quickly to sit opposite the desk.

'I'd like to eliminate him. Now that she,' he gestured at Eva's worried face, 'has surfaced, I think the threat – whilst minimal – is enough to warrant it.'

'But are they even connected anymore?'

'Why take the chance?'

'And her?'

'Maybe we should let Joseph Smith decide.'

For the second time that day, Eva found herself running. Only this time it was to escape. After leaving work early she'd gone home and curled up in bed. But by the evening she had allowed herself to believe her own lie about feeling ill and decided to walk to a late night chemist for some painkillers; no amount of water had been able to soothe the now continuous thumping inside her skull. It was almost 10pm, it was a Wednesday – the streets were wet with rain but empty of the usual crowds of revellers who would populate this area from tomorrow through to the end of the weekend. But as she left the chemist and crossed the road to make the ten minute journey back to the flat, the hair had begun to stand up on the back of her neck. A figure seemed to be shadowing her, stopping when she stopped, running when she ran, sticking to her like glue. It was impossible to tell whether it was male or female. She considered turning around and shouting a challenge but the streets were completely empty and the chances of anyone coming out of their home to help her were slim to none. She crossed the wide road in front of the station, walked by the glass canopy where she had bought her coffee that morning and jogged quickly up the small hill that led home. She felt her shadow follow, she even heard the footsteps. They weren't trying to hide.

Eva could hear her heartbeat thudding heavily in her ears. She was exhausted and drained, as if recalling past events had somehow opened up everything she had stored away after another very similar experience all those months ago. She drew another breath down into her lungs and forced herself to remain focused. In Paris, she had ended up bouncing off Leon's car bonnet after she had convinced herself she was being pursued and reacted like a frightened animal. This time, she would behave differently. She didn't like to make the same mistakes twice.

At the top of the hill, the road curved to the right and Eva quickly made her way down the turning that would take her back to her own flat. Unexpectedly, she turned left, slipping inside the narrow alleyway between two shops. She flattened herself against the wall. Her breath was fighting to escape in large, anxious bursts but she forced herself to be controlled. Sure enough, seconds later the shadowy figure slipped past the alleyway. From the brief glimpse that she had Eva recognised it was a man. But he was wearing a sweatshirt with the hood pulled up and a dark woollen hat covered most of his hair and the forehead of his profiled face. Eva waited several seconds for him to pass and keep walking and then stuck her head out of the alleyway.

What she saw made her heart skip a beat.

The man was standing just a couple of metres away under the darkness of a street lamp with no bulb. He was still, looking directly towards the alley in which she stood, the shadow of his hood creating a dark, faceless pool from which she knew two eyes were focused in her direction.

Eva stood frozen to the spot. Her heart was hammering frantically. The man didn't move. It was a surreal scene worthy of the finest Hollywood horror.

What was he going to do? Eva glanced around at her options – go further up the alley and become trapped, run at him and risk finding herself a stabbing statistic or run away from him and wait for him to chase her; wait to feel strong hands close around her neck and choke the life from her. Just like Paris.

Suddenly, voices broke the silence of the wet, cold streets. Drunken male and female voices heading towards where they were. The hooded man reacted briefly, glancing in the direction of the noise, and then slowly, almost unnaturally slowly, his head rotated back towards Eva. She still could not see any of his features. He looked almost as if he had none. Eva was frightened.

Then, without warning, the man turned and walked in the opposite direction, his hands in his pockets. Eva watched him go. The gaggle of Wednesday night revellers hustled past the alley, obscuring her vision of the departing man. None of them noticed the lone woman who had retreated, shaking, into the shadows. When they had moved on, she scanned the street for several minutes but could see nothing at all.

Her flat was just minutes from where she was standing. She could move, or she could remain cornered in that cold alleyway. She started to run. When she reached her front door, she drove the key home and flung open the door. It squeaked on its hinges. She leaped inside and felt for the handle behind her. A gust of wind blew in her face and, suddenly, she felt as if she was being pushed back, the door wrenched from her grasp. She felt a scream settle in her throat as she expected to see that empty hood appear around the door. The gust of wind died away. Quietly, Eva closed the door.

Once she had downed a glass of brandy to steady her nerves, Eva sat on her Swedish designed sofa and tried to stop shaking. The entire experience of the last hour was unpleasant, but what had shaken her most was that the man had done nothing. Perhaps he had been interrupted by those kids, but she wasn't sure. He had not tried to mug her, he had not tried to hurt her, he was apparently not trying to commit an opportunistic crime but just to intimidate. That meant there was another reason for his presence. Once again, Eva felt things slipping from her grasp. The steady, normal life she had constructed for herself over the past year seemed to be going up in smoke. Something was happening, she could feel it. Something she had no control over.

Her mind flicked back to the dying man at Waterloo Station earlier in the week. That seemed to be the point at which things had started to change.

She poured herself another drink and leaned back into the sofa. Then she stood up, walked to the kitchen and flicked the heating switch on the boiler before returning to the sofa and her drink. She tried to remember the man's face but it was difficult. She thought of his battered hat lying on the floor and felt sadness that someone in such a state could still do something as quaintly well mannered and old fashioned as wear a hat.

Where had he come from?

Again, Eva heard the word that he had said to her as he died, 'kolychak'. She realised she had said it out loud.

She leaned over and opened the notes app on her phone and typed it into the lined yellow page. She stared at it. It meant nothing to her. But it had meant something – at the time. Or had she imagined that in the drama of the moment.

She stood up, walked over to a vintage chest of drawers and pulled it open, the pale wood so smooth under her touch, contrasting with the clean modernist lines of the sofa. It was a contrived 'look' but she quite liked it. She retrieved a piece of paper and a black pen and wrote the word, first in large capital letters and then in standard sized text. She propped the sheet of paper on the arm of the sofa next to her and continued to stare. She was sure she knew that word. She had heard it before. But where had she heard it and what did it mean?

When she finally persuaded herself to go to bed an hour later, she took her laptop with her. She had bolted, locked and chained her front door, checked every window and even picked up an empty wine bottle and a kitchen knife, a small arsenal of weapons, 'just in case'. And she could use them, she knew that now – she had killed two people in Paris.

In the warm light of the cosy bedroom, she began to search the internet for the word 'kolychak'. She passed the term through several search engines but soon felt her mind begin to slow. The brandy was relaxing her body and she now realised how very tired she was. She looked at the screen but couldn't read what was on it. She closed the computer and shut her eyes.

Stefano Cirza stared in horror at the man in front of him, who held a metal claw at his throat. At the end of another late night in the lab, a feeling had crept over him that he wasn't alone. It was the same instinct he'd had several nights previously. When he had finally seen the stocky black man standing silently watching him, it had dawned on him he had indeed not been alone that night either. In fact, ever since that night

he'd instinctively felt someone was in his life, silently watching, and now this man had let himself in with a code known only to Stefano and his research assistant – who had been on an extended holiday for the past three weeks.

When the eyes of the two men had met, neither had moved for several seconds. But then, before Stefano could summon security, the metal claw was at his throat.

'W-what do you want?' he stuttered, every nerve ending on the back of his skull alight.

'I am sure you already know.' The accent was most definitely African but, other than that, Stefano could not tell.

'Who are you?'

'My name is Joseph Smith.'

With a sinking feeling, Stefano realised that the ease with which the man had revealed his name did not indicate a positive outcome. One in which Stefano was left breathing.

He felt the metal implement begin to graze his skin and he wondered why the man didn't just carry a gun. Why bother with the theatrics of such a cruel thing?

'What is that?' he asked, nodding as far as he could without the metal piercing his skin. Perhaps he could appeal to the man's better nature, make a connection with him.

'Bagh nakh. Tiger claws. They are from India.'

Stefano started to speak again but the other man interrupted. 'No,' he said and took a step back, removing the tiger claw from Stefano's throat.

Stefano tried to calm his heart but he knew what was coming.

Smith stepped forward and drove the metal implement through Stefano's thigh, slashing it down so that it was possible to hear the tearing of skin and muscle as it was ripped from the bone.

He covered Stefano's mouth to stifle the scream. 'If you give me what I need I will slash your throat so you die quickly. If you don't I will butcher your body so that you feel every single cut.'

Stefano clutched at his thigh, the blood was running warm and sticky through his hands. His eyes met those of his aggressor once again.

'I want to live!' It was a cry that bubbled up from Stefano's very core. He did not want this choice. It wasn't any choice at all.

There wasn't even a flicker of empathy in those black eyes. 'You cannot. Now make your decision.'

Shaking, Stefano closed his eyes. That it should come to this. Had his ex-business partner died at the hands of this man too – was that why he had disappeared? When he opened his eyes again, there was an acceptance of sorts. He was not a coward and he would die with as much dignity as he could. The pain in his leg from the first cut was bitter and he knew he could not take that over and over again.

He began slowly to lift a chain from around his neck. On it hung a small metal box. His entire body was shaking almost uncontrollably. The other man steadied his hands. Stefano opened the box and handed over a boxy key. He tried to speak but Joseph Smith was too fast.

FOUR

WHEN SHE OPENED her eyes, she felt she was dead straight away. There was a lightness to her limbs and a heaviness in her heart that told her she hadn't managed to escape this time with her life. She didn't live in fiction; she wasn't superhuman and her dreams of being something more had all been snatched away.

And then the pain started.

First, a gnawing sensation in her stomach that grew in intensity like a rising decibel and suddenly was so loud that she felt as if her entire body might split in two. She was bent double, screaming now.

Agony.

She couldn't end the pain, she knew that. There was no way to stop this anguish that had sliced through her and opened her up from stomach to heart. She would be stuck, forever – screaming.

Eva awoke with a start. She was sweating heavily. She reacted instantly to the darkened room and lurched for the light switch, knocking a book and a bottle of water on to the floor as she did so.

She pushed herself upwards against the headboard and ran a hand through damp hair.

The room around her was entirely still; outside the windows, a velvety darkness enveloped the peaceful sleepers of London.

She realised she was shivering, reached for a white robe that lay on the chair next to the bed and pulled it over her shoulders.

Her first nightmare in more than six months.

Eva had the distinct impression her dream had a vaguely religious undertone, that she had somehow dreamed herself into a state of purgatory.

She leaned back against the pillows and sighed out loud. While no one else had held her accountable for those two deaths in Paris, she seemed unable to allow herself to forget them. She was her own worst enemy, judge and jury.

One had been a fight to the death – if Eva hadn't fired that fatal shot, she would have been killed, without a doubt. As for the other, it was an unknown assassin wielding a needle filled with the virus that would have killed her exactly as it killed him if she hadn't pushed the plunger home into his flesh. He had died quickly and she had never forgotten the look on his face as his organs collapsed and the virus took control of his body, reprogramming his own immune system to kill.

'I had no choice,' she said out loud. Her voice sounded uncharacteristically weak and strained.

I'm *actually* going crazy.

She dismissed the thought, threw back the bedcovers, pulled the robe around her and belted it tightly. The air in the flat was cold and she could see her breath as she walked through her bedroom, along the boards of the hall floor and into the large open plan living room and kitchen. She had specifically chosen a flat with a minimalist feel – clutter did not work for her. She stood at the kitchen island and waited for the kettle to boil. For some reason, she felt as if she was not the only person in that room. It was almost as if she was waiting for someone – or something – to speak. But no one did. Nothing moved.

Eva turned back to the stainless steel kitchen area and retrieved her favourite mug from one of the cupboards; a heavy, insulated piece of stoneware designed to keep tea warm for 'up to an hour'. The clock on the kitchen wall read 5am. It was virtually morning. She gave up on the idea of going back to sleep, of entering that purgatory place again, and made herself tea with two strong caffeinated teabags. Milk, no sugar. Grabbing an apple from the fruit bowl, she made her way back into the bedroom.

As she walked through the darkened hallway, all the hairs stood up on the back of her neck.

Eva walked faster, quickly closing the bedroom door behind her.

When she reached the bed, she put the tea down on the bedside table before taking a large bite of the apple. For a moment she contemplated wedging a piece of furniture against the door but decided the fearful little girl apparently inhabiting her imagination did not need any encouragement.

She climbed back into bed and pulled the still warm covers over her chilled skin.

After a few sips of tea and the rest of the apple, Eva reached for her laptop and opened it. Instantly, it jumped to life, showing her the search engine she had been using the night before to look for information on 'kolychak'.

She stared at the screen.

There were two hits at the top of the list she was pretty sure had not been there the night before. Nothing relevant had appeared last night, she was almost 100 per cent sure of that.

But there was something there now.

Eva's stomach flipped.

She navigated her way onto the first page.

The headline read: *'This country remains committed as a party to the Geneva Protocol, and a party to and depository government of the Biological and Toxin Weapons Convention.'*

The rest of the page appeared to be written in the Cyrillic alphabet but she could clearly see the world 'kolychak' in English lettering, halfway down the screen. She stared at the page. It looked like a photocopy of a document, a pdf. It had an official stamp on the right hand side at the top and had been signed at the bottom – two signatories – and another stamp, this time so small and round that it was impossible to see what shape the ink was meant to convey.

Eva opened a second window and searched for 'Biological and Toxin Weapons Convention'. She was taken to a page that revealed the full name of the convention: the Convention on the Prohibition of the Development, Production and Stockpiling of Bacteriological (Biological) and Toxin Weapons and on their Destruction. It had been signed simultaneously in Moscow, Washington and London on 10 April 1972 and entered into force on 26 March 1975. She read on.

'The Convention bans the development, production, stockpiling, acquisition and retention of microbial or other biological agents or toxins, in types and in quantities that have no justification for prophylactic, protective or other peaceful purposes. It also bans weapons, equipment or means of delivery designed to use such agents or toxins for hostile purposes or in armed conflict. The actual use of biological weapons is prohibited by the 1925 Geneva Protocol and Article VIII of the BTWC recognizes that nothing contained in the Convention shall be construed as a derogation from the obligations contained in the Geneva Protocol.'

It was clearly a Cold War consequence, some 40 years old but, when she navigated back to that first screen again, there was 'kolychak'. A word she had heard very much in her own present.

Eva opened a third window and, this time, she searched for the name of the convention alongside the word 'Russia'. This brought up numerous pages where concerns were expressed, with various degrees of strength, about the country's compliance with the convention. It seemed that Russia – and formerly the Soviet Union – had covertly operated an offensive biological weapons programme in contravention of the convention for more than fifteen years. Many commentators appeared concerned about whether or not this programme had ever actually been dismantled.

Eva went back to the first page she had found and copied the text surrounding the word 'kolychak'. She located a free translation website and put it through the system.

The result was garbled but she could see that kolychak was one of the weapons plants that had been causing concern to international commentators and that the document with the signatures on it indicated it had been closed more than two decades ago.

Eva reached for her tea and realised it was cold. More than an hour of searching and she had returned exactly to the point at which she started.

She threw back the covers, picked up her mug and padded through to the kitchen. It was still dark outside and the night was silent. She flicked the 'on' switch on the heating as she waited for the kettle to boil and then made herself a second strong cup of tea. This time, when she went back to bed, she left all the lights on.

Back in front of her laptop, Eva tried the second search engine hit that had popped up in response to 'kolychak'.

As soon as the page appeared on her screen, she frowned.

'Kolychak private banking will protect and grow your wealth.'

The page was silvery grey with a royal blue logo that showed a crest of some sort. It did not look particularly Russian.

Eva clicked through to the 'about' page.

'Kolychak private banking offers investment advice and opportunity. Our wealth management offering is unprecedented, both with respect to our network reach and our proven success.'

And that was it. The page was cryptically absent of any information that could definitively tell Eva what the organisation was.

She copied and pasted the words 'kolychak private banking' into another search window and the single accurate hit that appeared was the same website she had just been on. There was nothing else at all.

Then she noticed the search had brought up a Maps result. She clicked on it and found herself looking down on an address in Paris. Kolychak private banking was located in Paris.

Her heart started to beat faster.

Opening up the Maps page, she tried to place the location.

She read through the address again and felt sure she had seen it before, written down – perhaps scribbled onto a piece of paper somewhere. She shut her eyes and tried to visualise the ghostly scrap of writing. She tried harder. Then, instantly, the image was clear in her mind.

Paris, 13 months ago.

FIVE

EVA AWOKE WITH a start. Bright sunlight was streaming in through the gaps in her curtains. Groggily, she reached for her phone. 9.30am. She groaned. She was already late for work.

Typing a quick text message to Sam, some lie about a burst pipe and a plumber, she quickly made the bed and headed for the shower. She flicked the switch on the powerful device with its enormous rainforest head and waited for the room to fill with warm clouds of steam as she cleaned her teeth. A haunted face stared back at her. She looked as if she hadn't slept for a week. Gradually, the mirror misted over.

Eva rinsed her toothbrush, stripped off and stepped under the huge silver showerhead. This hotel style bathroom was what had attracted her to the flat in the first place. She loved good bathrooms. Chrome fittings, a roll top bath, pale wood fixtures and a round contemporary basin that was satisfyingly smooth. She had lived most of her life in London with cracked avocado bathroom sets and mouldy grouting and she was fed up renting from landlords who seemed to think that was ok. She had chosen this flat because it was expensive, which made her feel it would at least guarantee a landlord who understood his legal responsibilities and wanted to take care of a (relatively) high rolling tenant. But, of course, it didn't. The expensive looking fixtures and fittings were as breakable as the avocado bathroom sets and she was already embroiled in running battles over the landlord's maintenance obligations.

The warm water energised Eva and she stepped out of the shower with a surprising enthusiasm for the day ahead. She combed her hair through, dried off and then padded through to the bedroom, enjoying the under floor heating that, for once, seemed to have come on when it was supposed to. She selected a pair of cigarette-style pants – black – a crisp white shirt and a close cut jacket in a matching dark shade. Then, she slipped her feet into some dark boots, dried her hair and spent at least 15 minutes trying to make herself look more human with the contents of her make-up bag. Finally, she pulled on the oversize coat, reached for her bag and dashed for the door.

It was 10.15.

By 10.30, she was sitting on the bus with a coffee.

'Oh, my God!'

Eva only realised she had spoken out loud because several people in the seats in front of her suddenly turned around to look at her.

She had to stop doing that.

But she had remembered something. She knew where she had heard that word 'kolychak' before.

He watched Eva's lithe figure as she jumped off the bus, strong legs carrying her through the closing doors and back to earth. She stood still on the pavement for several seconds before a large man going the other way knocked her, hard. Unusually for Eva, she didn't react. She looked dazed, almost shocked. And, he realised distractedly, she looked good. He wondered what had happened to her upstairs on that bus. This was not her work stop; in fact, she had jumped off the bus in the middle of the city, in a location miles from where she worked and miles from where she lived. What was she doing?

As he watched, Eva retrieved her phone from her bag and raised it to her ear. When the call apparently connected, she seemed to speak quickly and forcefully and then hung up, frustration written all over her face. Straight away she made a second call but, apparently, the results were the same. Worry creased her features – and something more: fear.

Then she was on the move and he had to walk quickly to keep up with her. She crossed the busy street, bustling with traffic, and narrowly avoided colliding with a black cab. She looked shocked and shaken as the driver sounded his horn and shouted a curse from his window, as if she hadn't even been aware she was on a road.

He was puzzled.

No matter what was going on inside, Eva usually portrayed the picture of a confident and well organised woman – at least to the outside world – but right now she looked utterly lost.

He gazed at her. She was only metres away…

Suddenly, she turned her head and appeared to look right at him. He moved away, averting his eyes and browsing his phone, glancing in her direction through sunglasses, and out from underneath his baseball cap, to see whether she had either seen him or recognised him.

She turned in the other direction but he was not reassured. That could mean that she was about to start running.

Sure enough, she began to move again, quickly through the crowds, until he realised she was heading for the tube station.

She flew down the stairs at breathtaking speed and traversed the barriers without ever looking back.

He realised that he had no ticket, nor a contactless card, and that the queues were too long.

He had lost her.

Eva stared down at her hands as she sat on the Northern Line train, heading south. At Charing Cross, she jumped from her seat, narrowly avoiding a collision with the woman attempting to get into it, and went in search of the Bakerloo Line connection. As she walked, she thought back to the realisation that she'd had on the bus. The word 'kolychak' had been spoken during a conversation via video link in the underground bunker in Paraguay.

Thirteen months ago.

There were four men from the Association for the Control of Regenerative Networking. After Daniel had announced his blackmail, one of them had said:

'You have no interest in being part of our ongoing organisation?'

And Daniel had replied.

'No, I don't have the patience to play the long game – not for kolychak or the rest.'

Eva frowned as she stepped on to the escalator and began moving upwards. 'Kolychak or the rest.' What did that mean?

And what was the 'ongoing organisation' those men were talking about?

Eva had tried to call Irene before she went underground but had been unable to reach her. She had once again tried Irene's secretary, who had simply trotted out the same line as the day before, and then she had tried Irene's home number. The number appeared to be disconnected.

Eva had almost lost it in the middle of the street. Something was happening, something bad. And it was linked to everything that had occurred thirteen months ago in Paris. The only other person she knew to be still alive who had any shared memories of that situation was Irene Hunt and Eva had to see her.

Irene lived in a Maida Vale mansion with her husband, Henry, and two children. Eva had once visited it under rather different circumstances – meeting the woman who she believed broke up her family. Years before, Irene had conducted an affair with Eva's father. After that, nothing had been the same.

Although it was some time since she had been to Irene's house, Eva thought she could remember the route from the station and she was determined to make contact. It was easy to ignore a phone call but a person on your doorstep, not so much.

When she emerged from the tube station, the bright sunlight was blinding. Normally, she would turn her face to the sun but today she ducked it.

She set off at pace across the wide roads, ignoring the large, aesthetically pleasing houses on either side, focused only on finding the gate she would recognise as Irene's.

Fifteen minutes later, there it was. The same gate, entry through the same garden and the same comfortingly solid front door.

She raced up the stairs and rang the doorbell. There was no response.

She rang it again, slightly too quickly.

The door was opened by a harassed looking woman. In the background, Eva could hear a baby crying.

'Yes?'

'Is Irene here?'

'Who?'

'Irene. Irene Hunt.'

'I think you must have the wrong address.'

The woman attempted to turn and shut the door.

'Wait!' Eva realised her voice was not calm. She took a deep breath. She smiled. The face opposite her was wary.

'I'm sorry, I've had to rush to get here. It's just that a woman called Irene Hunt – and her husband Henry – they lived here. I came to see them just over a year ago. And I really need to find out where they are.'

The woman just stared at Eva. She almost looked sympathetic but there was more suspicion in her eyes than anything else.

'I'm really sorry, I can't help you. We have lived here for more than five years now.'

Eva stared at the woman, taken aback.

'I was here just over 13 months ago and she was living in this exact house. I'm sorry but that can't be true.'

She couldn't have made a mistake, could she?

Suddenly, the woman was angry. 'Look, I don't know who you are or whether this is some kind of wind-up but this is my home and you're standing on my doorstep making me feel worried about what you're going to do next. I have an infant upstairs. If you don't mind, I'd like you to leave.'

Eva stepped back. She hadn't meant to intimidate. 'I'm sorry, of course.'

Immediately, she turned and walked back through the garden area, noting the same distinctive water feature she had seen on that night she had come here with Leon. It was Irene's house. She had not made a mistake. There was no way that woman could be telling the truth, no matter how genuine she might have seemed.

When she was outside the front gate, Eva shut it and turned to look at the house again. She closed her eyes and pulled back the memory from that misty night when she had come here looking for help, when Leon had kissed her, when she had confronted Irene for the first time.

When she opened her eyes again, she was standing in front of exactly the same house. Even the curtain arrangements hadn't changed.

Eva glanced around her at the wide streets, suddenly aware of being very alone. A fleeting thought crossed her mind that, given the way events unfolded last time, perhaps she needed to start carrying a weapon. She began walking back towards the tube. Maybe a pair of scissors. Or even a knife. She certainly felt like she needed something. Irene had disappeared, 'Jackson' was calling her again and, after six months of good sleep, her nightmares had returned.

The police who had found Stefano Cirza's body were horrified by the state in which it had been left. It looked almost as if he had been savaged by a wild animal and the gore... that was too much for some. There had been white faces all round and hastily distributed sick bags. Most of the flesh seemed to have been removed from his right thigh, which was horrific enough, but the neck wound had almost severed his head entirely. It appeared to have been delivered with such force there was suspicion that perhaps an animal had indeed been to blame. It would explain the inhuman claw marks at least and the ferocity with which he had been attacked.

What the police could not piece together was why this man had been the victim of such a heinous crime.

He was a doctor, a scientist, and his work was innocuous as far as anyone could tell. He was not working on biological warfare, he was not dealing with any particularly lucrative pharmaceuticals and he had done nothing other than research human genetics.

The young officers charged with trying to understand what was behind the attack had found the man's research interesting. It was a novel idea and, yes, what he had developed was pioneering. However, there seemed no reason to kill him for it. None at all. It could have been bought at a relatively cheap price.

When they had managed to reach his research assistant, a difficult conversation on a long-distance line had revealed there were buyers interested and that the whole process was under way to bring such a 'genetic key' onto the market. Some sort of mapping technology was also mentioned but there was no evidence of that anywhere in the lab so the officers focused on the key. They considered whether an English business partner the assistant had mentioned could be to blame but he had apparently disappeared in mysterious circumstances.

The officers thought that using one's own genetic code to provide the key to a digital lock was innovative. The key could never be lost and it could never be faked. Stress hormones detected in the blood sample used to activate the key would shut the whole system down. So, unlike eyeball or fingerprint recognition, the owner of the key could never be coerced into providing access. It would appeal to anyone who had something to hide, whatever the reason. From what the police could make out, there was only one issue with the research and that was the lack of a fully completed test. That was what Stefano Cirza had been working on before he died. And that also puzzled them. Why stop him before he had finished what must be the most essential task of all? His product was surely worthless without the final approval.

When they had finished with the blood on the floor – it always amazed them how much blood the human body really contained – they realised some of Cirza's computer equipment was missing. Which convinced them this was a crime that must really have been about his work. The only unexplained element of the whole scene was a small metal box on a chain, clutched in the victim's hand. The box was empty.

SIX

By the time Eva arrived home, the pressure in her head felt immense, unbearable almost. She shoved her key in the lock, threw open the door with unintentional force and jumped as it bounced off the wall behind and flew back at her. She steadied herself. *Calm down.*

Inside the flat, she closed the door and walked quickly into the bedroom. After pushing a chair that reclined in a curved 'S' shape over to a large wood wardrobe in the corner of the room, she gingerly stepped on it. It wobbled precariously. She glanced around for a better stepladder but the design brief for her furniture had been 'contemporary' rather than 'practical', so this would have to do.

When she was steady enough, she reached up and felt for a large canvas bag she knew was pushed down into the recess of the top of the wardrobe. Her fingertips made contact with the rough fabric and she tried to create a hold for herself then pulled sharply. The bag was too heavy. She ran her hand over the bag until she found one of the canvas straps and hooked her fingers underneath it. Then, she pulled with all her strength. Gradually, the bag started to move. Finally, she had it balanced unsteadily on the edge of the wardrobe, right above her head. She pulled it towards her one last time and leaned quickly out of the way as it thudded to the floor.

A small cloud of dust rose up.

Eva looked down on the sports bag as she stood on the chair.

This bag had been Jackson's. When she had left Paris, everything from her hotel room had been thrown into it and zipped up. It had not been opened since.

Eva jumped down from the chair and dragged the bag over to the bed, where she took a seat on the edge of the smooth covers. For several seconds, she stared at the bag in front of her. Then she ripped open the zip and began pulling out the contents. Papers flew into the air as she emptied the bag at high speed. She realised there were tears flowing down her cheeks as she continued hurling everything from the bag on to the floor. She had never wanted to look at any of this ever again. And yet she had not thrown any of it away. Why could she not just move on?

He sat in the car outside her house and debated his next move. It was early afternoon but darkness was already beginning to fall and he was unsure about the best way to proceed. If there was one thing he had learned about Eva Scott, it was that she was unpredictable – always. Of course, she felt fear like every other person but it didn't seem to stop her. Even from stepping into situations that might end her life. It wasn't a superhuman type of bravery, though, from what he could make out, more like an instinctive need to move forward at speed. She was either very careless or had an inbuilt recklessness. Or perhaps she was just damaged.

In his lap, his phone jumped to life and began flashing a warning light that indicated someone was trying to call him. He looked at the name on the display but couldn't bring himself to answer the call.

He glanced again at the building where Eva lived. The best thing he could do for her would be to end her involvement right now. Otherwise, she would continue to be dragged through an ordeal she had neither chosen nor deserved – again. But that meant either convincing her to let go of whatever trail she felt she was on to or... well, or forcing her to let go of it. He knew either would be almost impossible for him.

A tap on his window distracted him from his thoughts.

He looked up into a beautiful face, with striking green eyes, framed by flame-coloured hair disguised under the fabric of a hood. He quickly wound down the window and then drew a sharp breath as the muzzle of a gun was poked through.

'Open the door.'

A glance to the left and right revealed there was no escape route from the hire car. He had been forced to pick an inconspicuous city car rather than the huge urban vehicles he usually preferred and, as well as being incredibly uncomfortable to sit in for long periods of time, this model had little power. If he lunged for the passenger door, he knew he would feel a bullet in his back. Maybe the back of his head. He looked up into those green eyes and nodded slowly.

'Ok,' he said, raising his hands.

She took a step back from the car, allowing him the space in which to open the car door. He dropped one foot and then the other from the car, took a step to the side so that he was standing in front of the rear passenger door and leaned against it.

'What now?'

He was a good third of a metre taller than she was and he was pretty sure he was much stronger. He glanced up at Eva's kitchen window; a bolt of electricity travelled through him. He could see the pale oval of a face staring down.

Then everything began to move very fast.

Eva watched the scene below her in a state of near paralysis. A man whose face she could not make out was being hustled into a van that had pulled up next to him at high speed. He appeared to try and fight and then he stopped. She could clearly see the dark shape of a gun in the hands of a hooded figure who pushed him towards the other side of the van. Should she do something?

She ran into the bedroom and grabbed her mobile phone.

When she returned to the kitchen window, both man and van were gone. She stared down at the street below. The door of the car from which the man had emerged was left open.

Grabbing a pair of boots and her house keys, she ran quickly downstairs. Outside, it was bitterly cold and she wished she had thought to pick up a coat. She ran across the quiet road and then stopped. She looked up at the houses all around. The windows were dark and empty. It was early afternoon on a weekday and most of the residents around here would be at work. But still, she could never shift the feeling there might be someone who would see something and draw conclusions over which she had no control.

She climbed inside the car and quietly shut the door behind her.

The air inside the car had a strangely familiar smell – an aftershave of some sort and strong French cigarettes. The keys were still in the ignition.

On the passenger seat was a small carry-on size bag, unzipped and virtually empty. There was a drained coffee cup wedged between the dashboard and the windscreen.

The floor on the passenger side was littered with chocolate wrappers, sandwich packets and fruit peelings, as well as several cans of an energy drink she didn't recognise. Had that man been living in here?

She looked around the car for further clues, opened the glove box, felt underneath the seats and checked the footwell and seats in the back. There was nothing to provide any indication about who the man was and why he should have been sitting in his car – coincidentally outside her house? – or any explanation for what had just happened.

She looked again inside the small piece of cabin luggage on the seat next to her, briefly wondering why she was going through someone's possessions and not calling the police. But really she knew why. Paris had blown away any trust she had in institutions. She would never again ask for help. For Eva, involving the authorities now meant handing over control to an organisation where corruption potentially flourished. Anyone who thought any collective body of humans could escape that kind of decay was a fool.

Control. There was that word again.

She picked up the cabin luggage and emptied it of its contents. A hotel key, several packets of chewing gum, a large bottle of water, a map of London branded with the logo of a hire car company and a small black hardbacked notebook.

Eva opened the notebook and flicked through it. Inside, was a mess of writing, none of which she could identify. As she stared harder at the page in front of her, she realised part of what she was looking at was the Cyrillic alphabet. Her skin chilled. Another possible connection?

She glanced up as she sensed movement in one of the wing mirrors and then swiftly switched on a smile as she recognised one of her neighbours walking towards her, his eyes focused on the car in which she was sitting. He approached the car. Her heart began to beat faster.

'New car?' he smiled.

'Ah, it belongs to a friend.'

'Oh right, a "friend."?' He grinned. In his mid 30s, crisply turned out but inexplicably always 'around', he always went that bit too far with Eva, made her feel slightly threatened. She didn't know why he had to introduce a sexual element into every conversation.

'Just a friend.' She smiled innocuously back at him.

'You still with that blonde boyfriend of yours?'

Sam, shit. She had been supposed to call him and explain why she had not shown up at work.

'Yes.' She just let the tail end of the conversation drift. She couldn't be bothered to make polite conversation if all he wanted to do was pry.

'Well, should that change you know where I am,' he said, laughing falsely and holding her gaze for just a little too long. He stood outside the car door.

Eva looked at him. She had the feeling he was contemplating something. He glanced around them at the empty street. Was she just being paranoid? Probably. But nevertheless she needed to move. She pushed open the car door and he stumbled back as it knocked him on the hip.

'Oh sorry,' she said, slamming it behind her.

She didn't glance back at him, it was obvious what he would be looking at. He wouldn't really have done anything, she was fairly sure of that, but if he had Eva could have coped. After Paris Eva had taken on a personal trainer. Together, they had worked out a four-times-a-week plan of training sessions focused on self defence, including Krav Maga moves used by Mossad. The plan had taken eight months to complete and it was only after she had reached the end that she had started to feel she might be recovering. Now she could act, instead of being at the mercy of blind luck.

She turned and walked back to the car. She opened the door again, reached for the keys she had seen in the ignition. As she did, she noticed a black top shoved down the other side of the car, between the passenger seat and the door. Her heart missed a beat. Had this man been her silent intimidator from the other night?

She looked again at the fabric of the hoodie and then at her neighbour. He still seemed interested in what she was doing but he no longer had the predatory look she had seen before she had hit him with the door.

'Hi Sam, I'm really sorry about not calling earlier.'

'Is everything ok, I've been really worried about you.'

Eva sighed and stared at her reflection in the windows of the kitchen as she searched for a response. She felt a sense of unreality that made her feel isolated and detached. Was it someone's intention that she should be isolated with the knowledge she had? Knowledge that only she and the, now disappeared, Irene shared.

At the same time she couldn't shake the sneaking fear she was inventing this. What if she was simply bored and looking for conspiracy where in reality all that was there was a series of coincidences? She hardly felt she knew where reality lay anymore. Which was frightening.

'I'm fine,' she said finally, 'I've just not been feeling very well. You know how illness makes you do funny things.'

'Of course. Do you want me to come over? I'll bring chicken soup.'

Eva smiled. 'I'm fine, thanks, Sam.'

'Ok, well if you change your mind.'

'I'll let you know.'

'Oh, just one other thing.'

'Yes?'

'I don't know if they contacted you but there was some talk about sending you to Berlin.'

'Berlin?'

'Yes.'

'Why?'

'I'm not sure, exactly. I just heard jealous whisperings about it around the office – gossip, no real details. But it sounds like they need you to interview someone.'

'And when am I supposed to be leaving?'

'Tomorrow, I think.'

Eva said goodbye and put the phone down.

Berlin. That was the last thing she needed. She had more than enough on her plate. Who was the man in the car, for a start, and had he been watching her?

But Berlin. She had never been to Berlin. Which meant she knew no one and she would need a map to negotiate its streets.

Why were they sending her to Berlin, for God's sake?

Perhaps she should just quit. She'd had enough of the petty bureaucracy and the office 'personalities' to realise she actually hated working in an office. The commute seemed inhuman, being cooped up at a tiny desk in a room full of resentful failures was depressing and what was she actually getting out of it anyway? Was this a career move?

She laughed to herself. Career. That was funny.

But, as she looked around the expensive flat, she realised she couldn't give up the job. Yes, Jackson had left her cash that ensured she was comfortable but she was just not programmed to live off savings. She would go mad. And maybe every job would be just like this one anyway – what was the point in going from office to office and just finding the same state of affairs in each one? At least here she had Sam and she knew how it worked.

And maybe Berlin would do her good.

SEVEN

'ARE YOU TELLING me the problem has not been dealt with?'

'I'm telling you we have it under control but I want to use this situation a little bit creatively.'

'Creatively.'

'Yes, you know, think outside the box.'

Outside the box. What an awful phrase that was. It was corporate bullshit of the worst kind.

The man with the fading Mediterranean tan took a seat at his expensive desk and angrily snipped the tip off a Cuban cigar. The young man on the other end of the phone was not his type of person. Was it the exuberance of youth that annoyed him or was it simply the half-arsed way that Paul seemed to operate? They had worked together for such a short length of time but he was still able to discern that this was someone who flew by the seat of his pants, who progressed via others' mistakes and failings, not his own talents. How he had come to be in possession of all this innovative technology remained something of a mystery. And one that he did not care to clear up apparently.

'Are you still there?'

He could hear the hard edge in the voice on the other end of the line and he wondered whether this man-child had it in him to do business the old fashioned way – with his own bare hands – or whether, if it came to the crunch, he simply didn't have the stomach. That's how the man with the Mediterranean tan judged a person, whether they outsourced the carrying out of their own threats. It was unlikely that Paul had ever taken a life but it was always unwise to underestimate people. That's why he supposed caution would be advisable for now, no matter how much the man irritated him. Just in case.

'Ok, explain,' he said finally, in a cold, hard voice.

'The Scott...'

'No,' the older man snapped, interrupting immediately. 'No names over an unsecure line.'

That was satisfying. The more silly mistakes the younger man made, the more justified his older colleague felt in the dim view he had taken of him. Youth never trumped experience. Or, rarely so.

'Oh. Sorry.'

He really didn't sound that remorseful but he did at least hesitate.

'Well?'

'I thought it might be more fun to test it by putting him in a situation where he believes he has to kill to survive.'

'More "fun".'

'Yes. And it will mean there's no connection to us if he fails.'

The man with the Mediterranean tan felt irritated again. Paul had been on the project a matter of months and yet he talked as if the decade of work it had taken to get to this stage was all his. He changed well laid plans without asking, he had no respect for existing authority.

'And how do you propose to do this?'

'Kind of fox and hare, I thought. Set the hare running and make the fox chase.'

'But for that to succeed the technology has to be ready – and to work. We both know that this technology – *your* technology – has not yet been properly tested. Are you saying it's now magically ready?'

There was a tight response on the other end of the line. 'No. But this can be the test.'

'Isn't it a risk to test it when it's incomplete, and to do it on someone so close?'

'It should work…'

'Should…'

'Yes.'

'And he's the right test subject?'

'I believe so.'

'What if it fails?'

'If it does not work, the location we've chosen is too remote for him to escape.'

'Is all this really necessary?'

'We need her to believe it, correct? Well, what better person to test this on – other than her? If it works this time, the odds are it is ready.'

The man with the Mediterranean tan leaned back in his chair, thoughtfully puffing on the cigar. This was the second phase, and it was just as crucial as the first, and the third that would follow soon. But, as was so often the case, there was no blueprint for any of this and they were using multiple pieces of innovative technology that were still largely untested. Whilst it was exciting, he also felt incredibly nervous. And a part of him wished for the days when you could see your weapons, your battlefield and your enemy.

He was also still unable to chase from his mind his unease over Paul's arrival. What really troubled him was why Paul had become involved and how he had known this network even existed. One had to assume someone, somewhere had asked that question but, if they had, the answer had not been revealed to him. Paul had appeared at the exact moment the operation had happened to falter – and with precisely the right tools to correct its path. He claimed to have created this technology and yet he seemed to know very little about it and one always felt as if he was making it up when questioned on the specifics.

And then there was his attitude in general, a lack of respect for human life, the way he approached everything as a game. What he was suggesting in this instance was unnecessarily cruel – sport at the expense of at least one human life for no other reason than to test a product. It was not uncommon but it was also not necessary. However, ultimately, the man with the Mediterranean tan didn't want to appear weak in the face of a more ruthless and, possibly, bloodthirsty junior.

'Are you absolutely sure this is the way that we should do this?'

'Trust me, it will all work out.'

Eva watched the cabin safety demonstration without interest. It had been months since she had flown anywhere but, even so, the robotic moves and fixed smiles were just repeating information she had already absorbed somewhere along the line. She leaned back in her window seat and watched as the plane taxied through the early mist of a London morning. She had been up since 5am, quickly packed a suitcase after a few hours sleep, and taken a taxi to the airport. The call had come late the night before from Janet, whose reasoning for sending Eva to Berlin was based solely on the fact she was the only person in the office with any real journalistic experience. Despite herself, Eva found that she felt excited. She realised she missed the thrill of researching and writing a good story. Not that this was a good story – carbon emissions. Of course, it was interesting but it was not one of those heart-pumping, palm-clenching pieces she thought she craved – she had never even heard of the person she was going to meet. Annoyingly, the brief time she'd had to do research hadn't turned up anything either. There was almost nothing online except a few academic listings. This meant the interview was either a puff piece with someone who was completely irrelevant or this person was so important that they had achieved that elusive state of online anonymity.

She was escaping London and so could leave behind, at least for 24 hours, everything that had so alarmed her recently. The man at the station, the apparent abduction from outside her flat, the hooded figure, Irene Hunt's apparent disappearance off the face of the earth and the odd sense she couldn't shake that something was wrong. Maybe it was a good chance for some perspective she thought as the plane began to pick up speed. Stepping back from this situation could reveal it as just a series of coincidences, as deep down she suspected it might be.

Eva leaned back in her seat and closed her eyes as the front wheels of the plane lifted off and gravity pushed her back against the seat. She always felt that, at the moment the last part of the plane lifted from the ground, there was nothing she had control over anymore. In fact, perhaps 30,000 feet up in the air was the only place she really ever relaxed.

When they landed in Berlin, it was to a surprisingly bright and sunny morning. The air was cold but less so than London and, without the chilled fog, the conditions were far more pleasant. Eva took a taxi to the hotel booked for her – a stark, modern building that appealed to all her minimalist tendencies. It was not too pricey, not too cheap, the perfect option for someone travelling on the budget of an NGO.

She checked in and found her room, an attractive enough space on the third floor, with a window that looked out on to wide roads and glass-sided buildings, the closest of which housed another hotel. The street was lined with cars; on one side a fleet of cream-coloured Berlin taxis waiting to pick up, and on the other a selection of private vehicles. At the front was a large black bus with 'VIP' emblazoned in the kind of silver lettering that indicated no one 'very important' was on that vehicle.

She deposited her suitcase on a chair, unzipped it and began unpacking, quickly hanging up a pair of black jeans, a dark dress, the only pair of smart trousers she still owned, a bright orange sweater and several lightweight shirts with tiny prints on them, one miniature lemons and the other swallows flying in regulated geometric lines. She retrieved her wash bag and walked into the bathroom where, once again, she found herself looking into a face that didn't feel like hers.

Her resting expression now appeared to be a combination of exhaustion and wariness. She looked like she hadn't slept properly for a week. Which, actually, she hadn't.

She put down the wash bag and unpacked toothbrush and paste, which she placed neatly in a glass holder by the sink. She took out her hairbrush and pulled it through her dark hair and then retrieved make-up that would disguise some of the exhaustion that she felt.

Once she had finished, she looked better. And felt better.

She left her room, slamming the door behind her, and decided to walk around the hotel. It was the kind of place she knew would have conference and meeting rooms, as well as a 'fine dining' restaurant with white tablecloths, sparkling silverware and a jus on the menu.

She found the reception desk and asked where she could buy a coffee and breakfast. It wasn't time to leave the hotel just yet. The receptionist indicated the 'Grande Gallerie', a modest space housed in what was essentially a glass atrium in between the lifts.

Once the waiter had handed over the Wi-Fi password Eva, like anyone alone in a restaurant, began to pay excessive attention to her phone. She scrolled through old messages, tidied up her emails and then browsed a few social networking sites. She decided to clear out some of the older texts and began methodically working her way through the list.

There, towards the end, were the texts she had received from 'Jackson' when she had been in Paris. Thirteen months ago. She had looked at these only twice after she had received them. There had simply been no time to find out what they meant. But now, she had time.

She scrolled through the two messages. The content looked like lines of code – it was certainly not English, nor any other similar language. But neither was it the Cyrillic alphabet she had come across several times recently. When she realised she was unlikely to make any progress alone, she took a screenshot of the message on her phone and sent it to Sam. He seemed naturally gifted with computer stuff so perhaps he could help her decipher what 'Jackson' had been trying to send her.

She didn't trust Sam to the extent that she would reveal why she needed his help, but she figured he was an innocuous enough person to ask in her current situation. Perhaps working on this might deter him from asking more of the searching questions he seemed to specialise in – when can we be exclusive, do you love me, that kind of thing…

Eva shifted awkwardly in her seat at the thought of it.

At first, the attachment refused to send. She noticed her phone seemed to have dropped the hotel's Wi-Fi connection. She waited and then, several minutes later, the bars returned and the message went through straight away.

As she was online, she decided to try her own translation, opened an internet page on her phone and copied and pasted the message content into a free translation website. There was no result. She was not surprised, she couldn't even see what language it was supposed to be, so she couldn't blame a machine for being unable to do it either.

Out of interest, she pasted the copied text into the search engine of the internet page. At first, the jumble of letters and symbols appeared to generate no response. And then she noticed it. She had been about to close the internet page on her phone but the word was there on one of the search engine hits – 'kolychak'.

EIGHT

As soon as she left the hotel, Eva knew she was being followed. She could sense the presence behind her even if she couldn't see it. She crossed the road on her right, glancing slightly further than the flow of traffic to see if she could make out a figure in her slipstream but none stood out. She continued walking along the pavement on the other side of the road. It was broad daylight in Berlin, there were people everywhere, surely approaching her at this time of day would be crazy.

But she was wrong.

Almost as soon as the thought came, so did the assault. She was shoved from behind – so hard it completely took her breath away. She fell, sprawling onto the pavement, her bag hitting the floor before her body did. She felt the palms of her hands graze the concrete and she hit the front of her skull, hard. Instinctively, she reached for her head and then her bag, which had fallen in front, to her right. She grasped the leather strap. A heavy boot stamped down on her closed fist, making her grimace, but she didn't let go. Lifting her head caused a bolt of pain across her skull; the sun was bright in her eyes and Eva couldn't see who the foot belonged to. She dipped her head again, quickly brought her left hand to join her right on the bag strap. She felt her body jerk forward as someone picked up the bag and tried to rip it from her grasp, pulling her along the pavement with the soft leather satchel. She glanced up, breathing hard. Now she could see the face. She didn't recognise it but she understood the expression it wore. She yanked the bag back, trying to free it from the man's grasp, but he was built like a machine. She knew she should let go but she couldn't.

So she started screaming.

Her assailant's eyes widened and she knew people around would be staring at them. What would he do? And then the man surprised her.

'*Bitte*,' he said, in a hushed voice, his eyes pleading with her. '*Please, just give me your phone. That's all I need.*'

Eva stared at him but did not release the bag.

'What?'

His grip on her bag had loosened.

'I don't want to hurt you,' he said urgently, 'just give me the bag so I can get the phone.'

Why did he just want her phone? If this was a mugging, why not the cash and credit cards, too.

'*Bitte!*' the man repeated and Eva could sense there were people running in her direction as the man began to glance left and right.

Eva, looking up at him from the ground, her neck vibrating with tension, shook her head.

NO.

His eyes narrowed and he went to reach for something in his pocket. Then, apparently thinking better of it, he simply dropped the strap of her bag and began to run in the other direction.

'I will see you again!' he yelled, over his shoulder, as he turned a corner into a side street. The oddly civilised threat hung in the air. Eva heard someone running behind her and the hotel's porter streamed past in his smart green uniform.

Several minutes later, the porter returned to where Eva sat on the pavement with several inquisitive commuters around her.

'Are you OK?' he asked, looking genuinely concerned.

'I'm fine,' she said, shakily. 'I take it you didn't catch him?'

The porter shook his head.

'Thank you for trying.'

A small crowd had gathered around Eva, who was staring at the smears of blood that had appeared on the concrete from her grazed hands.

There was a quiet ripple of German conversation and Eva felt herself being helped to her feet.

She looked at the owner of the strong pair of hands that had hoisted her up to a seated position.

A man with bright blue eyes, a narrow face and black hair slicked to his head. He gazed at her for a second and she stared back. Her heart double beat. He looked as if he was about to say something and then, without warning, he made a grab for her handbag and started running away with it in the other direction.

'Hey! *HEY!*'

Eva was taken by surprise. However, she set off after the man at a run. Without her phone, her passport and her bank cards she really would be helpless here.

'Come back!'

People along the street turned and stared as the two ran past, but this time no one stepped in to help.

Perhaps they could see the odds were stacked against her.

As she ran, Eva could feel herself becoming breathless. She was used to jogging, but not to this fast-paced sprinting. In a different situation, she might have wondered whether it was a good idea to be chasing someone down the street like this – and perhaps stopped and given up.

But she had eight months of self-defence training behind her.

And she was seeing red.

Or rather, she was seeing clearly.

This was no ordinary mugging. This was something to do with… with it all, with the man at Waterloo Station and, most of all, with the word 'kolychak'. Perhaps the text messages on the phone were what they wanted, perhaps not. She felt she would never find out what was going on if she stopped chasing this man now.

And so she pushed all the energy she had through her limbs, forcing her body to switch up another gear, even though all her muscles burned.

Ahead, the running man was coming to the edge of a busy main road. He threw a glance back in her direction and, when he realised Eva was the only person in pursuit, he slowed his pace.

And then he stopped running. Unexpectedly, he turned to face her.

Eva slowed down too until she was just steps away.

They stared at each other for several seconds.

He was short but powerfully built.

'Give me my bag!' she yelled, over the traffic noise, breathlessly, forced to rest with her hands on her hips to try and support her lungs, which felt as if they were about to collapse.

'You're brave to chase me,' he replied, apparently having no difficulty breathing.

Eva regretted the cigarettes she had smoked recently, as she attempted to fill her lungs.

'Probably unwise,' said the man, 'but brave.'

She ignored the threatening tone. 'Just give me the bag and I won't make any trouble for you.'

The blue eyes laughed back at her. '*You* won't make any trouble for *me*!'

Eva took a step towards him. 'You're holding something that doesn't belong to you. You're a thief.'

She wondered where this casual antagonism was coming from. This was dangerous – reckless. It was not just the confidence of knowing she could defend herself, this was attack. Something else was driving her now.

'Give me my bag,' she said, trying to sound bigger than she was.

The man laughed again and took a step backwards towards

the edge of the stream of traffic. Eva inhaled sharply, he was a hair's breadth from being clipped by the cars steaming past at high speed.

She glanced around. They were close to a set of traffic lights. Presumably, he was waiting for the lights to change so he could run through the traffic. She saw him glance sideways.

Then she ran at him.

Surprised, he took that too-soon step back towards the road, just as a large lorry came speeding the other way, too close to the pavement. The huge wing mirror clipped the back of his head at high speed, the sound of bone cracking seemed to echo off the surrounding buildings. The man was thrown to the ground as the lorry began to screech to a halt. Eva's bag launched into the air and landed almost at her feet. Behind the first lorry, a second was too close to stop and ploughed into the back of the trailer in front. Eva watched, horrified, as the tail end of the vehicle in front began to swing around in her direction, shunted from behind. She heard a voice screaming inside her head and bent down, just about managing to close her fingers around part of her bag before she ran at speed in the other direction. She kept moving, expecting at any second to feel the enormous vehicle hit her in the back. She was braced for the impact – but it never came. She kept running for several minutes; all she could hear behind her was the sound of crunching metal. When she finally stopped, two streets away, she heard an explosion.

Eva stood dazed for several seconds, gulping down air into raw, empty lungs and trying to calm the frantic beating of her heart. She shut her eyes as, in her mind, she saw the tail end of the lorry swing at her again. She shook her head.

Stop, she thought to herself. Stop thinking. Just stop.

She forced herself to empty her mind and take deep breaths. Then, she realised she was being watched. A man in a small papershop – perhaps drawn out by the distant noise – was watching her, expressionless.

She met his eye and smiled, then forced herself to put one foot in front of the other.

She swung her bag over her shoulder and continued onwards, trying to make her awkward, wooden gait less obvious. But she felt as if her body was frozen in shock. She was like the Tin Man.

She exhaled, for the first time in several minutes she realised. Quickly, she pulled a pair of sunglasses out of her bag and covered her eyes, which no doubt were bloodshot and wide. As she made her way back towards the direction in which she had come, she straightened her hair, wiped the sweat from her upper lip and forced herself to move as if she had no idea what had just occurred on the adjoining street. There was no way she could allow herself to be connected to that.

It wasn't actually that difficult – despite the incredible noise the crash had made, there was no screaming and shouting, no panicked running in the direction of the street. Most people would not assume the worst until they were presented with it – at least at first. Although she knew the sense of calm wouldn't last, at that moment everything around her seemed normal, so Eva forced herself to pretend she was part of the scene and not the devastation she had left behind.

Despite the sunglasses, she felt self conscious. Should she report what had happened to the police, tell them her part in all of it? She should, she knew she should. But she wasn't going to.

Walking through the doors to the hotel, she jumped as the porter put his hand on her arm.

'Are you OK? Do you want me to call the police?'

'*No*,' she said, a little too forcefully, 'thank you, I'm fine.'

He noticed the bag. His eyes widened in surprise. 'How did you get it back?' he said, obviously assuming she could not have done it herself.

'The kindness of strangers,' she mumbled and walked back through the hotel lobby towards the lifts.

She shared the lift with three businessmen in expensive looking suits. The mirrored panels of the elevator revealed that, despite her best efforts, she looked dishevelled.

Back in her room, Eva stripped off and stood under the shower for twenty minutes. Then, she began again the process of making herself look human – a change of clothes, more make-up, a blow dry – so that not a hair was out of place. She ordered a large brandy and a pot of coffee to her room, as well as a sandwich and a bowl of fruit. Finally, she sat down and prepared herself for the interview with the climate change expert. As if nothing had happened.

He knew he had compromised himself. As soon as that van pulled up next to his car on the street in London, he knew. But until the blackout blindfold was removed from his eyes two days later, he didn't quite know how much. He had been kept in the dark the entire time. He had not been allowed to eat, drink or use the toilet and he felt weak, disorientated and tense. Exactly as he was meant to feel. But there was also something else, a chemical haze around his senses that he couldn't place. And a pain under the skin of his head, as if something had been inserted there.

He blinked as he tried to adjust his eyes to the sudden influx of light after all the time in the darkness. It was too difficult, so he shut his eyes again.

He could hear voices in the other room but, whoever had removed the blindfold had then left. Obviously, as yet, they had nothing to say to him.

He tried to make out a sound he recognised, something that would tell him where he was. But he had been senseless for too long and he was struggling. He felt the urge to panic rising inside his chest. His ribcage began to expand. He clenched his fists and pinched his eyelids together until the need to react had passed, then he focused on making his breathing slow and regular.

What did he know? He knew he had been here for two days because he had heard the birds singing twice. But he did not know where 'here' was. When they had taken him off the street, they had gone to great pains to ensure he couldn't tell what kind of vehicle he was being transported in, or where he was going. By his guess, he was no longer on British soil.

He slowly started to open his eyes again, testing each eyeball against the harsh light filtering in through his raised eyelids.

When his eyes were fully open, he could make out the room around him. It was light-filled and was expensively furnished. It was an odd place in which to be tied to a chair.

But he didn't recognise it.

He strained to hear the conversation filtering in through a slightly open door on the other side of the room.

They were talking about Eva.

NINE

EVA HAD WRAPPED up her interview within an hour and a half. It was straightforward, she had been well prepared and, when it came down to it, the woman had very little to say. Eva had managed to extract the basis for a sound piece of writing, complete with some appropriate quotes, but it wasn't exactly going to be one for the portfolio.

What she hadn't anticipated was being met, after the interview, by one of the NGO's Berlin-based translators who had insisted he had intructions from the 'guys back in London' to take her out to a Russian restaurant on Boxhagener Straße. As he repeated in the face of her refusals, he took all London visitors to the restaurant when they were in Berlin, 'it's tradition.' Eva had politely declined – several times. She wasn't in the mood for anyone, particularly someone quite so irritatingly effervescent; but apparently she had no choice. The man had smiled and said jokingly 'it's part of your job to report back on the borsch,' and the painful realisation dawned on Eva that nothing would deter him. If she wanted to spend the night alone, she was going to have to be rude – he had given her no other choice.

In the end, manners had prevailed; she had smiled, agreed and he picked her up in a taxi from the hotel at 7 pm.

Now, she was sitting across from him, gazing at a giant wall painting of a Russian doll and attempting to spoon her way through a bowl of thick beetroot soup.

'So, do you like the borsch?'

'Uh huh,' she nodded, and spooned in another mouthful. It was earthy and sweet at the same time, but it was also heavy and she never seemed to see the bottom of the bowl.

'Such a flying visit to Berlin. You should stay longer, there is so much to see.'

'I don't have much say in when I come and go – it was really just to do the interview.'

'And did you get what you needed today?'

She nodded and took another spoonful of the beetroot soup. 'It was fine.'

Apart from being mugged this morning – twice, she thought to herself.

Just as she thought she could see the bottom of the soup bowl, a waiter stopped at their table and deposited a tray with two tall glasses full of clear liquid.

'You must try this vodka, it is one of the best.'

She put her spoon down and looked at him. This was the fourth time he had said that. What with the bottle of wine he had ordered to accompany the soup, she was feeling ever so slightly drunk. If she was honest there was nothing she wanted more, right now, than the numbing effect of alcohol. Whether giving in to that desire would be wise was another matter.

'Here,' he said, handing her the glass. 'Za zdarovye!'

He downed the shot of vodka in one go and then slammed the glass down on the table, in a great display of showmanship.

Eva picked up her glass and sipped from it.

'Oh, come on!' he said ebulliently, 'this is a *Russian* establishment. In honour of the nation that drinks like men, you must down it!'

Eva was about to protest – both at the slur against womankind's ability to handle alcohol and at another onslaught of pure liquor – but she had run out of energy. She was exhausted and could already feel the recklessness of passing her tipping point settling over her. The events of the last 72 hours had begun to fade into the comfort of alcohol. She couldn't pretend that wasn't welcome. So the shot was downed and Eva slammed the glass on the table in the same way her dinner companion had done. She felt the liquid running down her throat, fiery with heat and booze. One final spoon of the beetroot soup and she pushed the bowl away.

'So, what is it exactly you do here, Andre?'

He smiled at her, eyes flashing, as he topped up her wine glass. He was a small man, perhaps in his late 30s, with a shadow of middle age already creeping up on him. His dark brown hair was flecked with grey, his face was youthful although showing the telltale marks of late nights and too many cigarettes, but he was pleasant and chatty, despite his slightly pushy demeanour.

'I'm a translator and facilitator,' was his reply.

'Who for?'

'Mostly for your employer.'

Eva took a small sip of wine. She had a taste for alcohol now.

'Do they need someone based permanently in Berlin? I thought most of the staff was in London, Brussels or Luxembourg.'

She could see instantly that he didn't like the questioning. It was obviously not his role to reveal anything about his position here. Which was a little odd.

'Let's not talk about me, Eva, let's talk about you!'

'No, I'm interested, really. What's it like working for them in a city like this?' Andre was not the only one who could be conversationally forceful.

He stopped and took a drink, assuming a thoughtful expression.

'Well, I suppose it is like working for them anywhere in Europe.'

'But I don't really understand what it is you do.'

'I look after people they send here.'

'Do they send many people here?'

Eva noticed Andre's expression darken and she could almost feel his irritation across the table. He really didn't want to talk about this.

'I mean, it seems an odd place to have someone permanent,' she said, pushing him further, 'rather than Brussels.'

'I think maybe it's just convenient,' he answered lamely, before completely changing the subject.

Eva watched him as he pretended to read parts of the menu to her in Russian, as if he knew what he was talking about. Or perhaps he did.

His forced joviality was about as believable as his fake tan and Eva had a strong sense from him that something didn't fit.

As the meal came to an end, she had been relieved at the prospect of escaping from someone who had told her virtually nothing about himself the entire time she had spent with him. Andre, however, had other plans.

'Have you ever been to Berghain?'

Eva shook her head as they sat in the back of the taxi. She'd heard of the Berghain and the legendary Panorama Bar, but never actually been to the vast East Berlin club.

'Oh man, it is just the best club in Berlin!'

Eva gazed out of the window. Was she really in the mood for a night of techno?

'Seriously,' continued Andre, enthusiastically, 'it's like one of the best clubs in the world, the sound system is incredible. If you haven't been you should take this opportunity! Their door policy is super strict – especially with foreigners – but I know people. We won't even have to queue.'

Eva knew she had enough alcohol in her system for the prospect of a club to be appealing, and there was a certain desire to block out what had happened earlier in the day rather than go back to her hotel room and think about it.

But was this really the way she wanted to spend her night here? It had been a while since she had enjoyed the hedonistic release of an all nighter in a dark, sweaty club. And from what she knew of Berghain, it was very much an all night – and all day – event. When you were out of practice, the thought of that seemed rather intimidating.

'Where is it?'

'Ostbahnhof. Not far.' Eva caught a nod between Andre and the taxi driver and the car turned a smooth right before speeding along unexpectedly quiet streets.

'Is it open?'

'Eva, it's Friday!'

Eva looked at him, surprised. It appeared she had lost track of the days.

She pulled her phone out of her bag and that was the second surprise of the evening – it was almost 2am. She had absolutely no idea where the rest of the night had gone, after those four shots of vodka, but at least that explained why she felt so tired.

She sat back against the squashy seat of the taxi and watched Berlin's city streets flash past. At this hour, the buildings looked dark and intimidating, but the city was still very much alive and awake, and she felt a combination of anxiousness and excitement as the taxi drove on into the night.

Being in a foreign city was always the same mix of thrill and fear for her – liberation and vulnerability all rolled into one. It had been the same each time she had visited Jackson in Paris, too.

Jackson.

Suddenly, the phone call she'd received filtered back into her mind. She still had not worked out what was going on with that, and she was no closer to finding out what 'kolychak' was either. Sam had not replied to her request for help and had she forgotten the muggings that morning? She felt herself sober up. Surely this was a mistake. After everything that had happened during the course of the day – and after only a few hours sleep and a skinful of alcohol – it seemed insane to go and drink the night away in a club.

She suddenly sat forward in the taxi.

'Actually, I think I'd rather go back to the hotel.'

Her sentence hung in the air.

The taxi remained on its path.

Andre looked at her.

'I said…'

'No,' he said quietly.

A slight tremor of anxiety travelled down Eva's spine.

'What do you mean, no?' she said quietly, looking at the face turned in profile in the seat next to her.

For several seconds, Andre said nothing. Suddenly, Eva lunged for the door but he was faster than her and his hand was around the handle of her door before she managed to open it.

They both remained still, he with his arm across her holding the door shut, she frozen by surprise and trying to control her rapidly spiralling heartbeat.

He let go of the door.

She sat back in her seat. What had she been going to do anyway, throw herself out of a moving car? Her instincts were obviously all over the place, thanks to the booze and the heightened emotion of her current situation.

'Honestly, Eva, it's something you really must see, it's such an experience!' He was talking again as if the odd and slightly sinister incident with the door had not happened at all.

She nodded at him. For now, clearly, she had no choice. Weighing up the situation, she concluded they were going to a public space and, once out of the taxi, Andre could no longer control her movements. If she didn't like the situation, she would leave. Quietly, as the cab continued onwards, Eva tried to work the situation through logically, sensibly and rationally. And at the same time, she could feel the recklessness of the alcohol coursing through her veins.

In the front seat of the taxi, Joseph Smith allowed himself a small smile. Eva had not noticed him when she had entered the car and, even though he had spent most of the journey watching her in the mirror, still she didn't realise how close he was to her.

He could see she was scared. Her strong features were set in a determined mask of resolution – determination not to show fear and a refusal to be cowed by whatever this situation was. He sensed that she did not like Andre, that she found him weak somehow, worthy of little respect. She was intuitive. He appreciated that.

However, fear was not all he had seen in her eyes; there was excitement there, too – a thrill at the danger of launching herself into the unknown perhaps. A foreign city, a strange man, an environment that had a reputation for denial of social convention – most people might have swiftly retreated but not her.

He looked at her again in the mirror, as she watched the city outside the taxi. She was attractive, there was no doubt about that, but she was not his type. She was too strong, too determined, she gave off too much confidence. Although he would enjoy the challenge of breaking a wilful woman like her, it would take too much time. Besides, Eva was already marked for someone else, and he didn't need the complication in his life of crossing that person.

He was here only to do a job, a job he had learned to love, for all its challenges. He would never work in an office; his assignments inevitably involved spilling blood. Failure could mean the loss of colleagues, exactly as had happened in Paris – a situation Eva had been partially responsible for. Since then he worked alone, very much alone. He needed no one to assist him and he rarely liked to leave witnesses. Most of his work was done in dark alleyways and quiet side streets, in basements or abandoned buildings. He was skilled at the pain he could inflict – as the scientist had recently found out – and even more adept at using that pain to achieve his purpose; which was often to further someone else's ends.

He had learned to shut off – both from his victims and from his own personal pain. He didn't dwell, he simply forgot. Nevertheless, he repeatedly remembered that moment in the Paris park, when the dark-haired woman sitting in the back seat of his taxi had been trapped underneath him, lying on the cold hard ground and entirely at his mercy. He had thought about that many times since it had happened. Usually, when he was alone.

And there she was now, right behind him, once again at his mercy – although she didn't know it yet.

As far as Eva Scott was concerned, he was just another taxi driver. All she had to do was make eye contact with him and he felt she would know in an instant – he would see the recognition – but she wouldn't look, he knew that. Because he was just a taxi driver. And who ever looks at the eyes of a taxi driver?

TEN

EVA HAD BEEN expecting a basement on a Berlin street, perhaps an abandoned warehouse or factory building, but Berghain was something else. An enormous, intimidating former power station in the east side of the city, it was possibly the biggest club Eva had ever seen. The stark building was lit up in flashing primary colours from the inside and a huge queue snaked from the front entrance, back several blocks.

She looked at the queue. 'I'm not a huge fan of standing in lines.'

Andre flashed her a side smile.

'I never queue.'

Eva looked at him doubtfully. She knew what it took to jump a line of this size and Andre didn't look like someone who had it. In fact, he looked like an accountant.

They walked past the penned-in queuers at the front and Eva could feel the piercing stares from each person she passed. She recognised that feeling of indignation. The rage of being queue jumped.

Nevertheless...

When they reached the front, an enormous bouncer stopped them. Andre spoke in German and Eva felt appraising eyes on her. The only thing she really knew about this club was that it was notoriously hard to get into – the door policy was whatever the bouncers wanted it to be and, if they didn't like the look of you, there was no appeal. But after a terse nod, they were waved in, branded with a Berghain stamp and that was it.

Eva was vaguely impressed.

Inside, the building was vast. They passed through the

enormous room that housed the coat check and then climbed
a giant set of stairs up to one of the main dance floors. Hard
techno pumped out from skip-sized speakers and the industrial
space was a mass of moving bodies. For a moment, Eva felt
overwhelmed by the sudden assault of noise and light on her
senses. She blindly followed Andre as he directed her around
the edge of a dance floor of football pitch dimensions, pulsating
with bodies, and to stairs at the side up to the top floor.

'Panorama Bar,' he yelled happily, as he turned to her at the
top of the stairs.

She nodded. He obviously loved this place.

The room upstairs was less crowded. Andre ushered her
towards a large bar in the centre of the room and bought drinks.
Two shots of Jägermeister in plastic, thimble-sized containers.

The music in Panorama Bar was not quite the wall of sound
the other dance floor had been, but it was still loud. The bar was
vast and oval shaped, lined with people waiting to be served,
sitting at bar stools or just nodding along to the bassline while
people watching. It was surprisingly well lit.

Eva had to admit the club felt good. There was none of the
extreme drunkenness typical of the UK at this time in the
morning and, although she didn't doubt there were plenty of
people enjoying more than just a drink, it didn't feel messy or
out of control. Yet.

'See,' Andre yelled, over the vicious bassline, 'I told you it
was worth coming!'

Eva nodded and wondered whether she had yet made the
decision to stay and join in or to quietly slip off back to the
hotel. She hadn't paid for anything, she reasoned, so, at the
very least, she could wait a while and see what this place was
about. It felt oddly safe, as if the wall of sound was a defence
and the people around some kind of temporary community.

'You know,' Andre was yelling again, 'Berghain isn't just a
techno club.'

He smiled at her with what was clearly meant to be predatory intent but he had a purple piece of beetroot stuck between two of his front teeth.

'Oh?'

She knew what he was about to say. She had read about clubs in Berlin where sex in the basement was common currency, gay, straight or bi. She had never been to one, but that wasn't to say she hadn't imagined what it might be like.

'There's more to this place you know. What happens in Berghain stays in Berghain.' He winked at her. Eva felt he wasn't doing the club justice by reducing it only to the more salacious sides of its existence.

She looked hard at Andre trying to figure what he wanted. It bothered her that he thought it acceptable to hit on her when she was here in a professional capacity. Or had she given up the right to that boundary when she walked through the doors of the club with him. That shouldn't be the case but he seemed like the type who might see it that way.

Then, just as he had done earlier, Andre switched from sex pest to professional in seconds.

'Want to dance?' A lightly casual tone to his yell over the music.

Eva looked at him. What a strange way to behave.

He led her back down the stairs from Panorama Bar into the middle of the enormous dance floor. Eva had forgotten how much she enjoyed dancing to this relentlessly heavy beat and Andre was right, the quality of sound really was incredible. The music required precisely no thinking at all, just an instinctive, animalistic response. Thankfully, Andre kept his distance and so she decided to sweat out some of the frustrations of the past week or so. There had been no opportunity for running since she left London so this was a good substitute. Between the combination of the lights, the music and the detachment in her head, she didn't notice when Andre suddenly slipped away.

In the darkness of the early hours, the man with the Mediterranean tan was not looking quite so bronzed.

He brusquely nodded his head to a side room, where a figure sat tied to a chair. Of course, he was used to events such as these. Nevertheless, a live captive always made him feel vulnerable. It was high risk. His colleague, on the other hand, seemed to relish every minute.

'He has been tied up in there now for, what... a day? We can't leave him like that much longer.'

He should not have listened to Paul, that much was obvious now. What were his credentials for this kind of work anyway?

'Have you suddenly developed a conscience?' When the younger spoke it was almost a sneer – caught just in time.

That reveal was surprising.

'No. But I value my carpets, my young friend, and so far he has pissed three times. Besides, there are other factors to consider here. The longer we hold him, the more vulnerable the rest of our operations are. It's unlikely he is working alone, I'm assuming you have realised that.'

A challenge. Territorial.

The younger man stalked several paces to the right.

'Perhaps if you told me more about what those other operations are, I could make better informed decisions. I could even advise you.'

The idea of being advised by one so inexperienced was an impertinence too far.

'No, you could not.'

The two men locked eyes. Seconds passed, neither looked away.

'So what are you saying?'

'I'm saying that you need to eliminate him, enough of these games, we need to move on.'

'He is the test subject, it has to be right. The scenario

is almost ready, I just need to install the implants.'

'Almost is not good en...'

The younger man suddenly slammed his balled fist down on a small oak card table. The sudden movement shattered the stillness of the air around him but his gaze never wavered.

The older man began to feel its intensity. He saw revealed in the person opposite the hidden dimension that he had suspected from the start – volatile, violent, emotional. This was not strictly business for him. He looked at Paul again and something in the air between them sparked. Without meaning to, he dropped Paul's gaze. As he did so, he realised the landscape of the relationship had changed.

The younger man moved away from the card table, which seemed to be almost reeling from the blow.

'I do agree, the delay is not ideal, but we could proceed without the cranial implants,' said Paul huskily, rubbing the side of his hand. A conversational olive branch from the victor. That again was unexpected. The deference, the revolt, the release of contained violence and then... reconciliation? That was not how it went. This man – Paul – did not behave normally, he did not follow the rules. Perhaps he didn't know them. Either way, nothing that he said or did could be taken as genuine.

The man with the Mediterranean tan realised he was hesitating to respond.

'Do as you think. How much longer?'

'It's rather unpredictable. It may be in the hands of fate.'

'Fate is a fallacy.' No hesitation anymore.

'You don't believe in fate?'

Another flash point.

'No, the futures of those two men lie in their actions. As do ours.'

There was no response.

'We have him right here,' said the older man, nodding his

head towards the room in which the man was tied to the chair. 'We should just kill him now.'

There was a small movement from the side room and both men looked through the spacious doorway at the incapacitated figure. There was no way the bound man could hear their conversation at that distance. Nevertheless, they both lowered their voices.

'But we have already administered the doses – he is almost ready. And we must make sure this works before we test it on her.' His voice sounded almost nervy.

'This is not my technology, Paul.'

The younger man did not need reminding.

'It is not mine either.'

The conversation fell away into an unimpressed silence.

When Eva realised Andre was gone, she briefly experienced a moment of panic. The enormous room seemed to expand and contract as her brain processed that she was alone. She stood still and looked around. Faces bore smiles, most people were clearly having a fantastic time, it didn't feel threatening. In fact, this was probably the kind of club you could come to on your own.

She met the eyes of a tall blonde man who was dancing on a raised platform. He held out his hand and she allowed herself to be pulled upwards.

For a moment, she felt self conscious and then, as the bass found its way into her limbs, she once again began to dance.

Eva had no idea how long she had been on the podium when she felt a hand clutch at hers from behind. She turned to look over her shoulder and felt her balance shift but could see no one. She steadied herself quickly, the lights and the noise were a sensory disruption but it would not do to end up on her back on the floor. English-style loutish drunkenness would probably not go down well in here.

Then, the human contact was broken and the hand

withdrew. She looked down at her closed fist, able to feel something small and solid inside it. Had someone just handed her a pill? She looked around again for anyone making eye contact but the grey light and flashes of strobe prevented her from seeing who it was and her senses had been numbed by the Jäger and loud music. Perhaps this was part of Andre's role as fixer in Berlin.

She climbed down off the podium, hand still clasped around whatever was in it, and walked to the back of the dance floor to lean against a railing that looked down on the entrance hall.

She opened her palm to a small piece of paper. She straightened it out.

'Do not leave Berlin. All the answers you seek are here.'

Eva stared at the paper as, around her, the club night continued to roll on. She suddenly felt very out of place in this world of hedonist escapism, given everything that was happening to her – as the alcohol wore off, reality muscled in and she knew she could no longer indulge, she had to sober up.

Quickly, she pushed her way up to Panorama Bar, where the light was brighter. She joined the queue for the bar, waiting for water, the note playing over and over in her head. Was this actually directed at her? There was every chance this was simply coincidence – some local artist or Berghain lover encouraging people to see what was at the heart of this strangely beautiful and dark city. But there was also a chance it was not.

Suddenly, Eva felt irritated. She needed water and then she needed to go.

She stepped forward to wave at the barman and someone grabbed her wrist.

'Don't touch my beard.'

Eva looked in surprise at face of the man she had barely registered on the bar stool in front of her.

'I...'

'Shst!'

He shoved her arm aside with some force and stared at her. He had a large, bushy beard, flecked with ginger and grey, and his eyes bored into her aggressively. Large earrings hung inside the lobes of his ears, stretching them to great wide circles in the flesh.

Eva clenched her teeth, lowered her arm, turned and walked in the other direction around the oval shaped bar.

'Idiot,' she muttered to herself, rubbing the point on her wrist at which he had grabbed her.

She felt an urgent desire to leave.

She walked back down the stairs towards the main club space. It would be light soon, she wanted to return to the hotel and pack, well before her flight.

Back downstairs the music had become harder and the club seemed to be picking up the pace. The dancing was more energetic and there were casualties now, collapsed against a wall or slowly chewing through their own lips as they swayed robotically on the dance floor.

This wasn't a world she wanted to inhabit anymore. The bearded ogre had been the wake up call that this place, like anywhere else, could have its unwelcome, dark side. And she was now on her own.

She made a beeline for the exit.

Outside, it was still just about dark. The air was cold. She looked at her watch. 6.30am. There was still an enormous queue for the club, longer than when they had arrived.

She pulled on her jacket. Although she knew she should find a taxi she wanted to walk first, she needed fresh air.

As she moved away from the noise and chatter of Berghain, she started to feel slightly uncomfortable but still she kept walking.

The streets of East Berlin had an entirely different feel to the centre.

'You want some help?'

A couple was walking towards her.

'Are you lost?'

'I'm fine, thank you.'

It never seemed sensible in the early hours of the morning, in a dark city, to admit to being either lost or in need of help.

They looked friendly, though, this couple, didn't they? Berlin-hipsters but harmless enough, walking arm in arm towards her. Although their stares were intense.

Then the woman did something odd. She turned over the hand linked through her partner's arm so that the palm was facing up. But she didn't open her fingers, they remained closed as if she was gripping something very small.

They continued to walk towards Eva, only paces away now. She took a step towards them and then tripped on a jagged piece of pavement and began to fall forward. As she fell, she noticed the couple had unlinked arms and the woman had raised her flat hand to her mouth. Eva fell to the floor as she heard the woman exhale. She looked behind her to see a white veil of powder had fallen where she had been standing. She looked up at the woman, whose hand was now empty. The couple stared at her for several seconds, as if waiting for something to happen. Eva stood up and looked at them. No one spoke. She walked away.

ELEVEN

A BLACK HOOD had been placed over his head some hours earlier. This was now removed, allowing daylight to flood his retina. He squinted into the sun; stared straight ahead.

The first emotion: shock.

Opposite him, stood a man he had long thought lost.

Behind him, the sound of a car engine revving and wheels turning in the dust as a vehicle made its way into the distance at high speed.

He didn't turn his head left or right. He didn't acknowledge his surroundings. He just stared at the face opposite.

When he had taken the job that had brought him here he had known it was a risk. Eva *affected* him. She left him, if not defenceless, then seriously compromised. And they had history. Then there was the oddly vague job brief, one he clearly should have refused. But this, he had not expected.

Perhaps deep down he had known that watching Eva would mean opening a channel to the man opposite, her brother. Maybe a subconscious desire for redemption had led him here.

The other man was blinking into the evening half light, as his own hood had also been removed. He started touching points on his head and face – the same six spots, repeatedly. Was he checking for injuries? He stopped suddenly, when he sensed himself being watched.

Slowly, he lowered his hands to his sides, knuckles clenched. Leon did not see any recognition in his eyes.

They stared at one another and he wondered whether neither could make out if the staring contest they were gripped in was hostile or conspiratorial. Was there still that shared bond between them or had events since shattered it completely?

He continued to stare at the dark-haired man in front of him who shifted on his feet. A movement of discomfort, perhaps he had been sitting for some time, maybe he had been injured, or he could be nervous. Leon's mind jarred; it seemed out of character.

He glanced around and tried to make sense of his surroundings. It was hot, which meant that he was no longer in the UK. A quick look down revealed army fatigues. He had no weapon. And he had no shoes.

She opened her eyes. A dingy light, the kind that shines in a basement. The air was damp and smelt musty. For several seconds, she felt calm. She looked around her as if it was the most natural thing in the world to open your eyes to a scene like this. But then Eva began to feel uneasy. She couldn't move her arms and she realised they were stuck, spreadeagled on either side of her. Groggily, she noticed that she was sitting up, each wrist tied to the edges of a bed.

She looked down at her legs, jutting out in front of her at right angles. She was wearing a pair of long black socks and stiletto heels she didn't recognise as her own. She bent her knees to make sure she could move her legs. Several seconds after she sent the command from her brain, her legs moved.

Funny, she thought to herself, and then her mind went blank again.

They had shadowed each other for what seemed like several hours. Leon had tried to start a conversation with the other man but there had been no response. He kept an almost calculated distance from Leon – when Leon stopped, so did he, if Leon jogged towards him he moved so as to maintain the space. Under normal circumstances Leon would have simply lunged but two things had made him want to wait it out: he trusted that face and he knew how lethal Jackson could be. Nevertheless, he urgently wanted to talk to the man who shadowed him. They had known each other for so long that, surely, there must be the same desire on both sides. And yet, they had not exchanged a single word in the last couple of hours and the other man kept his distance. Perhaps he, too, was unsure of the familiar face he saw in front of him.

Although the timing of the situation had caught him off guard, Leon wasn't surprised to find himself where he was – he had made a lot of enemies during his 'career'. However, he could not have anticipated this particular opponent. And it was now clear that's what Jackson was.

In the fading light of the day, the face of the other man puzzled him. So very familiar, so long lost. And yet he felt so little affection for it. Was that purely self protection on his part? His failure had resulted in Jackson's death after all. Or at least that's what he had thought – until now.

Leon briefly glanced up at the darkening sky. He knew he was exhausted; he had been exhausted when they arrived.

He had considered running, escaping, but he knew that turning away would be a rookie mistake. He began to wonder if there were other options besides to fight. There was never just one choice. If only he had time to think. But he didn't. Leon realised that, for the first time, he was facing an enemy who had a mental advantage – and so the power to take from him the one thing he had ever really owned; his life.

'She's compliant enough.'

'Don't you think we should give her more, just in case?'

'No. Combined with the drugs they gave us to use on her it could be too much.'

'But I don't want to take any risks with her. We don't know anything about her, the fixer was vague.'

'She was wandering around drunk, on her own, in the early

hours of the morning; what more do we need to know?'

Eva sat completely still, watching two people she thought she recognised having a conversation in a language she didn't. She felt almost apart from her body. She could see what was going on and perhaps didn't like it, but there was no connection to any emotional response.

She watched as the woman turned away from the man, frowning and shaking her head. She caught Eva's eye and, instantly, Eva realised where she had seen her. It was the couple who had been walking towards her when she left somewhere earlier that – day? night? – she smiled at the woman in recognition. The woman looked pained and glanced the other way.

'Look, she's too conscious for this, you can see it in her face. She will *remember*.'

'We can't stop this now.'

'I'm not saying we should stop, I just think maybe she needs more.'

'Why?'

'Because she looked at me like she recognised me. She might be able to identify us.'

'She won't remember, that's the whole point.'

'I don't see why they can't make do with hookers. And why all these additional drugs?'

'This way is more dangerous, it's a thrill for them. I don't know about those,' he indicated several clear plastic bags of liquid, 'that's not up to us.'

The woman turned towards her partner. 'But it's dangerous for us, you know that – especially if we don't know the whole story. We have to protect ourselves.'

The man hesitated. He was tall and thin and smelled of clothes that hadn't been aired properly. Or, perhaps, his damp aroma was simply because he spent so much time in a basement.

'I'm not sure.'

'Come on,' his partner urged, 'it's our interests that matter, not hers.'

'Ok, fine, if you want to then give her another dose.'

Eva watched, quite comfortably, as the woman reached for a small plastic bag and made to tip a white powder into the palm of her hands.

'Don't blow it in her face this time!' said the man suddenly. 'It will go all over her.'

The woman – small and blonde – slowly nodded in agreement. She found a curved tumbler and poured a small amount of water from a tap situated on a white basin fitted into the corner of the room. Then, she dropped the white powder into it.

He hadn't seen him coming. Perhaps it was the hunger, the disorientation, or the fact he had taken his eye off the ball, for just a second, to consider his options. But he had not seen it coming. That was not like him and there were few other men who could take him unawares, not with his training. He was now fielding blow after blow. A punch to the side of the head made his ears burn and ring. A low stab with a clenched fist to the solar plexus forced him to bend double in agony. For some reason, he felt unable to defend himself, he couldn't even stand up. When it came down to it, he realised this was the one person he couldn't – wouldn't – fight. And, of course, that had been intentional. That was why Jackson was here.

As the blows rained down on him, Leon felt this was the moment he had spent so much of his life trying to escape. Disconnection of body and soul. Perhaps it had been over as soon as he saw the man's face and recognised, in those features, the anger over his betrayal all those years ago. Inevitable.

And now that it was over it was almost a relief. He would no longer have to deal with the constant struggle between right and wrong that had recently become his daily internal monologue.

He deserved this. Maybe it was even what he wanted.

As acceptance descended, he felt his body relax and the air around him seemed to tense, to vibrate at a slower pace. He was waiting for the final blow, the one to extinguish the light and leave him in the comfort of darkness.

And then, in the pale light of a fingernail moon, he suddenly saw something change in the face of the man opposite. It flickered, almost imperceptibly, but it was there – almost as if a mask was being lifted to reveal the real face underneath. And that stirred something in Leon. He began to fight back.

'I have no idea how he got the knife.'

'*Well, he clearly didn't buy the face.*'

Silence.

'I don't understand,' said Paul finally, 'our man must have been carrying it – against the order I gave him.'

'I think your problem is that you underestimate people,' replied the man with the Mediterranean tan, 'the technology doesn't work, we should report it.'

'No!' the younger man was indignant. 'You don't understand, this should be foolproof. It was just because we couldn't put the implants into him.'

'It is faulty – or unfinished.'

Paul lit a cigarette and turned away. 'Do you think he really saw beneath?' he asked, childlike. 'The drugs and mapping alone should have been enough for such short exposure.'

At first, the older man didn't respond. Then, finally, 'he must have, what other reason could there be?'

Angrily, the young man threw his cigarette on to the floor and ground it down with his heel. He lit another.

'He should have been the one to die.'

'The risk you took was too great. We should have executed him when we had the chance.'

The older man was right, Paul knew that. But he had been so

sure that such a painful, humiliating and emotionally draining revenge was the satisfaction he needed. To watch Leon unable to fight, paralsyed by his own guilt. Guilt that he had seemingly never felt for the death he had visited on others – others who had once meant so much to Paul.

But it had not worked. The technology had failed – or rather he had left it incomplete, made a mistake.

Silence hung in the room as Paul lit another cigarette and the older man continued gazing at the screen of a wafer-thin laptop.

'What are you doing?' asked the younger man, finally. He felt as if the ground was shifting beneath him and he needed the balm of normal conversation.

'Checking the grid.'

Paul continued to smoke in silence.

'Where are we with the corporate identities?'

The question was posed in a completely different tone to the way the man had spoken to Paul earlier. A point had been made and they were moving on. This, Paul liked about his new colleague. What he didn't like was that, at some point, what happened today would be used against him. In the short time he had been here, Paul had realised the other man stored up events as weapons against others. Against anyone who could do him damage. He had a harmless, Gentleman Criminal, exterior but he was, in reality, ruthless, efficient and deadly.

Paul set aside the plans formulating in his mind concerning the escaped man. He would still be able to deal with the situation, it would just take more time and imagination. He had not lost. It was not over. He began to compose himself. For now, he had to keep a neutral front.

Quickly, he put out the cigarette and took a chair at his position at the table, accessing his own laptop. He spent several seconds working his way through electronic files.

'Most are already registered and running.'

'Most?'

'Ninety-five per cent.'

'And the rest?'

'Within days.'

'Are they proofed?'

'I…'

'As in, will they stand up to full scrutiny?'

'They are based on the exact model developed.'

'So they are impenetrable?'

'Yes, they should be. Completely disassociated corporate entities. No connections can be made by sector or location.'

'All of them?'

Paul looked at the grid. The lines splayed out from each name on the page but went nowhere. There were no connections made between them, no links.

'According to the grid, not a single one.' Paul was careful to choose his words properly – he must answer based on what was in front of him and not his own opinion or the responsibility for getting it wrong would land on his shoulders. He was learning.

'And where do we stand in terms of ownership?'

'We are on target.'

'No alerts?'

'No.'

'Any interest from the FCA?'

'None.'

'Authorities abroad?'

'No.'

'So the activity has gone unnoticed.'

'It would seem so.'

Paul nodded silently. He marvelled at the preparation that had gone into this – the foresight of paying off a myriad of insiders for ten years before they might be required to do anything. And he wondered, most of all, where the money for this had come from. He understood vaguely what was happening – to the extent he had been told before he had even begun this journey – but there was obviously more.

Paul knew he needed additional information to piggyback on the situation. He also knew that he was walking a relatively precarious line. Soon, his own contribution would really be tested – the reason they had taken him on. And, if he was going to achieve the results he needed to, that contribution would have to live up to expectations. Which, so far, it hadn't. So far, he had failed. And, in this company, that was a dangerous position to be in.

'Infrastructure contracts?' The questioning continued.

'Ahead of schedule. All key utilities and public service provision.'

'And the shares?'

'We already have volume to wield a controlling interest in most.'

'Do you know, I really hate the vagueness of "most"?'

He did know that.

'We have a controlling interest in 85 per cent,' came the amended response. For the first time, the older man looked satisfied. 'This is good,' he said quietly.

TWELVE

THE SUN WAS burning the bare skin on his forearms. He could feel the stinging sensation of cooking flesh as he lay motionless on the ground. He opened his eyes and tried to push himself into a sitting position. Dust rose from the dry earth with the movement; he began choking on it. His arms gave way and he fell back to the ground.

As he lay on his back, Leon became aware of being watched. He turned his head to the right.

Dead eyes glared back at him.

The other man lay motionless.

Momentarily, Leon wondered whether he was actually dead but there was no way he could have survived the knife wound, a cut made sharply under his ribs, splitting the flesh and piercing his heart.

As Leon's eyes focused, he saw a dark area around the body where the blood had seeped into the sand. He looked again at the face opposite.

It was not Jackson.

A dull pain in his ankle interrupted the thought process. Gradually, the pain grew less dull, growing in intensity. He gritted his teeth as the sensation seemed to radiate throughout his body, waves of warm agony almost too much to bear.

After several seconds, adrenaline gave him just enough strength to drag himself upright and he could see the bloody mess of flesh just below the ankle bone. The other man had tried to slash the tendons in his ankle but the knife had cut millimetres to the left. It was a piece of luck, nothing more. But it had allowed him to live. Leon pulled the leg of his combats back for a better view; the flesh was crawling with insects. He could feel their fast-moving bodies, consuming his rotting flesh; realisation dawned: danger. Infection. Frantically, he began to clear the wound of seething movement. How long had they been feasting on his broken skin?

His movements were laboured. He must have at least one broken rib, he thought, and there would surely be more damage visible once he got behind an X-ray machine.

With enormous effort, he cleaned the wound as best he could, wrapping it in a strip torn from his shirt to protect it. Then he was on his bare feet, looking around. His head was spinning, his eyes unfocused. The fear that he was beyond help, that death might be imminent, washed over him. He had to get help. He had to get help.

He felt his pockets but they were empty. He looked around him.

There was nothing other than the man who lay dead, his face a mess of angry purple bruising where Leon had been unable to hold back his anger. Quickly, Leon limped over to the deceased and searched his pockets. He took the knife and searched for a phone but there was none. He did, however, find a bulging money clip, an Omega Seamaster watch and a tiny remote control, single button, of the kind that would open a garage door. Other than that, there was nothing but a single black business card – 'Veritas'. He took it too and, once again, felt an urgency to move.

He glanced around.

The landscape felt African to him. Perhaps north African.

It was arid, dusty and dry and the sun was incredibly strong. It was high in the sky, so he must have been lying there all morning.

He turned his face to the sun and began limping towards it. There was no way of knowing where he was, or which was the best direction to take, but he must begin to move, to make decisions and, hopefully, find help along the way. If he did not, he would die.

He did not want to die.

Before, it had felt inevitable but now... after what he had seen. No.

Every step brought sharp pain in his right ankle and severe discomfort each time the bandage touched raw flesh underneath.

As he tried to force clarity through the pain radiating from all over his body, he realised he could see on the horizon the dark outlines of buildings. He began to move faster, dragging the injured leg that would not move quickly enough.

He had to get help.

Slowly but surely, the horizon loomed closer. He was approaching a settlement. It looked small and remote but there would be a mobile phone. There was always a mobile phone.

When she awoke that evening, Eva could remember almost nothing of what had happened to her since she left the club the night before. She was lying in bed fully dressed but when she started to undress she found she was wearing a pair of long black socks underneath her jeans. She stared at herself in the mirror. She looked like a character from a porn film. The socks finished at her thighs, although one had rolled down when she removed her jeans. The look was at odds with the rest of her underwear.

They are not mine.

Her heartbeat began to flutter. She didn't own a pair of socks like this.

She sat, fell back onto the bed. Her head began to swim.

Who had put them on her? Who did they belong to?

Confusion and disbelief began to whisper and then scream in her ears. What had happened to her? Why didn't she know? Automatically, she raised her hands to cradle her head, to try and trigger some memory. But there was nothing there. There was just nothing there.

As she lowered her hands, she noticed she had bright red marks around her wrists. She gazed at them and began to rub them. The flesh was sore, it had been cut in places.

She looked from the black socks to her wrists and back again. It was like a nightmare. If she could just remember.

'Remember,' she said to herself, rocking slightly forward, '*remember!*'

But her mind was just a dense grey fog.

She began clawing at the black socks, tearing them from her legs. She bundled them up and threw them into the bin, then ran to the door of her hotel and checked it. It was not locked from the inside.

She stumbled backwards.

Could someone really have broken in and done this to her? Could she somehow have done this to herself? Eva had had more than her share of painfully embarrassed awakenings after a drunken night out but this was something else. This was more than drunk texting abusive messages to an ex or throwing up in the street. She had never blacked out like this before.

She forced herself to calm down by sitting on the bed and taking deep breaths for several minutes. Then she checked the rest of the room to make sure there was no one still there. She indulged all her wildest worries and looked for hidden cameras, condom wrappers, any sign that she might not have been in there alone. She checked her bag for her phone and wallet, both were still there. What on earth had happened to her?

She was half-inclined to call Andre and ask him whether he had seen her leave but one thing she did remember was that, by the time she left the club, he was nowhere to be seen. But that was all she could remember. Almost at that exact point, her memories stopped.

Slowly, she stood up and headed for the shower, trying not

to allow rising waves of anxiety to take hold. Had she taken something? Had she been spiked?

She had felt absolutely fine when she left the club. Perhaps a little drunk – drunk enough to think it was a good idea to set off into the city on her own to find a taxi in an area she didn't know – but she hadn't felt drugged or high, which was something she should have been able to identify. Eva began running the shower and clouds of steam billowed into the bathroom. She turned the heat right up and stepped under the scalding stream of water. She began scrubbing furiously at her skin. She wanted to be outside it. Why had this happened to her?

Panic continued to pluck at her mind.

Again, she had to physically force herself to slow down her breathing and her thoughts. She did not feel as if she had been raped. She would know.

She began to breathe normally.

She turned the heat down on the shower.

She stopped scrubbing at her skin, closed her eyes for several seconds and reached for the shampoo.

That's right, she thought to herself, if something like that had happened, I would feel it. There would be damage – bruising at least. Wouldn't there?

She looked down at her thighs and felt the flesh around her middle and back, but nothing hurt. In fact, other than her wrists, she didn't even feel she had been touched.

Try to make sense of this, she told herself, don't fall into fear and become overwhelmed. But her mind felt clouded.

She began to force herself to think backwards. The last thing she remembered was the moment Andre had disappeared. Or was it? No, she knew she had left the club and she knew she had been on her own trying to find a taxi. So, what had happened between that point and this? Eva tipped her head back and allowed the warm water to soak her hair. Another memory began to surface. Two people – a couple – walking towards her in the dark, and the woman...

Eva stopped shampooing her hair. She remembered the strange movement the woman had made with her hand, lifting it to her mouth, opening her palm and apparently blowing something at Eva. That was odd.

But it was also a clue. More of a clue than she'd had several seconds ago.

Eva felt her mind begin to settle; the ground returned to beneath her feet. She had something to go on, she could take some action.

Nevertheless, she was still shaking.

She quickly finished her shower, wrapped towels around her trembling body and cocooned her hair then walked back to the bed. There, she took her laptop and typed 'drug you blow in someone's face' into Google.

She hadn't, of course, expected anything to come up, but there were pages and pages on it.

The results made her heart beat faster. Numerous links discussing a VICE documentary about a drug called 'scopolamine' – the 'world's scariest drug'. It could be administered by being blown into someone's face. It was a drug that rendered someone incapable of exercising free will. Victims became docile and helped the perpetrators of the crime being carried out against them. Women had been drugged and gang raped or rented out as prostitutes, tourists relieved of all their cash at ATMs.

The drug came from Colombia, but most of the information the search engine generated suggested it was already quite widespread across Europe, so there was every chance there would be some here in Berlin.

But why use it? And why her?

Eva curled up on the bed. She looked at her phone and saw all the texts and missed calls from Sam and others wondering why she had not come home that day. When she got out of the shower, she'd noticed a note from reception telling her she would be charged for another night after apparently failing to hear all the polite knocks on the door. That was fine. She wanted to stay exactly where she was. Until she worked out what had happened to her, she didn't feel she could go anywhere.

Several hours later, Eva began to experience flashbacks to a basement space and the distinct impression she had been tied to a bed, maybe even handcuffed. She looked at the black socks she had retrieved from the bin and then spread out on the bed opposite. They were cheap, bad quality and, clearly, only for one purpose. The fact she had been dressed in them, and fastened to something, was terrifying. But she had a choice about how to react to this now and she could not help herself if she fell apart. She still didn't feel as if she'd had sex with anyone, and she knew she would feel it if that was what had happened. But could she really be sure… the uncertainty brought the panic back. She quietened both. No, she could not be sure but she had to be practical. She was alive; apparently uninjured. Concerns about anything having been transmitted to her could be allayed with tests. And besides, there was little she could do about that right now. What she really needed to establish was why this had happened and whether she was still in any further danger. She wished she could remember something else – anything – but from what she had read about scopolamine that was unlikely to happen. Ever.

She used the internet on her phone to search for scopolamine and Berlin. There was nothing reported on any of the digital news sites but several forums popped up with entries from local Berliners afraid of the arrival of this new and scary drug.

Some were in German but, of the English entries, she was particularly interested in posts on a forum offering support to those who felt they had been spiked – there were several people convinced they had been a victim of the drug. They were always women, they were around the same age as she was, and they were usually walking home at night, although none was in the area she had been in, most seemed to be further east.

More worrying were posts from people who seemed to be searching for a woman who had gone missing in the same circumstances, in the same area. For them, there were even fewer answers than she had, Eva realised.

He had borrowed a phone from a teenage boy at the settlement – who seemed to have nothing to his name other than that devise and whose eyes had almost bulged out of his head at the sight of the bills in the money clip. Thanks to the dated piece of technology, Leon had made enough calls to get himself out. He sat in a state-of-the-art medical room as his injuries were noted and categorised, checked and treated. They had offered him strong pain meds but he knew he couldn't afford to be even slightly off his game and, besides, that always seemed to trigger a relapse in his drinking. He had to reach Berlin and he had to return to the job he had been doing when he had been taken – that was even more important now. The man he had seen had been real enough, his bruises were a testament to that. But his face… it just didn't make sense. None of it made sense.

Eva was screaming when she woke and the thundering on her hotel door added to the terror she felt in the darkened room. She struggled to clear the sleep from her head as the banging on the door continued and it took several seconds to realise the voice was asking – in English – whether she was alright. She gulped down several breaths of air and quickly reached for the light. Under the sheets she was dressed so she walked quickly to the door, looked through the spy hole and, seeing a man in a jacket with a name tag, pulled open the door.

'Are you ok, Miss Scott?'

'Yes, I'm sorry.'

'It's just that we had a call from one of the other residents. They said it sounded as if you were being attacked.'

'I'm fine really. I'm sorry, it was just a nightmare.'

'You were sleeping?'

'Yes, what time is it?'

He looked at her strangely. 'It's 5pm.'

Eva had slept for most of the afternoon. She looked at the man. She could think of nothing else to say.

It was obvious he was waiting for something from her – some other explanation, an apology, perhaps a tip – but she was so tense she could hardly breathe. She desperately wanted to shut the door.

Finally, he nodded and she watched unmoving as he began to back away.

Eva pushed herself to action and quickly shut the door. As the locking mechanism clicked home, she leaned heavily against it. She shut her eyes and slid slowly down the door until she was sitting on the floor. She cradled her head in her hands, a low moan coming involuntarily from her. Why was she so panic stricken, she didn't feel as if she could cope.

She screwed her eyes shut.

The image was still there. The one she had awoken with.

It was a basement room. Her legs – in those socks – on a bed. Then there was nothing but black and screams. The couple she had seen outside the club, slumped on the floor, eyes lifeless, blood everywhere. And then – the thing that scared her most – the last image branded on her mind in that dark hotel room. A face.

Joseph Smith.

THIRTEEN

HE LOOKED AT himself in the mirror as he dressed in the bedroom of his suite. His face was shadowed and his eyes still bore the telltale dark circles of going without sleep for far too long. He couldn't remember the last time he hadn't looked like that. He had left a half-centimetre of stubble covering his cheeks and chin. It changed his appearance very slightly, no bad thing. But he had not gone for a full disguise. Whilst his instinct was he should be dead – that this had been the intention – he was aware of the threat to his safety now and, as far as he was concerned, awareness was all he needed to keep himself alive. Or perhaps, after all this time, he simply wanted to be found.

He pulled on a pair of charcoal grey trousers, cut close to the broad muscles of his thighs, and buttoned up a crisp white shirt. He was travelling business class to Berlin and he wanted to appear the faceless businessman. Except the suit was Tom Ford, as were the shoes.

He stopped and looked again at the mirror. Piercing dark eyes stared back at him. There was a moment of weariness, of the kind he had begun to experience more and more as the years had gone on. A feeling this could not be *it*. That there must be more. The thought itself sapped his energy, so he banished it as quickly as it had come.

He pulled on the suit jacket which, of course, fitted perfectly. He could understand why people would pay tens of thousands of pounds for 'couture'. It was like wearing your own skin, only better.

He briefly wondered what Eva would make of seeing him

in such an expensive suit. And then, even more intensely, he wondered about the moment when they were face to face. Would the light of recognition flare in her eyes or was he too changed and had too much happened?

He found himself fantasising the moment. How her dark eyes would widen – in surprise, disbelief, shock? Her hand would probably fly to her mouth as always happened when she was surprised. And then... and then what? He had no idea whether he would meet resistance or acceptance. He didn't want to think about it.

The phone rang and, in two large strides, he was beside it, receiver in his hand.

'Yes.'

'Your taxi is here, sir.'

'Thank you.'

He put the phone down and scanned the suite for anything forgotten. He'd had nothing when he arrived, so there was little to remember. All his essentials had been sent to him covertly, in the usual way, and the rest he had purchased in London's finest stores, even though it galled him to waste so much money on everyday items. But he was following a pre-arranged plan and, because of that, he was not entirely autonomous.

He pulled the keycard from its holder by the door and the suite fell into darkness. He hadn't even drawn back the curtains the entire time he was there and he realised, suddenly, he wasn't sure whether it would be light outside. He shook his head angrily. Five years ago, that would not have happened, he would never have become so preoccupied with his thoughts.

He was changing.

Eva sat and stared at the piece of paper in her hand.

'Do not leave Berlin. All the answers you seek are here.'

She put it down on the thick, satiny brown coverlet on the double bed, writing side up. She folded her legs underneath her and continued to stare at it, but no answers appeared.

Eventually, she slid down so that she was lying on her side, still looking at the piece of paper.

She closed her eyes. She was tired, her body ached, but her mind was restless.

It was now 7pm. She still couldn't get Joseph Smith's face out of her head. But why had she dreamed about him?

She had assumed the elements of her dream that had been drawn from reality were just fiction, but what if they were not? What if that had been a memory? A drug like scopolamine was an unknown quantity, she had never taken it before so she couldn't judge the most likely scenario. Which made her feel shaky and nervous. It did not help that she still felt drugged, the edges of her consciousness smudged.

Eva pushed herself back up so that she was sitting and then stood. With sudden energy, she began changing out of the leggings and T-shirt she had originally put on, into dark, tight jeans and a lightweight jumper – an almost fluoro shade of orange, in sharp contrast to her current mood.

She pulled on her coat and boots, grabbed her small, battered satchel, threw her phone and purse into it and strode towards the door, pulling the key card from its holder as she did so.

As the lights went out, the piece of paper that had been lying on the bed fluttered to the floor and landed writing side down.

Seconds later, she was striding along the thick, patterned carpet of the hotel corridor; she knew she had to move fast. If she didn't go outside the hotel, fear would overtake her and she wouldn't be able to do it.

She stood in the lift with two businessmen and a woman wearing a clinging gold dress, which shimmered in the bright lights. Eva tried not to choke on the vanilla-scented perfume, filling the lift so full it was almost tangible.

At the ground floor, she let the other guests exit before her and followed. Footsteps strong, stride firm. She was going to do this. Her heart felt as if it might explode.

She could see, through the glass doors of the hotel, it was dark outside.

Her memory-less brain terrified her. But she couldn't be in that room anymore. Or inside her own head. It was not a happy place.

As she crossed the lobby, she slowed her pace. Where was she even going? But she didn't stop. She just needed to be outside.

She pushed her way out through the hotel doors, stood and took some deep breaths. She glanced around – no one was paying her any attention. Of course they weren't, why would they?

Eva's reality had sometimes suffered at the hands of mild paranoia – she had never crossed the line into being unable to distinguish between the two but there had been times when it was blurred. Her life had been a series of lies, important people had concealed the truth from her at key moments. Sometimes this made it difficult for her to trust that the world was what it seemed to be. Wasn't it all a matter of perception anyway?

Eva tended to take what people said with a pinch of salt, which could isolate as much as protect. But recently – especially today – there was cause to indulge paranoia. And she had. However, now she had to distinguish her instincts from fear, even if it was instinct driving her out into the night. That was the thing about instincts, they often didn't seem to make sense.

With one last glance to left and right, Eva crossed the road from the hotel and set off along the pavement towards the nearest S-Bahn station. She had spent the last two hours alternating between fits of panic and fear, until she could not take it any longer. It had occurred to her that some clarity might be provided if she could go back – retrace her steps to the point where she left the club Berghain. It might trigger a memory and that was what was really driving her mad – the lack of information about what had occurred.

The next morning, she would have to return to London. She could not spend any more time or money on this trip. Which meant she had a matter of hours to do this or it would have to be forgotten forever – and, frankly, that was more frightening than the idea of being attacked again. At least, if the crime were repeated she might be able to find some answers.

The thought of being outside – vulnerable again – had terrified her. But the longer she sat in that hotel room waiting for someone else to solve the problem, the more afraid she would become.

The entrance to the S-Bahn station looked like an underpass to get mugged in.

Great, Eva thought, pulling her coat tighter around her.

Like many locations she had come across in Berlin, there was a random, inexplicable air of aggression or danger, as if something unspeakable had once happened in the spot and left behind a ghost of a feeling. Or perhaps she was imagining it.

She walked quickly into the station and began putting coins into the slot of the ticket machine. She bought a single to Berlin Ostbahnhof. She would have to do the rest on foot. Then she began to walk to the platform.

And that's when she began to feel uneasy.

For some reason, she kept walking towards the other end of the platform, keen to move away from the station entrance and maybe conceal herself behind a pillar until the train pulled into the station. She was sure she could hear it coming now. The faint rumble that indicated, in any mass transit system in the world, that a train was on its way. She checked which side the train would come in and then looked nervously up and down the track. Why were the hairs standing up on the back of her neck?

She pulled her sleeve back from her arm and looked down. Goosebumps. *Instinct.*

She found a wall to lean against and casually glanced down the platform towards the exit. Had she heard footsteps behind her as she walked to this spot? Or was she simply imagining that because she was scared? She pulled her sleeve back down to her wrist and took a step away from the wall.

At that moment, the whooshing and rumbling of the train became louder. It was almost at the station. She took another tentative step towards the edge of the platform, steadied herself as a silent gust of wind made her wobble slightly. She was just a pace from the edge of the platform now, ready to step into the warmth and light of the train. Where there would be other people and she could stop listening to paranoid thoughts circling around in her brain.

What happened next was so fast and so violent that Eva had no time to react. A pointed force smashed her hard between the shoulder blades, forcing her body to contract backwards and projecting her forward at the same time. She felt herself being pushed in the direction of the train track. Out of the corner of her eye, she could see the yellow train approaching. She resisted the force from behind, compelling her towards the tracks, but she was dizzy and her balance was shot. Then, with one final shove, the force released her and she fell forward. She turned as gravity dragged her down, her shoulder clipping the front of the S-Bahn train which bounced her straight back on the platform with its forward momentum. She skidded, stumbled and then fell against the wall separating the two directions of the platform. And there she sat like a rag doll.

'There has been a lack of caution. We have taken too many chances.'

There were four people in the conversation, two in the room and two via video link.

The man with the Mediterranean tan was projected large on to the screen. He looked angry. 'I don't think you realise the pressure we've been under. The deadlines have been incredible – unrealistic and almost completely unmanageable. You have parachuted someone in at the last minute, it has disrupted everything.'

'But… you have managed it haven't you?'

'No! I told you, we're already behind schedule and the additional issues – the failure of this technology – have left us in a very compromising position.'

'Are all three of them free?'

'Yes. For now.'

'And what do you think they will do next?'

'Heaven knows!' the man was becoming exasperated. He disliked this cold, logical approach, the appraising and the rationing, a life lived like that was a life lived at half speed. Action was what mattered. Besides, if he had not been forced to incorporate Paul into his plans, none of this would have ever arisen. 'Honestly, how do you expect me to predict what they will do next?'

There was a tense silence in the room and across the video connection.

'It's your job,' was the cold response.

'Not strictly true.'

Again another silence. He knew he was pushing it.

'This is a serious threat,' came the voice from the screen, 'and you are both responsible. You will resolve it.'

The man's voice had assumed an unmistakably authoritative tone. Perhaps he had had enough pretending in this partnership. They were, after all, not really partners.

'I don't understand what you expect me to do about this.'

'You must make it work. There is not much time.'

FOURTEEN

THE DRIVER OF the S-Bahn train had been almost hysterical. Eva had heard him shouting at someone. She had heard his panic from her hiding place in the dark recesses of the entrance to the ticket hall, where she had pressed her shaking body into a half open doorway and waited for the noise level to die down. She had no idea what he was saying but she could hear the high pitch of his voice and the way his sentences were punctuated with semi-hyperventilated inhalations of breath. She clutched at her shoulder and held it tight as she waited for the chance to escape to her hotel. She didn't want to cry and ask for help but this pain was very real. Her biggest concern was she might have punctured something internally. The rest would heal but, presumably, that could kill her.

Why was this happening? She shut her eyes and tried to block out the waves of pain washing over her from the tip of her shoulder across her back and neck. But she couldn't and she began to cry softly.

He had, of course, visited Berlin many times but never so conspicuously. Usually, his MO was staying below the radar, being as inconspicuous as possible, but this time there was no point. They knew he was there, he knew they knew and, from the information he had, there was little sense in trying to conceal his movements or where he was going. Stand up and fight – face them. Finally. He was glad that was the path chosen, it suited him far better than being on the run.

'Mitte, please,' he said as he entered one of the cream-coloured taxis waiting in line at the airport.

The driver nodded at him in the mirror and pulled the car out into the lanes to take them into the city. It was dark outside and the cover of the velvety blackness always gave him more comfort than the bright, harsh, revealing light of day.

He had chosen to fly into Berlin Tegel as he was familiar with the strange, circular airport and, without luggage, he had known he could go from his seat to the taxi in less than 15 minutes. Normally, he hated the exposed nature of these small airports, where anonymity was virtually impossible, but on this occasion he had been grateful for it. Now, as he sat in the back of the air conditioned taxi, watching the lights of the city flash past, he felt the flaws in all his planning pinching at the edges of his consciousness. He knew that, for all his predicting, foresight and rigid organisation, there was one unpredictable factor in all of this – Eva.

He had never been able to read her. Whether because she followed her instincts rather than doing what she should do, or was just very good at keeping her real feelings concealed, he didn't know. Either way, she had taken him by surprise more times than he cared to admit – even without meaning to – and, as she had neither formal training, nor apparently any intention to mislead him, that made her mercurial to deal with.

It was that instinct. He thought hard as the cab took him from leafy suburban streets and further into the heart of the city. For most people, instinct had become a dumbed-down reaction, something that was subject to guilt and fear, to the manipulation of advertisers and personal drive for wealth and personal status. Few people could hear their inner voice these days – or few cared to listen. This made them powerless, easy to read and simple to manipulate.

But not Eva. Somehow, Eva was fully plugged into her instinct – or most of the time at least. And that meant she could read people and situations almost as well as he could. Luckily for him, she didn't know this and she occasionally hesitated.

He wondered whether it was the life she had led – such adversity and so much to deal with from such a young age. Not for Eva the mind-numbing ties of an early marriage, the security of a predictable childhood, a regular job, a life that made her feel safe. She had existed outside many of society's structures from what he could see and yet, as a result, she seemed to know herself better. As the taxi pulled up to the address he had given the driver he realised that it made him feel emotion – which was unusual for him – sadness perhaps, that there was a chance that the events she was caught up in, that he had involved her in, could mean that she might never get the chance to live that potential. And that he might have to be the one to take it away.

Eva quietly closed the door of her hotel room and thumped against it. Immediately, she gasped in pain. More tears sprung to her eyes. She felt desperate. The last 48 hours had been too much. She almost couldn't take it. How could anyone handle so much?

At the back of her mind, she heard a calm, logical voice 'you need to go to a hospital.' But she couldn't think straight and she didn't want to leave the safety of her room. Not now. Not yet.

She staggered over to the mini bar and, using her left hand, pulled open the faux oak wood panel disguising it and then the door behind. She reached for a miniature bottle of Jack Daniels, one of the only spirits other than brandy that she could drink straight, and twisted the tiny cap off with her teeth.

The liquid was cold. She felt it pour smoothly down her throat and then its cool warmth spread through her chest and into her gut. She threw the bottle into the bin and reached for the miniature gin, repeating the same movements in the space of seconds. The gin was not pleasant and she choked slightly as the sour liquor made its way into her body. But the effects were welcome. A slight dulling of the pain in her shoulder. An easing of the anxiety in her mind. She let the miniature gin bottle drop to the bed and took three deep breaths. Her mind was racing. Her nerve endings felt as if they were on fire, adrenaline seared through her system. At the back of her mind she knew that these reactions were not all her.

She walked over to the door. Checked it once again. Then she searched the room. She packed her suitcase. Methodical movements, *doing*. The only way she knew to calm herself down. Other than running. And she could not leave the hotel again in darkness. Not now.

Finally, as the mist of emotion settled into an alcohol induced calm, she tried to think back to the S-Bahn and work out what had happened to her. There was no way she had fallen, none whatsoever. She had felt something hit her in the back, between the shoulder blades, and something – presumably someone – pushing her towards the train tracks. What puzzled Eva was that there must have been witnesses. There must have been cameras on the station, it was all very public – and yet, from what she could make out, everyone at the station was as confused as she was. They all seemed to think she had jumped. Then there was the fact that pushing someone in front of a train wasn't exactly a subtle way to kill. Definitely not as efficient as a quick shot to the back of the head in one of the many dark and lonely spots in this city. Plus, she wondered whether the train would even have killed her – did they travel that fast?

Instinctively, it felt to Eva like a warning rather than an attempt on her life. Maybe it was even an attempt at disabling her, slowing her down. But why? And who? She had come to Berlin on an innocent business trip, entirely unconnected to other events that had begun to happen to her – the phone calls from Jackson, seeing that poor man being kidnapped outside her house – so why should everything suddenly be coming to a head in Berlin?

She remembered the piece of paper she had been given in Berghain and spotted it on the floor. It was now writing side down on the carpet. She stared at the small white shape and, as she did so, her eyes seemed to unfocus and then focus on it again. She looked harder and realised that, with the paper this way up, there was something marked on it she hadn't noticed before. On the back was a symbol, one that made her heart begin to beat faster again. It was hand drawn but it was definitely the same symbol she had seen throughout everything that had happened to her in Paris. It was an acorn.

It took Eva several minutes to recover from the shock of seeing the acorn on the back of the paper. It had been drawn in a very light green colour, so as to be almost invisible, and certainly not obvious from looking at the words on the other side. As soon as she saw it, her mind cleared of everything else. It was surely a connection between what was happening now and what had happened before. To Eva, acorn meant ACORN – the Association for the Control of Regenerative Networking – whose logo had appeared on everything from the antidote vaccines in the basement in Paraguay, to a building she had visited in France – in fact, the building at the same address as that of 'kolychak', the bank her research had turned up only days before. There were connections forming. Lots of them. Eva's mind hesitated over the credibility of the connections, she began to wonder whether she shouldn't be more suspicious.

Then her phone rang. Sam. She ended the call. Instantly, the phone rang again, its harsh tone sounding loud in the room, as if it could be heard in the corridor beyond.

There was a sharp knock at the door. Eva froze. She silenced the phone. She took several steps towards the door, and looked for a spy hole, but there wasn't one.

'I can see your feet, Eva.'

Sam's voice! Eva took a step back, puzzled. He was in Berlin?

She turned to the mirror and tried to disguise the effects of the tears she had shed and the injuries she had suffered. She reached for the paper with the acorn on it and shoved it into her pocket. Cautiously, she opened the door. It was definitely Sam, who walked in brusquely, immediately spotting the empty miniatures and shaking his head disapprovingly. But he did not have the air of the Sam she knew.

'What are you doing here?' she asked, in surprise.

'Well, that's a nice way to greet your boyfriend.' His voice had a hard undertone she had never previously heard directed at her.

She closed the door. 'Why didn't you tell me you were coming?'

He seemed to be looking around the hotel room.

'You'd probably have taken off somewhere if you knew I was on my way. Wouldn't you?' He fixed her with a hard stare.

'Have you come all this way to say that?'

'You were supposed to come home yesterday.'

'I decided to stay on.'

'Do you *know* how irresponsible it is not to show up back at the office? That interview has a deadline, people are worried about you.'

'The deadline is five weeks away, Sam, it's not exactly a stop-press piece. And we both know there isn't anyone in that office who would be genuinely worried about me, they're just colleagues.'

He stopped looking around the room and turned to face her. 'I was worried about you.'

'Why?'

'You haven't responded to my messages and you haven't been in touch. I thought you were having some kind of breakdown.'

'Why on earth would you think that?'

He hesitated for the first time since he had confidently stormed into the room.

'I know you,' he said softly, apparently deciding to change his approach, 'you're vulnerable, things have happened. I just didn't want to think of you here, dealing with stuff alone.'

He took a step towards Eva and reached for one of her hands. She didn't move.

He was lying. She could *feel* he was lying. His words were designed to make her believe he was right – that she was vulnerable and needed his help. It was the equivalent of telling her she was overreacting, over emotional; it was intended to have a crippling effect on her ability to discern what was actually happening.

She did not sense any genuine affection from him, perhaps she never had. But what other reason could there be for his showing up here like this? She had to be careful not to become too suspicious of the motives of absolutely everyone, despite everything that had happened. She could easily end up on the wrong side of crazy.

'I just want to take care of you, Eva. I know things haven't been easy but I think, sometimes, you see life much more negatively than you need to. I can help, I can be there for you.'

Eva looked at him. The aesthetically perfect face, the apparent warmth streaming from his eyes, the hands held out towards her.

She felt nothing. Absolutely nothing.

In a large white cube of a house, high up in the Hollywood Hills, a memory stick was delivered via fast courier. A woman in pale denims took it and signed for it – she had been expecting the delivery. The sun was just setting over the west coast of America but still she made herself a large coffee. If this was what she had been told to expect she would not be sleeping tonight. Her work for such clients was not something she chose to share with anyone. It was not entirely legal – not so much what they asked of her, which was purely analysis – but what was revealed to her in the process. She worked in finance, she specialised in financial mechanisms, control and complex structuring. But these days it was not just legal, visible organisations that needed to understand how to make, and hold, money.

Yes, this work was lucrative. No, it didn't trouble her that she didn't know who it was for. She did it for a combination of the income and the insight. It was never ordinary. Like all her clients, the focus was on liquidity and control, but what was fascinating about this particular work stream was the disregard for law and regulation – and the need to circumvent it. That was very liberating although it could never be approached entirely without caution. Sometimes she wondered what these brains could do if employed legally rather than in a criminal capacity but she knew the answer was simple: they would do much less.

As the sun began to set, she took a seat at the breakfast bar in the kitchen. She sipped from the freshly made coffee and, for a second, listened to the sounds of her husband preparing the children for bed.

Then she opened the laptop reserved specially for this work – it was physically and electronically locked away, inaccessible to anyone but her with a password impossible to guess at and identification that only she could provide.

She opened the small padded packet and retrieved the memory stick inside. It was blue and looked scratched, as if it had already seen much use. She opened the envelope but there was nothing else – no note, no instructions. That meant she would simply be required to report back on the usual: viability, potential and risk.

She inserted the stick into the machine and watched as it began to start up. It contained a single folder with a single document. At the end of the document was a link to a private cloud storage facility, as well as a username and password. But she did not require those at present.

She started at the top of the document and worked her way down – it was five pages long.

At page three, her eyes widened in surprise.

At page four, she exclaimed out loud.

At page five, she realised she would have to read the entire document again.

Her coffee went slowly cold.

FIFTEEN

AFTER SAM HAD gone, Eva sat on the bed, head in her hands. She had not been able to invite him into her room. He made her feel claustrophobic. Everything that had happened to her since she arrived – the mugging, the Scopolamine, the S-Bahn – she needed to start making connections. But Sam's presence was odd. And annoying.

She exhaled heavily.

There were times when she felt she was never going to get there – with life. Other people managed 9-5 jobs, a daily routine, a degree of predictability. Apparently she would do anything to avoid that – even look for trouble. She couldn't live like that forever. Her train of thought was interrupted by a soft knock at the door. Sam again?

She moved quietly to the door and, this time, took care to stand far enough away so her feet could not be seen.

She stood, silently, her heart beating hard in her chest.

She cursed the lack of a spy hole.

On the other side of the door, there was no movement. Eva tried to lean in and listen against the hard wood but could hear nothing.

After she had stood for several minutes waiting for something to happen, Eva walked back to the bed and sat. She was just retrieving her phone, to plug it into the charger, when she heard the unmistakable sound of a keycard opening the room door.

She froze.

Her heart began to pound.

There was a mechanical click, followed by two high pitched

beeps, and then Eva heard the handle being pushed cautiously down.

She sat rigidly on the bed.

That wasn't Sam.

The way her room was designed meant that, in between the door and her bed, was a thin strip of wall housing the wardrobe, a safe and some shelves, as well as a mirror on each side. Because of this wall, there was no way she could see what was happening on the other side of it.

She listened hard and heard a quiet swish as the door was pushed open.

Shit.

Her heart rate was at a painful level. Her chest felt tight. Did the hotel have a turn down service? She thought quickly. She'd heard no 'housekeeping!'.

No, this did not feel right.

She looked around for a weapon. The glass water bottle on the desk at the end of the bed was her only choice. It might be enough of a distraction that she could run. She took a silent step towards it and picked it up as she heard the room door quietly shut. She positioned herself at the end of the wall separating the bed from the door; she held her breath. The only advantage she had was the element of surprise. When she saw a shadow fall across the carpet to the edge of the wardrobe, she hit out with the bottle. It made contact with something and was then dashed from her hands, bouncing off the edge of the desk but not smashing.

But Eva couldn't see it anymore as she had been turned, forced face down into the muddy brown bedclothes and was being pinned there by a firm grip. She cried out as the pain of the injury sustained earlier, combined with the position she was being held in, became almost unbearable. Her vision began to swim.

She stayed still, breathing hard, aware of a pair of hard thighs pressed against the back of her own, hands holding her wrist tight to the small of her back and sharp fingernails digging into her opposite shoulder, keeping the top half of her body pressed against the bed.

'Are you going to behave?'

It was a woman's voice.

That was a surprise. Eva hesitated. She might once have thought a woman assailant meant a better chance – but, in her recent experience, it did not.

'Who are you?' she asked, her voice audibly shaking.

'I'm someone who doesn't take kindly to being attacked with a fucking glass bottle.'

Eva tried to shake her hands free. 'You broke into my room, what do you expect?'

'You didn't answer the door.'

'AND?'

'And so I broke into your room.'

Eva listened to the voice, husky and strong. She was fairly certain it wasn't one she had heard before.

'What do you want?'

There was hesitation, then the grip on Eva's wrist and back was released. Slowly, cautiously, she straightened up and turned to face the woman. For some reason she felt embarrassed, inadequate, in a way she knew she wouldn't have done if she had just been physically overwhelmed by a man. For several seconds, they stood opposite each other, tension tangible between them.

Then, suddenly, the woman stuck her hand out. 'I'm Anya.'

Eva looked at the hand. It was a comedic gesture in light of the preceding series of events.

Eva pulled together her mental resources and tried to control the trembling tone in her voice.

'What do you want, Anya?'

'You.'

The last meeting had been incredibly difficult and the man with the Mediterranean tan was beginning to feel the pressure. Years of work and an extraordinary amount of resource had gone into this and it was unthinkable that three people might jeopardise it. Three people who should all have been dead by now. He glanced pointedly over at his younger colleague, who was tapping into a silver laptop on a different row of the tiny private jet.

There was more to Paul than he let on, that much was obvious. He was not a career criminal, he did not belong. It was still not clear why he was even here. He was obviously intelligent but he was emotional. Overly emotional, and inconsistent. Like an addict or a vengeful child. Money was the only motivation that made any sense.

Then there was the extreme anger that occasionally flickered across the man's face, which spoke of something buried deep inside him. That was the part of him that was truly frightening.

'What are you working on?'

'Moving the corporate identities.' The response was clipped and terse, as if Paul had realised his game was almost up.

'Are we close to meeting the next milestone?'

'Why don't you look at the spreadsheets?'

The man with the Mediterranean tan was not surprised by this sudden rudeness. This is what Paul did, he suddenly flipped. Nevertheless, the older man could hold his temper no longer. 'You don't speak to me like that.'

The reply was a long, cold look.

'Who exactly do you think I am?' continued the older man.

'The past,' Paul said, without blinking.

Apparently, he had run out of patience for pleasantries, too.

There was silence in the cabin as his remark seemed to bounce off the cushioned walls. Whatever his agenda was, he clearly felt that the current arrangement was slowing him down. He was revealing himself, whether he meant to or not, and that could mean only one thing. He'd had enough.

But he wasn't the only one.

'Your failed technology is the reason we are in this position.'

'It is groundbreaking innovation, there must be room for failure, that's how it works.'

'And how would you know, you're not even a scientist?'

'It is my project, it is mine, I own it.' The younger man sounded petulant, instantly defensive.

The older man suddenly realised why.

'You stole it.'

Paul looked up. He stared but did not respond. How much of a threat was this, he wondered.

A hostess appeared with a tray of two squat tumblers of liquid, one clear, one amber. They said nothing as she walked across the thickly carpeted cabin and placed one in front of each of them. The older man smiled his thanks, the younger simply ignored her.

When she had gone, they began speaking again.

'You didn't develop this at all, you stole it. And that's why you can't complete the testing. You don't know how to.'

Paul slowly closed the laptop and looked at his colleague.

In that instant, the man with the Mediterranean tan realised that, for the first time in decades, he felt afraid. Paul was reckless, cruel and he apparently had far less to lose.

The older man began to feel the odds were stacked against him, as if Paul had actually been brought into the project to remind him he was aged, out of date. Perhaps he had.

That was a precarious position to be in.

Slowly, the younger man leaned towards his colleague.

'Are you threatening me?'

'No.' Despite the pulsating anxiety running through him, the older man refused to be intimidated into apologising. 'It's an observation.'

The younger man continued to look at him as he drank the straight vodka.

'Good.'

Eva regarded Anya suspiciously.

'I don't understand.'

'You need to come with me.'

Eva realised her legs were shaking. She sat on the bed. *Why me? Why this, again? I'm exhausted.*

'If you were in my position and someone had appeared in your hotel room and physically assaulted you, would you?'

'No.'

Eva raised her hands in an 'I told you so' gesture.

'I'm not going to kill you, Eva.'

'Well, I've only got your word for that. Which is completely meaningless, seeing as I have absolutely no idea who you are.'

Eva rubbed the spot on her shoulders where she had been pinned. Thankfully, it was the opposite side from where she had bounced off the train. 'You have a hard grip for a woman.'

Anya didn't acknowledge the statement as either a compliment or an insult. One positive was that at least Eva knew she had no serious internal injuries after what had happened at the S-Bahn station. When Anya had pushed her onto the bed, the only pain had been in her shoulder.

'It's important that you come with me.'

'You said. Why don't you tell me why?'

Eva was aware she was being rude but she had few filters left.

'I can help you.'

'I thought you were going to say something along the lines of "don't leave Berlin, all the answers are here".'

'So, you got the note.'

Eva looked up, surprised. 'That was you?'

Anya nodded. She had an athletic figure, stronger and broader at the top and slimmer from the waist down. Layered blonde hair hung either side of an oval face bearing a tense but firm expression. She had large brown eyes and strong cheek bones, with unfeasibly smooth skin for someone who apparently used her body in her line of work. Overall, from the way she stood to her unnerving gaze, she didn't look like a woman used to being messed with.

Anya herself didn't interest Eva as much as the note – specifically the acorn on the back.

'Why did you send me the note – what does it mean?'

'We can't talk here.'

'I'm not leaving this room with you without more information,' said Eva, more definitely this time.

A muscle flickered to the side of Anya's right eye.

'I can't give you more information here.'

'Well, I guess we're stuck.'

A stand-off.

Then, Anya reached inside her slim fitting jacket. Eva expected a weapon but, instead, there was just a card.

Anya flipped the card over and Eva saw it held just a single number. She handed it to Eva, who took it and turned it over in her hands. On the other side, a graphic representation of a cube in line drawing. Not an acorn.

'Call if you change your mind,' said Anya and she turned and walked towards the door.

She stopped in front of the door and turned to Eva again. 'Call,' she said forcefully.

And then she left.

SIXTEEN

AFTER ANYA LEFT, Eva fell into a fitful sleep but, around 2am, her eyes flicked open. She took a couple of deep breaths and orientated herself. A familiar feeling of unease kept her still for several seconds. She hated waking suddenly in the night; she could never escape the feeling that there was a reason for it – a noise, a movement, an instinct of some sort. She lay there in the dark and listened; all she could hear was the sound of her pulse thudding in her ears.

She sat up and quickly pressed one of the metallic pads that controlled the lights in the hotel room. The room was immediately illuminated by a set of cold, awkward spotlights. She looked around. Nothing. From her position on the bed, she stared at the dividing wall, the one blocking her view of the door – and of anyone who might have done what Anya did and simply let themselves in.

She sat and listened. If someone was in the room would they not have reacted as she turned on the lights?

Eva took a deep breath and cautiously started to peel back the bed sheets. The air was cold and immediately her skin puckered into goose bumps.

She slid down the side of the high bed, so plumped with mattresses that it would have suited the fairytale Princess and the Pea, and she began to take small, silent steps across the thick carpet towards the edge of the jutting wardrobe.

The carpet was soft but to Eva's ears it sounded as if she was crushing autumn leaves. The more seconds she spent not being able to see the other side of the room, the more her imagination created alarming pictures of what might be there.

One more step and she was standing at the edge of the small partition.

She hesitated. Perhaps waiting for a face to appear on the other side, perhaps just tempted to go back to bed and pretend there was no danger.

Oh, for God's sake. She took a large step around the partition, fists clenched, body rigid and ready for a fight. Her heart was now singing in her ears, a high-pitched staccato of fear that was making it difficult for her already fatigued body to respond as she might have wanted.

But there was no one there.

Joseph Smith stood outside the bland, wooden door and waited. He had spent 15 minutes in Eva's hotel room and the whole time he had been itching to wrap his hands around her neck. But that was not why he was there, not this time. He had made the decision to leave as soon as he heard her waking up. He had negotiated the chair by the door and the various obstacles she had left on the floor – on purpose? – and then had trodden on something that cracked under his weight. Instantly he heard her breathing become more shallow and quicken and realised she was waking up. He had seen the light go on underneath the door, as he waited outside, but she had not opened the door to her room. If she had done, they would have come face to face. She may not have noticed him as her taxi driver several days earlier, but up close she would certainly have recognised him from their encounters in Paris and South America. In neither location had their interactions been anything but unpleasant – for her.

But, although he had been quick to dismiss Eva Scott first time around, particularly as she was female, she remained alive and that gave him pause. For no one else who had been involved in events in Paris was still alive.

He had yet to establish how she had escaped death at the very last moment. The mercenary had been charged with making her demise look like an accident – shooting her, then pushing her over the edge of the Iguaçu Falls in one of the Land Rovers. And yet, here she was. The mercenary had disappeared for months after the incident and rumours were that Eva had killed him, not the other way around. But from what he could make out, only one body had been found strapped into the Land Rover, the bloated corpse of Daniel Marchment, and mystery had remained over what happened to the other two.

Finally, Joseph had found police records showing Eva had been rescued by a busload of tourists but of the mercenary there had been no mention. He had failed to appear at his Paris flat, his usual post office box remained unchecked and he had not responded to any of the aliases Joseph had been ordered to set up to tempt him out of wherever he was hiding. And then, suddenly, he had surfaced – in the UK, close to Eva.

When she woke the next day, Eva felt heavy, exhausted and spent. She looked around her hotel room and contemplated that this was the day she was meant to check out. The thought of leaving made her instantly anxious. The anxiety was not helped by the fact that the room was a complete mess. Although she had suffered from obsessive compulsive disorder for many years – the kind that requires lots of objects to be constantly straightened and items placed in orderly clean lines – sometimes this simply disappeared and, instead, she just created chaos. It made her wonder if she could really call it obsessive compulsive disorder at all, or whether it was simply a habit. She pushed herself up in the bed and checked her mobile – always the first thing she did on waking. A couple of texts from friends and a message from her dad. Interestingly, nothing from Sam. She wondered if, after their encounter, he had done something reactive, gone out on a drinking spree, ended up in the arms of another woman. She might find him more interesting if he had.

And there, she thought to herself, lies the reason that I am nearly 30 and still single.

She opened the news app on her phone as a distraction and browsed through all the sensationalised goings-on. There were, she knew, elements of 'real' within every story but the truth? No. Reporting was never truly impartial. Maybe other than the weather. And that seemed to be woefully off the mark most of the time.

There were a couple of articles about politics that vaguely held her attention and one investigative piece on financial cartels that she read with interest. The way cartels operated fascinated her, whether it was a business cartel or a drug cartel. An agreement to cooperate – often between opposing sides – for the sake of reaping cash rewards. In every walk of life principles always seemed to have a purchasable price.

Eva had often thought how closely the behaviour of governments resembled organisations such as these – when very occasionally there was a glimpse behind the curtain. Collusion to supply weapons, suppress research, ignore emissions targets to ensure that profit came first. All legitimised simply because the people doing it wore suits instead of carrying guns.

Fifteen minutes later and the room looked as if it had been made up by the hotel cleaning staff. Eva was looking at her neatly packed suitcase with a puzzled expression. On the desk next to the case lay a lipstick, its shell in several pieces. She was trying to work out how the shell had become so cracked, as she didn't remember the pain of treading on it or hearing it break at any point when Anya had been in the room.

It was one of those puzzling anomalies, so often dismissed – unless it turned out later to have meant something more, in which case ignoring it became a cause for regret. At that moment it meant nothing to Eva. And it would not be the first time in the past 48 hours that her memory had let her down. The thought of that blank space where the memories should have been caused a surge of panic. Eva took several slow, deep breaths. She stared at the lipstick for another few minutes, then picked up her keycard, walked out and shut the hotel room door behind her, leaving the lipstick and her suitcase on the desk.

She was going to have to get her confidence back, she couldn't continue to be controlled by fear. As she was currently motivated by being incredibly hungry, this seemed as good a time as any to start rebuilding it. In daylight, the idea of the streets held far less menace than they had the night before and she had Anya's card shoved deep into the pocket of her jeans, which somehow made her feel comforted. Nevertheless her spine was rigid with tension.

She pushed through the hotel's front doors and was met with a sunny morning, skies blue, the air crisp and fresh and the sunshine bright. She was trembling slightly as she stepped outside the safety of the building. Ignoring her shaking knees she walked north, away from the hotel, for several minutes. To drown out the fearful voices in her head, she repeated the chorus lyrics of one of her favourite songs. Over and over again.

When she found the café she was looking for, she ordered an enormous coffee, then bread and eggs, which she ate slowly by a window overlooking a quiet street. She felt something like contentedness after she had finished, the food was numbing. It was the first decent meal she had eaten since the Russian restaurant and that had not been particularly satisfying.

After another ten minutes browsing the news app on her phone, Eva began her walk back to the hotel.

'Eva.'

She had been too wrapped up in her own thoughts to notice she had a shadow. The voice registered in her mind even before she saw the face and, as a result, when she raised her eyes to his they were already wide with shock. She instinctively took a step back from him, without realising she was stepping into the road. He locked a hand around the top of her arm, pulling her back towards the pavement, as a car sped past, sounding its horn.

'Leon.'

She said his name in a flat voice. But, inside, she felt an odd mix of excitement and fear. He looked much the same, although more tanned. But he was also bruised and she could see the marks on his face where stitches had recently been removed. He still had the same animalistic quality, the burning blue eyes, a contrast against the thick, dark hair and that large frame almost blocking out the sun from where he was standing. She couldn't ignore the fact that half of her initial reaction appeared to be pleasure at seeing him. Of course, there were other things she couldn't ignore, either.

'What do you want?'

His face showed no surprise at the lack of friendly greeting. He had, after all, tried to kill her the last time they met.

'I need your phone.'

As usual, he ignored social conventions such as small talk.

Eva took a step away from him – sideways this time – and instinctively touched the point in her bag at which her phone sat, subconsciously giving away its location. Then, she moved to walk away from him, intending to run at speed back to the hotel. But she didn't get far. Leon grabbed her arm and forced her to stop, almost lifting her from the ground.

'Give me your phone.' The piercing blue of those eyes.

'Why don't you go and fuck yourself?' She was angry now. Bizarrely, she felt it was the lack of manners that caused this fury to burn so strongly inside her. He hadn't even asked how she was. They stared at each other and then she aimed a kick at his leg, her foot landing on his left ankle. It seemed to be a weak point, as he cringed and loosened his grip. Eva pulled herself free, turned and began running. But Leon was faster. Once again, he took hold of her, this time hustling her into a small park, empty at that early hour, where he pushed her towards a climbing frame and wedged her between the cold metal poles and his own body. His favourite tactic, she thought angrily, when she realised she couldn't move.

'Just give me your phone.'

She began to struggle.

'I'm going to start screaming if you don't move away.'

'*Just give me your fucking phone.*'

'FUCK YOU.'

Their faces were inches away from each other and their eyes were locked. Eva felt his breath brush the skin of her cheek. She could barely control her heart beating in her chest.

'You haven't changed,' she said, through gritted teeth, 'still a thug.'

Nothing on Leon's face moved. She had never met anyone who could so effectively disguise their emotions. It was infuriating.

He continued to hold her tight against the climbing frame, his hard body as impassable as the thickest concrete wall. However, Eva sensed he didn't really know what to do next. He didn't appear to be his old, efficiently merciless self – that Leon would surely just have taken the phone by force. So she kicked him again, in the same spot on his ankle that had produced the reaction before. The light in the blue eyes flickered as, again, he weakened. It was enough for her to duck under his arms and begin running towards the edge of the park. She turned her head as she ran but, this time, he did not follow. He just stood and stared.

SEVENTEEN

As SHE RAN back to the hotel, Eva fumbled in her pockets for the business card Anya had given her. Her heart was beating out of her chest and she kept throwing glances behind her, to make sure Leon, with his lean boxer's physique and those hands that could so efficiently break a human neck, was not following her. Inside her mind, a whirlwind of questions. Why was he here, why did he want her phone – he was the second person to try and take it from her – why was he wearing a suit? And most pressing of all, how had he even survived the drop from the cliff, last time she had seen him? From experience, she knew Leon was a man of few words, even when his interests were aligned with hers – which, from the encounter in the park moments ago, they clearly were not this time.

But she was certain this wouldn't be the last time she would see him. It troubled her a great deal that she experienced not only fear but also excitement at the thought.

As soon as she found Anya's card, she dialled the number.

'Eva.' It was answered on the first ring.

'I need help.'

'We'll come and pick you up.'

The line went dead.

Eva exhaled; she felt the adrenaline from the confrontation in the park start to wane. She slowed her pace. What am I doing, she thought to herself. I have no idea who Anya is.

Eva looked at the screen of her phone, informing her the call had been ended, and put it in her bag. She had felt as if she had been presented with making a decision between Anya or Leon, and Anya, with her (comparative) lack of physical aggression, seemed the lesser of two evils.

But was that really her only choice? Was either of them actually anything more than a rock or a hard place?

Shit.

Eva pulled the phone out of her bag and looked at the time. She had to check out of the hotel in an hour. Perhaps she should just go to the airport and board the next flight to London. There was no need for her to see Anya again and she was sure she could outwit Leon enough to make it safely onto her flight.

But then what?

Sit at a desk in an office and think about whatever it was she might have uncovered in Berlin. Something that might help her to finally let go of the obsessive thoughts about her brother and the man at the station in London – and that strange phrase 'kolychak'. Wait for whatever was happening – and something was happening – to bring chaos to her life when she was unprepared for it?

Sometimes, she thought to herself as she took the lift back to her room, sometimes the only way out is through. You can do everything within your power to force yourself to make the right choices, to be in the right situations, to be the right kind of person, but sometimes, in spite of all that, you just end up somewhere else.

Almost as soon as Eva had finished having a shower, dressing and repacking the last of her suitcase, there was a quiet knock at the door. She glanced briefly at her wet hair and realised there was no time to dry it. She reached for the door handle. And then stopped. Was this actually Anya? It could be Leon. Or, she realised with a start, it could be Sam.

Sam. Shouldn't she at least let him know she was leaving? But when she thought about the way he had spoken to her last night, the resistance she had felt towards him, and the cloying suffocation of his affection, she just couldn't face it.

'Who is it?'

'Anya.'

Eva opened the door and the statuesque Blonde walked into the room.

'What made you change your mind?'

Anya clearly did not pull punches. Direct eye contact, even voice tone, body language that indicated she was braced for any eventuality.

'A blast from the past.'

Anya waited but, sensing she wasn't about to get anything else from Eva, she held her hand out for the suitcase.

The two women said nothing as they walked silently along the corridors of the hotel.

In the lift, Eva said 'I need to pay my room service bill.'

'I've paid it. We need to get you out of here as soon as possible.'

'Why is that?'

'After what happened to you this morning...'

'You know about that.'

Eva couldn't say she was particularly surprised. Somehow, Anya had obtained a key to her room, so surveillance was likely. But how much? And why had they not helped her? Eva wondered whether she should be feeling more unnerved than she did. How much was she being manipulated? All she felt was a raw burning around her ears, as if she was hyper aware of what was going on. She rubbed her ear. A dark spot appeared in front of her right eye. She shook her head.

'We have been keeping an eye on you.'

Eva looked at Anya. The dark spot was gone. 'Who is "we"?'

'That will have to wait.'

'I don't think so.'

Eva slammed her hand against the emergency stop on the lift and it came to rest between the third and fourth floors.

'You know that we'll have to deal with reception now,' said Anya, quietly, as the lift intercom began to buzz.

'Tell me who you are and what your interest is in me – in this.'

Anya met Eva's gaze quite evenly. She seemed utterly unruffled. 'I'm a friend, Eva, really – we are a network of friends.'

'That's not enough.'

'What is it specifically you want to know?'

The lift intercom was buzzing repeatedly now, with an intermittent voice being broadcast across it in German and then English.

'I want to know what this network is, and, specifically, who you are.'

'We are an international network of insiders, known only to each other.'

'Sure you are.'

'Do you want this information or not?' asked Anya coolly.

'Go on.'

'We're like the back-up plan, when official channels can't necessarily achieve what needs to be done to meet an objective – that's when we step in and help out.'

'You're the "black ops".'

'This isn't a film, Eva.'

'Frankly, it sounds just as fictional.'

'I can't tell you much more right now, you're just going to have to trust me.'

'Would you trust you?'

Anya didn't respond.

Both women jumped as a grinding noise indicated the lift doors being forced open by someone. Eva could see one pair of feet on the carpeted floor, currently at her nose height. She was sure she recognised those shoes. Suddenly, Sam's face appeared in the gap. He took a quick look at her and then –

uninvited – began to roll himself in through the space. Eva inhaled sharply.

'Do you know him?' Anya asked.

'Yes, he's my boyfriend,' replied Eva, although she was slightly surprised at Sam's behaviour.

'What are you doing, Sam, just call the hotel staff.'

But Sam was through the gap. He took a pace towards Eva and loomed over her. 'Shut up.'

Shocked, she shrank back.

Sam turned towards Anya. Eva could see the other woman was confused, half on guard but half ready to welcome someone who, although unidentified, was more likely to be friend than foe.

Perhaps it was that which caused her to miss the knife.

Sam turned, bent his knees slightly and swung his right arm and fist at Anya's stomach. Blood spurted out across the lift. Drops landed on Eva's hands. She stared open-mouthed and, somewhere in the back of her throat, there was a gurgle that almost passed for a scream.

Anya went down clutching at her stomach, her face as white as a sheet. She pulled something from an ankle holster as she fell to the floor and fired a small black gun up at Sam, shooting him through the shoulder. He took a stumbling step back from the impact, also looking slightly shocked, and then he lunged again at Anya.

Instinctively, Eva threw herself in between the two. She knocked Sam sideways, punched him in the side of the head, jabbing her fingers into the softest part of his throat when he came at her again and hitting out at the panel of buttons on the elevator until one of them caused it to move again.

Sam was reeling backwards as the doors opened behind him and he staggered, and almost fell, onto the cold, hard floor. Then, he regained his balance and grabbed Eva by the hair, pulling her over to him, where he could gain a better grip. He squashed her against him and she caught the distinctive iron smell as the wound in his shoulder started to bleed.

Eva glanced back. Anya was lying in a heap on the floor of the lift. People in the reception had begun to realise something was happening. They looked at Anya and then at Eva and Sam. Eva thought she saw panic in Sam's eyes. *Run*, she willed him. *Just go.*

But he didn't. Instead, he grabbed her and held to her neck the same blade he had just used on Anya.

'Nobody move!'

A hush fell across the busy reception.

He hustled Eva sideways across the room and towards the reception doors.

'If you move, I'll stab her in the throat.'

'Sam, stop. Let me go.'

Eva was struggling to make sense of what was happening. This was Sam – docile, puppy dog Sam. He was millimetres away from cutting her throat. Was this revenge, anger, obsession? Somehow, she didn't think so.

'Sam...' she began, trying to exercise the control she'd apparently had over him back in the UK.

He flicked her head, so that his mouth was right up against her ear. 'I mean it, shut up or I will cut you.'

She shut her mouth. Glancing sideways she could see that his eyes were bloodshot. He was obviously in pain. This was not the same person.

Who was he?

Eva struggled to stay on her feet, trying to keep her throat from his knife as he dragged her out through the hotel doors and into the street. Sam's wound was leaking blood, not gushing, but enough to leave a trail of drops on the pavement. Although she couldn't see him, his movements indicated he was frantically looking first left and then right, as if trying to spot someone. He began to drag her away from the hotel entrancc. Eva heard the unmistakable sound of Berlin police sirens in the distance.

'Shit', Sam muttered, and then pushed her up against the wall of the adjacent building. 'Stay,' he said, keeping the knife at her throat, as he reached for his phone.

She glanced down at the screen. Sam quickly turned it from view. Had she seen what she thought she had?

Eva stood still, trying to process the two words on Sam's screen. She realised she was watching a man with a briefcase and curiously square glasses who was walking towards them. He seemed to have no reaction to what was happening in front of him – had he even realised? She looked at him but he looked away. People never wanted to become involved in someone else's shit.

And then, suddenly, the man with the briefcase turned towards them. She saw the muzzle of a silenced gun and Sam's body jerked from hers. The knife grazed her throat as he fell.

'Where's Anya?' The man was running towards her.

Eva heard the screeching of tyres on the street.

'*Where's Anya?*' he said again, more urgently this time.

'She's in the hotel,' said Eva, pointing back in that direction, 'in the lift.' She was dazed and breathless. What on earth was going on?

'Only get into the black car,' said the man, as he set off at pace towards the hotel.

A yellow van screeched to a halt on the opposite side of the street and the door sprung open. Eva began to run back towards the hotel. *Only get in the black car...* which black car?? There must be thousands in this city. And then she saw it, a black car driving stealthily towards the hotel, pulling up to a stop across the road. She ran over to it, just as the man emerged from the hotel with Anya over one shoulder, dragging Eva's suitcase with one hand, her handbag – with her phone in – balanced on top. Eva ran and took the case from him but he seemed angry.

He saw the yellow van and shouted at her 'GO!' and pushed her in the direction of the black car. Both doors on their side of the road opened. Eva jumped for the passenger seat as a hail of bullets came in their direction from the yellow van. Anya was now in one of the passenger seats behind her, the man next to her. And in the front seat was Irene.

EIGHTEEN

EVA WAS STARING out of the window as the streets of West Berlin gave way to those of the East. Irene Hunt was driving the car in silence. From the seats behind, Eva could hear the sound of medical supplies being ripped open and a noise like liquid bubbling up. However, she couldn't bring herself to turn around and find out if Anya was likely to survive. Equally, she could not look at Irene. In fact, all she could do was sit and stare out of the window. It was as if a layer of white noise had settled around the outside of her brain. Disjointed thoughts came and went, half finished, uncertain and accompanied by underlying anxiety, building and building. Her heart was thudding in her chest, she felt she could hear it struggling from one beat to the next, as if the tension building up in every muscle, every vein, might overwhelm its ability to function.

Then a thought occurred to her.

I have to get out of the car.

She heard it repeat through every recess of her brain.

I have to get out of the car. NOW.

She reached for the door handle.

'Eva!'

Irene's shout was tense and high pitched.

Eva stopped.

She looked at her hand on the door handle of the passenger side; she had been about to open the door and step out. The car was still moving.

She removed her hand from the door handle and glanced over at Irene.

'You're in shock, Eva. Just sit still.'

It was an order but Eva found it comforting. She could just sit still, she could do that, yes. It was fine to let someone else take over until her brain returned to normal speed. She felt as if it was swelling, anxiety and confusion creating a ballooning mass that at any moment could burst the fragile bone of her skull.

Eva sucked in a thin breath, through bluish lips.

She forced herself to sit back in the seat and tried to calm her frantic heartbeat with normal thoughts. She watched as they drove along Friedrichstraße, past the original Checkpoint Charlie, crossing from west to east as few had wanted to do in the years Berlin had been divided by the giant Wall.

As the car continued its steady pace and the architecture began to change around her, Eva forced herself to think, not about her own situation, but the struggle for freedom that had taken place in this city, not that long ago. If the people could survive that kind of brutally incomprehensible regime then she had no right to crumble under whatever was happening to her now. It was a tenuous comparison but it was all she had.

'What can you tell me about that back there?'

Her voice was calm. Amazing what the power of reflection can achieve, she thought to herself, as the physical symptoms of her panic began to subside.

She felt Irene's gaze on her. The other woman was looking at Eva's hand, which was resting not far from the passenger door.

She withdrew her hand to her lap.

'I'm fine, Irene, really.'

Irene turned back to the road. 'To be honest, I'm surprised that your first question wasn't about my presence here, Eva.'

Eva glanced across the car.

Irene and Eva had never made things easy for one another. Both headstrong, both stubborn, both used to having their own way.

'Did you know I tried to get hold of you in London a week ago?'

Irene nodded at the road. 'Of course.'

'Apparently, you never lived at the house where I visited you with Leon.'

'You know I can't discuss that with you, Eva.'

Eva felt resentment building. 'Need to know' had never really worked for her. As far as she was concerned, she needed to know everything.

She was interrupted by a gasp from behind.

'Irene, she's bleeding out,' said the man sitting in the seat behind Eva. 'We must get her to a medic.'

'You know I can't drive any faster than this, Sassan, we cannot draw attention to ourselves. Anya will be fine.'

Eva stared at the side of Irene's face. It wasn't the first time she had seen this woman, and her will of iron, in action but it was the first time she had been in a car with someone bleeding profusely and Irene had just refused to do anything to help.

'Don't look at me like that, Eva, you saw what happened back there. We can't sacrifice all of us for the sake of getting her to a hospital.'

It was cold logic of the worst kind but it was, unfortunately, the truth.

They arrived at an address in East Berlin which Eva felt sure wasn't far from the Berghain club. Several people appeared from the gloomy looking building and silently removed Anya from the car.

'Will she survive?' asked Eva. A knife wound to the stomach surely required more than a home first aid kit could supply. Irene didn't answer the request for reassurance. She was giving nothing away – not about why Irene was here or why Eva was.

People who played games for a living, Eva recalled, ensured no one ever knew which side they were on. These people only associated with those less powerful if they were either a threat or useful. Which meant she had been brought here because she was either of the above. Which was not comforting.

On the outside, the sprawling townhouse had a ramshackle, run-down air but, inside, it was a different story. The interiors could have been plucked straight from the pages of a high-end design magazine. Clinically whitewashed walls, smooth edges and sharp corners were softened by design features, a 70s style hanging lamp, a curved couch, a thick rug that looked so soft Eva just wanted to take her shoes off and stand on it in bare feet. It was a beautiful conversion but it made little sense to Eva that she should have been brought here. It was the wrong location.

Irene made them both a coffee and signalled she should sit down at an industrial-sized dining table.

'I doubt very much whether you know what's going on.'

Eva shook her head slowly. 'Tell me.'

'Unfortunately, we are almost as much in the dark as you are.'

Eva sipped her coffee. 'I doubt that.'

'It's true, I'm afraid.'

'So, why have you brought me here?'

'I – and people working for me – have kept an eye on you over the past year or so, as well as that phone calls you and I have had, and things seem to have changed for you recently. For a short period of time you appeared to settle into life, to take a step back from all the questions I know remain unanswered for you. But that isn't the case anymore, is it?'

Eva said nothing.

'You seem to have returned to your old recklessness.'

My 'old recklessness'? thought Eva... was that how she was defined in a file somewhere, as 'reckless'?

Irene continued. 'I want you to explain where this change in behaviour has come from.'

She was hesitant to cooperate, particularly as the question

seemed odd given the circumstances. It could have been asked in London months ago. But Eva was tired and fed up with feeling isolated.

So she told Irene why she had tried to contact her back in London – the connections with the word 'kolychak', the dying man at Waterloo, and the fact she had remembered where she had heard the word before – in a subterranean basement in South America. She told Irene that kolychak was a defunct weapons plant – and a private bank – and that the bank's address was one they both knew from Paris. She felt she was telling Irene what she already knew, certainly the other woman showed no surprise at any of it.

Eva did not mention Leon. And she didn't know why not.

'But I'm guessing you know all this anyway,' she said, as she finished her account, her voice trailing away as Irene continued making notes.

'It's interesting to hear how you've come to these conclusions,' said Irene, ignoring Eva's attempt to place the other woman somewhere on the knowledge spectrum.

'But, Irene, something is happening isn't it? You can at least confirm that – and it's connected to the events of last year. It's not over...'

Irene met Eva's gaze.

'No.'

In this light, she seemed to have aged only slightly since Eva last shared a room with her and the small changes to her face were perhaps more attributable to the constant pressure she existed under than to the passing of time. Eva wondered how Irene's personal life was faring – she knew there was little balance to be found between a job like Irene's, with its unofficial hours and 'work until you drop' culture, and a family life.

'What's going on, Irene?'

'Obviously, I wish I could tell you.'

Eva stood and walked across the immaculate kitchen, leaning against a beautifully restored Aga on the opposite side of the room. 'Here's the thing, Irene.'

The other woman waited, expressionless.

'You know, as well as I do, that if something is happening here, it's connected to what we were both part of in Paris.'

Nothing.

Eva continued. 'And you also know I already have a great deal of knowledge about that situation, much more than I have told you – perhaps information that you *don't* have.'

There was the carrot.

'If you don't share what you have with me, why should I share what I have with you?'

And there was the stick.

Even though Eva couldn't quite see Irene's eyes, she knew they were narrowing.

She put her hands behind her, against the cold metal of the huge oven. Her right hand wandered onto the large hot plate on top. If the appliance was on, her skin would have stuck to it.

'We all thought that operation was over, Eva, you know that.'

Do I? wondered Eva.

'Until today, there would have been nothing to *share*, as you so collegiately put it.'

It was not the truth, Eva knew that. She was silent for several seconds. 'What about Jackson?'

'There has been no word on your brother.'

Eva moved back to the table and took her seat opposite Irene. She raised her eyes and locked them onto Irene's. There wasn't even a flicker in the stare of the older woman. But she was, no doubt, a practised liar and Eva had the distinct impression that, if she did know a) Jackson was alive and b) where he was, every effort would be made to keep the siblings apart. Why that should be the case, however, she couldn't guess.

'How did you find Leon?' Eva ventured.

The time had come to mention him; she knew instinctively, if she didn't do it right now, it was for reasons she didn't want to think about.

Irene didn't even blink at the mention of his name.

'He started watching you.'

'Me?'

'In London.'

'I didn't notice…'

'Not surprising. You have an incredibly sharp instinct but you're no match for him.'

Although she knew Irene might be right, Eva felt irritated. She *was* a match for Leon.

'It was when we were watching him we realised we weren't the only ones.'

'Who's the other party in this?'

The question once again went unanswered.

'They took Leon on your street.'

Eva's mind moved and locked onto a memory. The man in the baseball cap she had seen bundled into a waiting van…

'He disappeared for several days and we couldn't find him. Then, he reappeared in north Africa, injured. But we have no way of piecing together what happened to him in that time. And, knowing him, frankly your guess is as good as mine.'

'What does he want with me?'

'You tell me.'

'I don't think I can. I mean, I thought he was dead – I thought he rolled off the cliff at the Iguaçu Falls in the Land Rover.'

'Did anything pass between you during that incident to indicate why he would suddenly want to make contact now?'

Irritatingly, Eva felt herself blushing. She knew Irene would notice.

'Were you lovers?' Irene didn't miss a trick.

'Once,' she replied, 'literally, just once.'

'And you continued to carry a candle for him after the event?'

Her turn of phrase was endearingly old fashioned.

'No, absolutely not.'

'Did you not feel used by him?'

'It was very much the other way around.'

Eva couldn't help noticing the slight discomfort Irene seemed to experience at the idea of Eva having used Leon for sex. Was that the line for Irene, she wondered. She could kill, maim, order death to be dished out left, right and centre but she could never use sex as a weapon, a tool, or simply as a release.

'What did he want from you when he saw you?'

'My phone.'

'Your phone?' Irene seemed surprised.

'Yes.'

'Give it to me.'

And then Eva hesitated. She realised she had identified a bargaining chip. 'I think I will hang on to it for now.'

There was the look once again from Irene, the look that could kill.

Joseph Smith stared at the three faces on the screen of the laptop on the table in front of him. The sleek, matte metal cast a glum reflection of the scene. Around him, the room was dark.

'Ok, I'm ready,' he said, eventually.

There was no reaction on the screen. Three men in suits sat staring at him as his words made their way across the international connection.

'It is new technology. It has been developed with the resources from kolychak.'

The word meant little to him.

'Ok,' he said and waited for them to continue.

'Check your iPhone,' another of the men spoke this time. 'You have been sent an "instruction manual" for the mapping. You will be required to brief others.'

'I understand the basic principles but what about the chemicals?'

'That will not be your role.'

'To whom will the task fall?'

'Not your concern.'

Joseph Smith began to feel the bile rise in his throat. He detested anyone attempting to exert authority over him and, in particular, these three men. He hated the way they flinched when he spoke, the taint of his rough Sudanese accent offended their ears. But he had learned over many years – and several very hard lessons – there was little to be gained in reacting to snobbery and prejudice. Better to simply note it, lock away the emotion it created and use it at some future point. For, if he was ever face to face with those men and he heard that note of disdain... their connections and their cash would do nothing to preserve them. However, right now, his future depended on them, as much as theirs depended on his. And in this situation, the wise man would stay silent.

'When will I be required to begin using the mapping?'

He found himself speaking in his best English, as if he had just stepped from the screen of a colonial era film, as if he were a slave trained to ape his masters' speech. Although he knew that would not be enough to gain even the smallest grain of respect. Perhaps just the opposite. He would never be their equal. He gazed at their ageing faces on the screen. The atrocities they had committed numbered far more than his. But all was so cleverly disguised behind a perfectly cut bespoke suit and a ski tan.

'You will be told when this is required.'

'I don't understand how it works.'

'It requires drug doses over a specific period of time and then possibly a drug bath and cranial implants.'

'How long does it take?'

'You don't need to know.'

'And am I just a performing monkey, apparently not intelligent enough to use my brain?' It was what he wanted to say but, of course, he did not. He just nodded at the screen as if subservience came naturally to him. As those three men probably assumed it did to everyone of his skin colour.

'You have the key?'

Joseph Smith remembered the tiny key he had taken – as instructed – from the lab technician. Stefano... Stefano something. He could not remember now. It had been the first time he had been able to use his tiger claw, the most awesome of weapons.

He was distracted, remembering the gore of it. He realised he was being questioned again.

'The key?'

'I have it.' He hesitated, then asked, 'What is it for?' He had no idea.

His question was ignored.

'Where is the girl?'

'No longer at her hotel.'

'But where is she?'

'I am not sure. She has been flesh-tagged but, for some reason, there is currently no signal.'

Silence.

'This is not good enough.'

'It is most likely she has been taken somewhere isolated to prevent any tracking. As soon as she steps outside, we will know exactly where she is.'

'What if that does not happen?'

'It will. From my study of her, she is a creature of habit when it comes to exercise. I do not believe, other than in extreme circumstances, anything would prevent her from her nightly run.'

'I hope you are sure.'

'I am.' And then, because Joseph Smith felt he had won

a point, he took a virtual step towards them. 'Is the grid complete?'

Instantly. 'That is not your concern.'

'But she is required for that, too?'

'Yes.'

'Then, it is my concern.' He was getting angry now, despite himself. He could see the ground he had won had been instantly lost.

'It is not your concern.'

The screen went blank.

NINETEEN

AFTER HER CONVERSATION with Irene, Eva was shown to a bedroom in the house. It was another slickly decorated space and Eva wondered who owned this property and where the resources were coming from to fund such ostentatious accommodation. Was Irene still working for the government? Eva realised she hadn't thought to ask. Anya had described her employer as an international network of insiders, 'the back-up plan, when official channels can't necessarily achieve what needs to be done to meet an objective.' Obviously, Irene and Anya worked for the same organisation. Which may or may not be government funded and driven – 'insiders' was an incredibly broad term.

Eva was troubled by the acorn she had seen on the back of the slip of paper in Berlin. Did it mean anything? She checked her pockets to see if she still had it but there was nothing there. After recent events she had no idea where that piece of paper was. It appeared to link Anya to the Association for the Control of Regenerative Networking – and by association, Irene too.

Or did it.

Eva realised that she couldn't even remember what the acorn had looked like. In fact she was beginning to doubt whether it had been an acorn at all. She had not asked Anya about it at the time – and now she would not be able to. She was 99.9 per cent sure that Irene would provide nothing to fill in knowledge gaps. For some reason her, usually sharp, memory felt very confused. She tried to visualise that piece of paper with the words on the front and the symbol on the back. But she could not.

And then there were the two words she was sure she had seen on Sam's phone 'Jackson calling'. Or had it been just '…ckson calling' and she had assumed the rest? Or had it said something entirely different. She realised she could not remember. Eva normally recalled memories as pictures. For that moment earlier in the day, just as for events two nights ago, she had none.

That was odd.

Eva considered her options. A mad dash to the airport, a white knuckle flight home and then sweaty night terrors alone in her flat.

Or she could rely on the small amount of trust she had once placed in Irene to try and piece together what was happening. What did she really have to lose?

Perhaps she really was reckless just as Irene had described her.

Her case sat next to her on the floor. Should she unpack? This wasn't exactly a holiday.

She stared at her case for several seconds and decided not to go through the motions of settling into the room. What was the point? Clearly she had little, or no, free will in this situation. She was effectively a prisoner, compelled into incarceration by fear of something apparently more dangerous. It was a protective incarceration – for her own good. Perhaps the worst kind.

She sat on the edge of the broad metal bed and stared at her hands for several seconds. There was a split in the skin on her right palm, where the knife Sam had held to her throat had lightly grazed the skin. Her hand automatically moved to the point on her throat where the blade had been, marked by a now slightly raised line, but the flesh had not been broken. She shut her eyes as she felt the room rushing up to meet her.

Sam.

She thought of him, presumably now lying lifeless on the pavement outside the hotel. Or in a body bag somewhere. She had no idea where to start in terms of trying to figure out why he had done what he had done. She felt a confusing mix of sadness and shock. Why attack Anya? And what had he been intending to do with Eva – was she the target or just the escape bargaining chip?

If only she'd had time to question him or could remember what she had really seen on his phone.

Had their relationship even been real?

Pointless thoughts, Eva scolded herself. Why waste your brain power on querying what you cannot know?

Opening her eyes, Eva steadied herself back on the bed with her hands. She had been in situations like this before – situations where she had no control over what was happening to her, and where people apparently behaved entirely out of character. When she had experienced this before she had wasted time trying to figure out why. Actually the more important decision was really what to do next.

So, what to do next?

She unzipped her suitcase, removed her phone charger, plugged it in to the wall and pulled her phone from her handbag. Then she dialled the hotel's number as she connected the phone to the charger. A rather harassed woman answered.

'Hallo?'

She didn't even say the name of the hotel.

'Hi,' said Eva. 'I left your hotel several hours ago and I forgot to check out of room 311. I just wanted to say I left the room key on the desk in the room and my room service bill was settled by a colleague.'

Eva stopped speaking.

Why was she making this call? It was as if, in this ridiculous situation, she was attempting to preserve a semblance of normality.

There was a short silence on the other end of the phone and then... 'you are Miss Scott?'

'Yes, that's me.'

'I think the police want to speak with you...'

'Are they still there?'

'No, but they left information for you to contact them.'

'Ok, I will, of course,' she said, not asking for the information. 'Could you possibly tell me what happened to the young man who was injured?'

There was a hesitation on the other end of the phone, as if the woman was consulting someone else. Eva realised she would have to hang up soon.

'The British man?'

'Yes, I believe he was shot outside your hotel.'

'He is dead.'

'I see. And do you, by any chance, know who came for his body?'

'I don't think I understand the question.'

'Was he taken away in an ambulance?'

'A private ambulance I believe. But why are you asking this? I really think you must speak to the police.'

'Thanks for your help.'

Eva hung up.

She had done nothing particularly incriminating by calling from her mobile as they already had her number on their records and would no doubt give it to the police. She seriously doubted there was any trace on the call, presumably everyone at the hotel was still so shocked by what had happened no one had yet started connecting it all together for the police. Well, she was relying on that anyway.

Reckless...

There was a soft knock at the door and the man who had shot Sam walked in with a tray bearing a sandwich, a bottle of water and a mug filled with what looked like tea. She had the distinct impression he had been listening at the door.

He put the tray on a side table but didn't smile at her. Eva made a mental note to lock the bedroom door when he had gone and then, glancing over at it, realised there didn't seem to be a lock. Just a small, round handle.

She moved her gaze back to the man and watched as he tested the balance of the table on which he was placing the tray.

'How's Anya?' she asked.

He finally made eye contact. His face looked grim. 'She will live. But your friend did her some serious damage.'

'He's not my friend.'

'Anya said you told her he was your boyfriend.'

'He was. He's certainly not anymore.'

'He's not anything anymore.'

Eva started at the bluntness. Grey eyes stared back at her unflinchingly. He *had* been eavesdropping at the door.

'No,' she said finally. 'I guess not.'

The man turned to go.

'Look, can you tell me anything more? Irene didn't seem to have much information but I always have the feeling with her that she's holding most of it back.' She laughed as she spoke but could see there would not be a jovial response.

'Honestly? I wouldn't tell you, even if I knew.'

Eva was surprised at the hostility but she didn't respond. Obviously, there was much about her role in this situation she didn't understand.

Or perhaps this man – what had Irene called him? Sassan, that was it – perhaps Sassan and Anya were... if that were true, he might blame Eva for what had happened to the other woman.

Which would be illogical. But emotions cloud logic.

Sassan stopped by the door and seemed to relent. 'All we know is that, whatever we are looking at, involves cartels – at the moment, there is very little else to go on.'

'Drugs?'

'No. Finance.'

Eva remembered she had been thinking about the issue only that morning. Which was an odd coincidence. Wasn't it?

'Is it connected to the Association for the Control of Regenerative Networking?' She was fishing.

'I'm sorry, I don't know what that is.'

She gazed at him and wondered whether he was telling the truth. Probably not; although his inability to disguise the emotional reaction to Anya suggested he was not as much of a robot as Irene. Not yet, anyway.

If he was telling the truth then this new team – whoever they may be and whatever their purpose – knew nothing of what had happened before. Perhaps that was because it wasn't relevant to what was happening now.

But then why the acorn…?

After the man had gone, Eva sat down on the bed again and drank the tea. It was very sweet and, whoever had made it, was obviously assuming she was still in shock. In fact, she felt quite the opposite, her body was alive with adrenaline, her thoughts were starting to rush, and she desperately wanted to go for a run. She glanced out of the window – it was getting dark outside. Was it madness to set off around streets she didn't know after what had happened today? Or, would she simply blend in unnoticed. Mentally, she knew the physical exercise was exactly what she needed. But, obviously, no one in this house was going to let her go. Whether she was a threat or useful, they would want her to remain firmly within their control.

However, it might be a good opportunity to test out just how much autonomy she really had here. And to make sure that she hadn't become so accustomed to crashing from one out-of-control situation to the next that she would allow someone else to steer the course of her life without question.

She would go. It was crazy, maybe even stupid, but she was going to do it.

Reckless... the word played around the edges of her brain again.

She put down the tea mug forcefully, walked over to her case, pulled out her running clothes and set them on the bed. She moved over to the window, closed the blind over the dark sky outside and began to change.

Somewhere at the back of her mind was a voice screaming 'after everything that has happened recently, what are you doing, this is madness!' but Eva was on autopilot. She needed to feel better. Running would make her feel better. It was the only way she knew to process everything. She was blinkered.

When she was ready to go, Eva flicked on a lamp sitting on the broad top of a sturdy moulded plastic desk. She found a pen and notepad and wrote a simple 'gone for a run, back soon' and left it where someone could see it. She was going to go around the block a few times – within shouting distance of the house – so was sure there wouldn't be any trouble. Of course, those were famous last words.

With a shiver of excitement, she slipped out of the bedroom door and made her way down the stairs, trying to avoid the creakier steps, until she was standing in front of the door to the street. There was a key on a hook that looked as if it would fit the locking mechanism and she took it and zipped it into the pocket of her running pants. Now, she really was beginning to feel reckless. But she knew this would make her feel better and it was something she could do for herself in a situation where she had no other semblance of control. I have to do this, she repeated obsessively. She stood still for several seconds and listened – the house seemed completely still, silent and empty. Then, from somewhere deep in its recesses, she heard a groan which developed into a scream. Eva froze. It was a chilling sound. She glanced at the front door again. Perhaps this wasn't such a good idea after all.

Then, she wrenched open the front door and stepped outside.

No one had stopped Eva as she made her way down the front steps from the house and on to a dark street lined with towering houses and blocks of flats. She had expected to hear her name called, or to feel herself being bodily dragged back inside, but, apparently, everyone was caught up in something else. Presumably related to the scream...

Outside, it was a half light between day and evening. It was cold but, to Eva, it felt refreshing. She took several deep breaths, filling her lungs, before setting off along the pavement at a gentle jog. She hadn't brought her phone with her so she would have to remember the route she took and find her way back without it – that, in itself, was slightly unnerving as she had become reliant on Maps apps to move around.

The road in front of her was straight and long and she thought she could probably run for fifteen minutes, circle back and then do another lap, repeat, and that should be enough – if it wasn't, she could just keep repeating until it was. There were a few people around walking home from work, one woman with a pushchair, but few lights were on in the windows lining the road. The area had a feeling of being recently gentrified but it was shadowed by something else.

As Eva ran, she felt her heartbeat start to fall in line with her regular breathing. Warmth spread throughout her body and she began to sweat. She felt her mind relax as the physical motion took over.

When, fifteen minutes later, she reached the end of the huge street she turned and began to run back the other way. She was a little unnerved by the darkness, so she had decided that, when she reached the house again, she would do one more lap and finish, run back inside and shower in the ensuite, eat the sandwich and no one would be any the wiser.

As she ran, she tried to be as observant as possible of the people around her. Most were walking with their heads down as the darkness became more complete and the cold really set in. On the other side of the road, she could see a couple walking slowly, holding hands, their breath making frosty shapes in the night air.

She glanced back to the road in front of her. At the solitary figure walking towards her. It was a man, well built – the kind of physique Eva liked, leanly muscled and strong. He had a slightly limping gait but was walking quickly, as if he had somewhere to be. His head was down, he seemed focused on the pavement. And then he looked up.

He began running towards her at speed.

Eva stumbled.

It was Leon.

Her heart was pounding. How had he found her, yet again?

She had to get away. Skidding to slow down, Eva swerved right and ran up the middle of the road, avoiding the pavement lined with walls or bushes she could be dragged behind. She could hear his pounding feet approaching and, even with the limp, she knew he could catch her. She swerved left sharply, back onto the pavement, and heard him swear and follow; his ankle was clearly giving him trouble. Maybe she could use that. The house was still too far away for her to outrun him. Inevitably, the pounding tread was coming closer. She stopped suddenly and turned, braced herself, faced him.

'What do you want?' she shouted, as he came to a stumbling stop several paces away from her. He wasn't even out of breath.

'I want your phone,' he said firmly and took two huge steps towards her, grabbing the front of her running shirt as he moved, pulling it tight so it trapped her shoulders and arms and then hustling her up against a wall. He started patting her down as if searching for it.

She fought him. He cursed at her. She managed to free an arm and hit him on the side of the head but Leon didn't even flinch. Instead, with his free hand, he slapped her back.

Eva stopped moving and stared at him breathlessly. Something changed in his face. The same thing she had seen in the park.

She was breathing heavily, hiccupping almost. But she was nowhere near tears.

He had stopped moving, he seemed frozen. But he hadn't let her go.

'Back off,' she hissed, into his face so close to hers.

'I can't, Eva.' The voice was oddly hollow.

'Why?'

'I just can't.'

'Are you ever going to tell me what happened back in South America?'

The question took him by surprise. He dropped his grip on her shirt. Eva was released but didn't move away.

'I don't understand,' he said quietly.

'You switched sides. Or you seemed to. Perhaps that was where your loyalties lay all along.'

He moved a half pace away but his eyes never left hers. 'I can't do this right now.'

The two continued to stare at each other. Eva was sweating, breathing heavily, Leon's dark features were stone-like. She waited for him to make the next move. Why doesn't he just break my neck and force me to give him the bloody handset, she thought. His standard modus operandi. But he just stood looking at her, as if he had no idea what to do.

TWENTY

ALTHOUGH EVA SEEMED to slip back into the house unnoticed, she had a feeling someone within those immaculately decorated four walls knew she had left and now returned. She realised, as she quietly shut the heavy front door, that she had been relying on their powers of observation and relentless interference when she had set off out into the street to run. If she had not returned, they would have come for her. Right?

It hadn't escaped her that she was slightly elated, as well as shocked and scared, after the encounter with Leon. Finally, she had been able to ask him 'why' – something that she had wanted to do since Paraguay. Not that he had given her a satisfactory answer. But sometimes asking the question was enough.

Eva glanced around the hall but still no one appeared. Perhaps this time they hadn't been watching. She doubted that somehow.

It briefly crossed Eva's mind to ask Irene whether she had any information on the night Eva had lost her memory; or about the possible truth in the visions she'd had in which she had seen Joseph Smith. If there had been surveillance to the extent Anya had indicated, they might be able to provide answers.

But Eva was hesitant. She still didn't know what had happened to her after Berghain, how much of it had been 'her fault'. Or even what 'it' was. And she still couldn't shift this lingering feeling of guilt. And shame. Irene had already said she thought Eva was reckless and perhaps she would just assume that situation was a natural consequence. Eva didn't want to see judgment in those steely eyes. And nor did she want to see evidence that Irene knew what else had happened – especially if it was something Eva would not want to hear.

She looked down.

In her hands, she held Leon's wallet. She had taken it from him – easily – when he'd had her in his grasp. Which was surprising. But then he had not seemed himself.

'I thought you'd probably ignore instructions.'

A voice brought Eva back into the room like a slap in the face. Irene, who had apparently appeared from nowhere, was standing across the hall.

Eva lowered her hands to her side and held the wallet casually, as if it was hers.

'I wanted some cigarettes.'

'You don't smoke.'

'Sometimes I just want one.'

Eva observed Irene looking at her running gear and felt herself caught in the untruth. That was stupid. She could lie better.

The light bulb in the hallway flickered above their heads, as if acknowledging the power struggle being played out below. Ostensibly, Irene was the one in control. But appearances could be deceptive. Both of them knew that.

'I'm going to have a shower,' Eva said, as she crossed Irene's path and headed for the stairs.

Irene's response was so quick that Eva barely saw her traverse the floor. But within a split second Eva had her back to the banister – before she had even finished speaking the word 'shower'. Although Irene was shorter and slighter than Eva, she had positioned herself on the step above, trapping Eva against the hard wood.

One hand was around Eva's throat. The grip was loose but tense.

'What the hell are you doing?' Eva was taken by surprise but doing her best to disguise it.

Irene had never actually touched Eva before. Or physically threatened her. It was a development.

'Don't *cross* me, Eva.'

Neither woman moved. Eva didn't struggle at all. Her main focus was regaining control of her breathing, which had accelerated instantly at the shock of such an unexpected attack. She squeezed the soft leather of Leon's wallet and it felt warm to the touch. She forced herself to remain still. If she struggled, Irene would only tighten her grip.

Finally, Irene began to let go. She released Eva's throat but Eva didn't break eye contact with her. For several seconds more the stand-off continued but neither made another move.

Then Irene's posture changed and Eva noticed her male assistant had appeared at the side of the room. Had he seen that?

'It's Anya,' he said quietly.

Irene turned and left with him, without a backward glance, her sensible heels tapping quietly at the floor.

Eva turned around and leaned forward, using one of the steps to steady herself. It felt as if she had been holding her breath since Irene had touched her. Perhaps she had been. Every nerve ending was alight, almost burned through – there had been no break in the adrenaline since the contact with Leon only minutes before. And Sam before that. She was beginning to feel like a character in a video game.

She steadied her balance. There was no time to fall apart. She looked again at the wallet and jogged back up the stairs.

After she had taken a shower, Eva emptied the contents of Leon's wallet onto the bed. It contained nothing personal at all – business cards, receipts, a bank card and several platinum credit cards, one of which was not in his name. This did not surprise Eva; she knew he lived about six lives other than his own. She began sorting through the business cards, then stopped. Her eyes widened in surprise. There, amongst four other smart and well designed pieces of thickly expensive cardboard, was a name she recognised very well.

'Dinner,' came a voice from the door, which flew open, banging against the wall behind it.

Eva froze. Should she gather up the contents of the wallet and attract attention to it, or should she leave it where it was and hope it went unnoticed? If it was Irene, it would have been pointless trying to hide anything but this was her assistant.

She stood up and turned round.

Grey, penetrating eyes met hers. He was holding a tray with food on it, a bowl that was steaming and a plate with bread and butter.

'Soup,' he said.

She hated soup.

'Thanks.' She almost smiled then stopped herself. There was no need to make him suspicious by suddenly turning on the charm.

'Here,' she said, reaching out her arms, 'I'll take it.'

He stepped forward and shoved it at her so the soup slopped over the edge of the bowl, then turned without a word, for the door.

Eva watched the door as it slammed.

A prime example of passive aggression. Or was it just aggression?

She disposed of the soup on the nearest flat surface and returned to kneel by the bed. She picked up the business card again; shivers travelled down her spine. It was Sam's business card.

Or, at least, it was Sam's name, but the branding was nothing like the organisation they had both worked for. It was minimal, black and slick. She flicked the card over. On the back, a single word 'Veritas'.

She said it out loud and heard her voice echo back at her,

slightly gravelly from the recently retreating adrenaline. Truth?

There was a second, similar card, although this one carried no name.

She put the cards on the bed and began looking through the receipts in the wallet. There was a cash point receipt for earlier that day for 200 euros from a machine near her hotel, as well as a receipt from what looked like a banking organisation.

The last receipt was for a train ticket to Perpignan in France. On the back of it were some numbers – which seemed to be tomorrow's date and a note of a time using the 24 hour clock. Presumably, the time and date of the tickets he had purchased. But where were the tickets?

Eva searched through the wallet but there was nothing else of interest.

She flicked on the bedside light for the second time in an hour. Eva absolutely hated sleeping in a room where the door didn't lock. Particularly in her current situation. She pulled back the covers and walked across the overheated room to check the chair she had propped up under the door handle to warn her of intruders.

She pushed and pulled it gently. Ok, still there.

She turned back to the bed. And that was when she saw him. Just a glimpse in the mirror. A talk, dark man standing in between the wardrobe and the wall.

He raised his hand.

She stared.

The room exploded around her.

'Is she alive?'

Through the ringing in her ears, Eva could just make out concerned voices she recognised as Irene and her assistant.

She felt herself being gently lifted and placed on a softer

surface. She opened her eyes, coughing. She tried to sit up. Someone pushed her back down.

'Don't try to move.'

'I'm fine,' she said, angrily pushing their arms away as adrenaline and panic began to surge through her body. She sat up. Apparently, the explosion she had experienced had been real. It had not destroyed the building but it had blown the right hand side away.

She looked warily at Irene, who was covered in dust and had a large, bloody gash across the top of her right arm which had torn right through the fabric of her suit. 'What happened?'

'Most likely a letter bomb. Old school. Only partially detonated. Otherwise, we'd all be dead.'

Eva looked back towards her bedroom, which was now above where she sat in the rubble. 'Is that fire?' she said suddenly, noticing smoke and a red glow emanating from the glass.

The two others turned quickly and saw the same thing.

'We need to get out of here now,' said Irene, quickly, starting to pull Eva to her feet. 'Your room was undamaged. All your possessions are being retrieved. Take them and wait in that car over there.' She indicated a large black people carrier, perhaps the same vehicle Eva had been in before.

'Don't we need to wait for the police?'

Irene gave Eva a long look.

'Wait, Irene,' Eva said, as thoughts suddenly rushed into her head. 'There was a man in my room, I'm sure there was. I saw him just before the explosion happened.'

'What?' Irene was shocked.

'A man, by the wardrobe.'

Then the second explosion happened.

It had taken her several days to form her conclusions on the single document that had arrived on that sunny evening. In her

Hollywood Hills home, the analyst once again read over what she had prepared as her response to what had been revealed to her. It was audacious, in fact it was almost ridiculously simple – and that, she suspected, was what would give it the element of surprise. There was such power to be found in being underestimated.

The document had recorded a network of transactions that had taken place – and continued to take place silently and without note. These transactions were all focused on the economy of a single country: the UK. Not too big and not too small.

They had been designed to take advantage of the economic progress of that state over the past 50 years, everything from privatisation of utilities such as water and gas to the principles of free market capitalism that had reduced state intervention and sought to let the market define its own winners and losers. The reality was that this approach had created a market where wealth was concentrated in the hands of the few. And that was what had allowed this – she hesitated at what to call it in her mind – … this 'plan' to be put into action.

You offer everything for sale. You risk it ending up in the hands of an undesirable owner.

It was really as simple as that. Everything that the UK had turned over to a profit motive, everything it had sold off, privatised or set up as a private enterprise in the first place was essentially for sale to anyone with the resources, no matter where those resources came from or what the motivation for purchase was. Despite the fact that the infrastructure of the country still relied on those entities, they had still been offered for sale to private buyers. And if the powers that be thought they could stop the buyers being a single entity by setting up regulators, committees and ombudsmen then they were sadly mistaken. Anonymity and disguise could be acquired for any entity. And they were essential for surreptitious control.

Although this particular entity was one that she doubted the powers that be were even aware of. It was faceless, it was nameless – and its reach was unchecked.

TWENTY ONE

EVA COULDN'T HEAR, other than a high-pitched ringing noise. She realised she was shouting when she felt the pressure of her voice in her throat but she couldn't hear anything. She was lying on a stretcher inside a moving vehicle. There was nothing she recognised, she didn't even have any belongings and she couldn't see a single face she knew. She was being attended to by a middle-aged man with a narrow, lined face and a shock of grey hair which made him look as if he had been electrocuted. Although she couldn't hear him, he seemed to be very concerned to stop her shouting. He pointed across the interior of what was, apparently, an ambulance and, on the other side, Eva saw a body. So badly burned it was almost black. But, apparently, still alive.

She closed her mouth.

The grey-haired man looked relieved.

Eva continued to stare at the body opposite.

Her heart was pounding. She realised the body was too tall – and far too male – to be Irene. What was left of the hair was not the right colour to be Irene's assistant. And nor was it Anya.

Eva's fragile flow of consciousness was interrupted by each jolting movement of the ambulance. Her thoughts were travelling too fast, she couldn't pin anything down. All she could think about was the body on the stretcher.

She tried to push herself up on her elbows but the movement of the vehicle in motion – and the arms of the paramedic – stopped her. It had to be the man she had seen in her room before the explosion. It had to be. She had to find out who he was.

Eva continued to stare across at the prone figure.

With a start, she realised its head was on one side. Her vision was blurring, her head was thumping. But she could have sworn there were eyes looking directly at her.

The vehicle began to slow down and Eva realised they were about to reach their destination. Where they would no doubt be separated and she might never be able to locate him because he had no face. She had to find out who he was, why he had been in her room.

She turned to the paramedic and tried to speak but her words sounded as if she was shouting into a balloon. He winced as she tried again; she realised it was futile.

She shut her eyes.

What the hell was happening?

The next time she opened her eyes, she was in a hospital room, dressed in a gown and tucked underneath several blankets, almost secured to the bed by them. The paramedic must have sedated her. Cold fingers of fear scratched at her consciousness. What was going on?

It was dark outside but there was a soft light coming from a lamp near the bed. There was no one else in the room, although she could hear voices from the corridor.

Hear. She could hear.

Eva lay still and realised she no longer had a harsh ringing in her ears. It had dropped to a low hum. However, now that the adrenaline had worn off, her body felt broken. She was sore in a way she had never been before – her skin burned; she knew that, if she tried to move, it would disturb every bruise and cut. But shouldn't she try?

Small lights danced in front of Eva's eyes as she tried to follow the thought through. Her body felt heavily medicated, she could barely keep her eyes open and the edges of her consciousness were blurred, unclear and lacking focus. She gave in to the heaviness and began to close her eyes.

Almost as soon as her eyes were shut, she began to dream. She was in the hospital bed in the same room, feeling the same pain. Her dream self looked across at the door and there was something there, silhouetted against the light. Her eyes focused and she saw it was the other body from the ambulance, tall, dark-haired and horrifically burned, but standing – in exactly the same position as the person she had seen in her room just before the explosion.

He stared from the other side of the room. He said nothing. He just stood half facing her, the rest of his body turned towards the door, completely still as if he was an actor waiting for a cue. She felt as if his head might rotate 360 degrees on his neck. Then, in the dream, he turned and walked out of the door to the private room and, as he did so, went up in flames.

Eva awoke with a sharp intake of breath.

Briefly, her heart fluttered into arrhythmia as she tried to place where she was and why.

It was just a dream.

She looked around but experienced no post-nightmare relief.

The image from the dream continued to run through her head, as if on replay. The turn of the man's head, the walk out of the door and then the hellish rush of flames as the body was consumed.

Eva looked at the door. Nothing.

She continued to stare at it, as if she would miss something if she looked away, but nothing happened.

The dream was unnerving. It did not help that she had nothing from her world to comfort herself with, to reassure herself that she was real and that the vision was just a dream – because at that moment she wasn't sure she could tell.

Eva felt immensely vulnerable.

She moved and found that sitting up was painful but not impossible. Her body hurt, but she could move.

She pushed back the sheets and disconnected herself from

the wires delivering rehydration and monitoring her bodily functions. Despite what she had been through, it was clear that she wasn't seriously injured or she wouldn't have been left alone like this. And there would have been more tubes.

She swung her legs over the edge of the bed and felt for the floor with her feet. It was cold and rough and her skin was tender and feverish.

Carefully, she stood and tightened the ties on the hospital robe, closing the gap at the back. She began taking slow, steady steps towards the door, until she realised she could walk without difficulty and then she stepped out into the corridor.

The hospital ward seemed to be a collection of private rooms and it was quiet. All the doors were shut. There were no windows looking into the rooms, which seemed a little odd. At the end of the corridor, Eva saw a nurse's station with one occupant reading in the light of a muted desk lamp.

The woman looked up.

Eva walked towards her.

It was impossible to read the expression on the woman's face. Eva began to feel nervous. Her feet were cold against the hard floor and she shivered.

'I wonder if you can help me,' she said, smiling as she reached the nurse.

The nurse continued to look at her. 'If I can, I will.'

She was English.

Strange. Wasn't it?

'Can you tell me where I am?'

'You're in a hospital.'

'I know, but which one?'

'We're on the outskirts of Berlin.'

The answer was evasive. Why avoid giving a straight answer to a sick patient? Eva noticed that her own skin was alive with goosebumps she couldn't attribute solely to the cold.

'There was a man. Or a person. They arrived with me in the

same ambulance. Do you know what happened to them?'

'No.'

'Is there any way that you could find out?'

'Unlikely.'

For several seconds, all that passed between the two women was a look. Eva felt as if she were trying to engage a brick wall. She considered demanding that the nurse help her, she was sure she could find a convincing reason – or at least make enough noise – to force a response. But she needed to conserve her energy. Besides, there was more than one way to get what she wanted.

'Thanks,' she said and turned and began walking in the other direction. Eva heard a phone ring as she reached her room and looked back. The nurse was now on the phone. She glanced at Eva and looked down at something on the desk in front of her, apparently not interested in what Eva did next. Which was not very nurse-like behaviour. Eva stopped and stared at the top of the woman's head. Was she even a nurse?

After several seconds, Eva collected herself. Whatever medication she had been given was making her slow. She veered left away from the door to her room and ducked down the corridor opposite, moving silently along the hard floor in her bare feet.

As she walked away from her room, the hospital became colder and darker. Eva didn't know if it was her drugged imagination but the place seemed to chill the further she walked from the nurse's station; she wished she had thought to bring a jumper. Or shoes.

She stumbled and swore as she stubbed her toe on a concrete block next to the wall on the left. She stopped walking, looked at it, puzzled. It looked like debris. Then she scanned the rest of her surroundings before glancing back in the direction she had come. It was almost as if the room she had been in was a film set and this was backstage.

She felt compelled to keep walking, so she turned away from the warmth and light and pushed open a door into the darkness of the corridor beyond.

At the end of the corridor, she could see a single room illuminated by a bright fluorescent bulb. Unlike the other rooms, this one had glass on all sides and in the bed, propped up into a sitting position, was the charred figure of the man she had seen in the ambulance. As she drew closer to the room, she could see he had no wires, drips or monitors attached to his body, and no one was attending to him. The only movement was the jagged rise and fall of his chest, as if he too had been drugged, this time into an uncomfortable sleep. She couldn't take her eyes off him as she walked down the corridor. He cut a shocking figure.

It was as if he had simply been left to die.

When she reached the room, she pushed open the door. No one stopped her, no alarm sounded.

The man in the bed continued his ragged breathing and then, as she looked closer, she noticed an eye peeling open.

It was a deep brown eye. So similar to one she knew from many years ago. She shook her head to try and clear it. The room was cold. The man was shivering. Eva pulled her arms around her. She looked at what was left of his hair, thick and dark, like... like...

No, surely not.

Her stomach dropped like a stone.

'Jackson?' she took a step towards the bed.

The burned figure was still. And then, slowly, he began trying to turn his head. There was a sucking noise as the melted skin on one side of his neck began to tear, as he turned towards her. His moan made the hair on the back of Eva's neck stand on end.

He could only open one eye. Nevertheless...

Eva felt her heartbeat spiral. The room started to spin. She stared hard at his face but her vision kept shifting.

'Jackson? Is that you?'

The one open eye was all she could focus on.

Was she going mad?

But she was sure she recognised that eye. It had to be… it was…

'*Jackson!*' she ran at the bed, losing her balance as her body failed to cope with the sudden movement and falling as the man in the bed began to emit a low moan.

She hit her head on the bed frame, which was rusted, but pushed herself back up into a kneeling position. She struggled to stand again. The body in the bed was making an inhuman noise now, keening, rocking from side to side.

Eva's nostrils were suddenly filled with the smell of charred flesh, she hadn't noticed it before. She retched; put her hand to her mouth; retched again.

'Please,' she said to the man, 'please stop making that noise.' She tried to look for somewhere to put a hand on his chest or arms, to try and comfort him, but the flesh was completely raw. Why is no one taking care of him, she thought unsteadily, those must be first degree burns. He will die!

Eventually, the man calmed down and was quiet. He lay still and, again, attempted to open one eye.

'It is you isn't it? Jackson?'

It seemed as if the man was trying to speak but the flesh of his mouth was burned shut. Eva stared again at that one open eye; years of pain and frustration began to well up inside her. She felt an urgency overtake her. '*Please. Just tell me if it is you.*'

Teresa had to admit the date had not gone particularly well. She had been hesitant to go in the first place and, frankly, the whole experience left her wishing she was of pensionable age so she could stop trying. 'Oops!' Teresa laughed out loud as she stumbled on her heels, climbing up the steep concrete steps to her Berlin apartment. She was tipsy, there was no doubt about that – but how else did one survive a bad date?

'Exactly!' she laughed to herself.

She had been single for several years and had never felt an urgency to start searching for someone. At least, until all her friends turned 30 and started marrying the first pair of trousers which came along. She knew at least half of them were miserable, and made more so on a daily basis by staying with their partners, but they never left. They just bitched and moaned, put on weight, silently resented their husbands' freedom ordained by biology, dreaded the day the kids left, and drank too much wine.

However, the pressure to at least start dating had affected Teresa, despite the long hours she worked and the fact she already had more than enough money to keep herself in the lifestyle to which she had become accustomed.

She had no financial need for a man, no desire for security. But she did miss the sex – it was so variable and inconsistent outside the confines of a relationship.

As she pushed her key into the front door, Teresa suddenly stopped dead. There were tiny scratches around the keyhole. Had they been there before?

She looked closely.

A shiver travelled down her spine.

She turned and glanced back down the dark hallway of her apartment block. The light flicked off its timer switch and, for several seconds, she stood in the dark as the hairs rose on the back of her neck.

'Shit,' she muttered to herself, turned the key and opened the door. Don't be ridiculous, she thought. As if anyone had broken in.

Nevertheless, she checked the entire flat before pouring a glass of wine and retreating to the bedroom to record her evening for posterity on her various social media accounts.

She scrolled through the feeds, chuckling delightedly to herself at several notifications which informed her a man she had been flirting with quite carelessly was responding in exactly the way she wanted. How easily manipulated they are, she smiled to herself.

She pushed off her heels – handmade, four-inch stiletto courts from a British designer with a burgeoning reputation – and began to undress. Despite the cold outside, the room was warm, so she left her robe where she had draped it over the chair and walked to her dressing table in her underwear.

Maybe a selfie, she thought to herself, as she sat down at the table – her make-up was so good it would be a shame for no one to have seen it other than the bad date and the taxi driver.

So she stood up, pushed her hair to give it volume and held her smart phone so that the screen was facing her. Her face filled the screen. She smiled at her 'reflection'. She pulled the phone away slightly, turned it diagonally, tilted her head to one side and tried out two or three different poses before settling on the one which conveyed exactly the right message and looked the least like she had taken it herself.

She snapped two or three images. She moved the camera back slightly, widening the frame.

She froze.

Captured in the last photo she had taken was the image of a man standing behind her.

TWENTY TWO

JOSEPH SMITH SWORE repeatedly to himself as he ran down the street from the woman's apartment. With her damn camera phone she had glimpsed him just before he had been about to wrap a pair of stockings around her neck. Although he had hit her hard, he had lost his advantage and she had been able to grab at her wine glass, which had been smashed to a single lethal shard. Now he had a gash running bright red with blood down one side of his cheek.

As usual, the pain had sharpened his senses; instantly cut through red mist. And he had looked down at the woman lying on the floor, almost as if he wasn't sure how he had arrived in her apartment or why she was looking up at him, a combination of terror and defiance in her eyes.

He had found, over the years, that, periodically, he had to do this. It was the same every time but he could not break the pattern. He was always carrying out the same revenge. A hurt from so many years ago. There is nothing more powerful than rejection, he thought, as he ran – it never leaves you. If it catches you at the wrong time in your life, it's like a wrecking ball sweeping the foundations from under you – that burn, the feeling of being out in the cold.

He had not known his father. Other than by way of cuts, bruises and beatings. And his mother had been weak, cowed by years of inflicted violence, yes, but ultimately focused only on protecting her own skin.

In the end, he had watched his father kill her. Crush the life from her neck as if he were screwing up a paper bag.

Her eyes locked on to Joseph's, held his gaze before

slowly draining of life.

She hadn't made a sound. It hardly took any time at all. Almost as if she was glad to go, to escape.

In fact, the last look he had seen in her eyes had been pity although, at the time, eleven-year-old Joseph had not understood why. With his mother's same instinct for self-protection, he had hidden and watched as she had died, had not intervened. And he cried in loneliness and fear after his father removed her corpse.

But soon that had turned to anger, when he became the front line for the assault his relentlessly wounded father waged on anyone he shared a house with.

Joseph then suffered for four years at his father's hands because his mother had not fought for her life – and, by association, for his. If she had lived until he left, he might have escaped with only broken bones but the wounds inflicted after her death never healed.

Instead, he became obsessed with taking life – copying his father in his own childish way by squeezing the breath out of living creatures he had power over, be they a bird, or a frog. Watching the light die in their eyes in the same way as his mother's had gave him a feeling of safety. If he was the one inflicting the damage, it could not be done to him.

The first time he had taken a human life he hadn't even intended to. But the woman had reminded him so much of his mother he had flown into a rage, which only subsided when he found himself still holding her by the neck, which he had almost snapped in two.

After that, he realised he needed the release, periodically, to keep his anger under control, to remain focused. It was almost like medication.

He usually chose women he thought would not be missed – people who existed on the fringes of the world, without social security numbers and families, work colleagues and savings accounts. But this time he had stepped outside his usual pattern and picked a different type of woman. And he knew that somehow Eva was to blame. He had wanted power over the woman tonight in a way he knew he could never have without forcing her. Just like Eva. It had been a mistake. Not only had she spotted him but she had not cowered from him. She had attacked him with the wine glass and, even though the blow should have been hard enough to knock her out, she had recovered, picked up a chair and swung it at him, screaming. Her reaction had frightened him. In his experience, women rarely fought back – those he had chosen before wouldn't dare. But this one did. And so he had followed his instincts and run. Now he would have to leave Berlin – slightly sooner than he had intended, but only by a day.

She was still screaming the same words over and over again when she was dragged backwards from the room by two tall men in dark bomber jackets. They were not wearing scrubs. There wasn't even a pretence at hospital garb. As Eva watched the neon hospital lights pass by, one after the other, above her head, she acknowledged this was not like any hospital she knew, she was not safe. But the fog was descending between her thoughts and her reactions, isolating her brain from the harm that could be caused by what she had just seen only increased her confusion. She could feel the skin on her heels burning, blistering against the rough floor as she was pulled across it and she felt the sting of the blow to her right cheek as she fought being pushed back into the room she had occupied. Her body registered the pain as, again, her head hit the metal furniture by the bed but her reaction was non-existent. As the boot made contact with her stomach, she finally stopped screaming, lying in a foetal position parallel to the bed. She stared ahead into the middle distance and didn't flinch as the boot came towards her abdomen once again. Finally, when the boot made contact with Eva's skull, she let go.

'I don't understand why we can't find her, she can't just have dropped off the face of the earth.'

'There is a strong possibility she didn't disappear on her own.'

'I know that,' snapped Irene. She was angry, very angry. It burned at her insides and she was barely able to control it. Or was that fear.

Eva must be found; it was not possible to proceed without her.

'Locate her.' Irene turned to her assistant and stared at him.

'I have tried.' He was patient but he thought he was being the voice of reason. 'She is most likely dead by now.' He had no idea what was at stake.

Irene felt a jolt against her insides. She'd had no tenderness for Eva before this had happened and now – well, now she disliked her even more. In the past she had become representative of everything that Irene had failed at. And now she was doing it again.

But Eva was complex. She survived. Like a cockroach.

'I think you underestimate her.'

The man laughed. It was a short, sharp sound with a distinctly patronising undertone.

Irene swung around. 'Why are you laughing?'

'I…'

'*Shut up.*'

He stopped immediately.

'Don't you realise,' continued Irene, 'what will happen if we don't find her? If she is dead?'

The man looked at her, held her gaze, but only just. He didn't know. That much was clear. Irene looked away. She had already revealed far too much of her own inner turmoil for one interaction.

She could not show weakness.

'Just go,' she said, shooing him from the room with her voice.

After he left, Irene shut the door, locked it and then slowly lowered herself into one of the metal chairs in yet another Berlin safe house. 'Safe' house she thought, bitterly, to herself; it had not proven to be particularly safe for any of them in the past 24 hours.

Anya and Sassan were gone, Sassan killed in the second explosion, Anya barely alive, and Irene was left with a team of unknowns. It was unnerving enough when she'd had help, now she was on her own.

She flipped open a slim, silver laptop and flicked the on button.

The screen jumped to life and she launched an application, then watched as the screen filled with her own face in one box and the moving image of someone else's in another.

'You're late.'

'There have been issues.'

'Unless everyone – including you – is dead, I don't want to know.' The tone was haughty and superior. Irene wanted to point out the ridiculous nature of what had just been said. But she didn't.

She abhorred being a subordinate. But this was the path she had chosen.

'Where is Eva Scott?'

'We don't know.' The admission was hard to make. Irene waited for an explosion.

'Do you, at least, have her possessions, the phone?'

'No, we searched the rubble and there was nothing. I think they must have been destroyed in the second explosion.'

Another silence hung in the air.

Irene again waited for expletives, the screaming she had

experienced previously, even a mild telling-off but there was nothing. Which was much worse.

'Find her,' said the face on the other end of the video call, then the connection was dropped.

Irene continued to stare at the screen, which was now filled only by her own worried-looking expression. She looked at herself in the image of the laptop's camera. It was not flattering. She had lined skin, her hair had lost its lustre and she was slightly thicker set than she had been at Eva's age.

What struck her most about her appearance were the enormous bags underneath her eyes, making her features look hollow and haunted. When had that happened?

Briefly, she thought of Henry and the children at home in London. He was presumably tucking them into bed right now. Once again, they would ask where was mummy and (if he wasn't feeling too resentful) Henry would perhaps say how much she loved them before reading a story and singing them to sleep.

Irene suddenly felt very alone.

For several days, Eva drifted in and out of consciousness and sleep, never really able to differentiate between the two. Her mind wandered aimlessly from memories to dreams – the flaming man at the door of her room, the charred body in the bed, Jackson as a child, the phone calls from her dead brother's phone and that word 'kolychak'. Every thought was soundtracked by the moaning of the man in the bed. The sound ran like a pulse linking every other wild and baseless thought that she had. It was the only constant.

Outside her mental confusion, Eva had little awareness of what was going on. She had been dosed with drugs that topped up what was already in her system to the point where her mind willingly submitted. The series of shock events she had experienced since the dying man at Waterloo had threatened to overwhelm her when she was conscious and these, combined with chemical encouragement, now sent her deep into the recesses of her mind. She was being subdued, rather than treated, and she was also being prepared. As she was never conscious long enough to complain, she remained suspended in a nightmarish animation, reliving all the most frightening moments of her life as well as each and every one of her fears.

She didn't notice when they finally changed her blood-stained clothing or when they moved her to a different bed. She had no reaction when she was wheeled from one room to another, this one full of machines and computers. And she had no idea when they began to cut into her skin.

The man with the Mediterranean tan closed his laptop and turned to face Paul, who was smoking self consciously. Or, at least, it appeared to be self consciousness but the older man was learning Paul had many talents and one of them was a Janus-like ability to be two-faced. What Paul felt and what one saw were often two very different things. Nevertheless, it was time Paul was made aware of the scale of the issues his complacency had caused.

'This is a mess.'

The words hung in the air as the two failed to make eye contact.

The man with the Mediterranean tan waited, watching his younger associate who, he hoped, would hold his hands up to what had gone wrong. Not only was Paul responsible for the technology that had backfired so disastrously but he had also made a bad call on what should have been a very straightforward execution. Paul would not learn from these mistakes unless he was forced to, unless someone highlighted them for him. Otherwise, he would continue to play his cruel games, inflicting pain for entertainment, torture to amuse. The older man knew pain was a weapon and should be used as such, it was not for fun or gratification. Pleasure gleaned from others' suffering... it was like playing God. That seemed to be asking for trouble.

'I suppose it is not entirely a mess.' Paul looked over at the older man. His expression was sly, clearly he thought he could get out of this situation as he had others before.

There was a moment of uncomfortable eye contact. Neither looked away. The older man recalled their spats recently in which he had begun to feel that Paul was dangerous and no longer within his control. Psychotic, even. He felt a small nudge of regret at raising the topic.

'I mean,' Paul continued, like a wily teenager making excuses, 'everything else is entirely operational, correct?'

The tone felt patronising. That was aggravating. Especially now he knew Paul was just a common thief who had gained a place at this table through deception. The only question remaining was why had he done it. Looking at the expression on Paul's face, the man with the Mediterranean tan knew he now had to do something to uncover the rest of Paul's story. Not knowing it had become too much of a disadvantage. It was a risk but he had to push the other man to anger, to that point where caution was destroyed by emotion. He could not think of another way to get Paul to reveal himself – soon it would be too late.

Paul continued talking.

'We have achieved the milestones that we were set, yes?'

No reply.

'I mean, there's very little that can stop it... is there?' Was that a slight note of uncertainty in that oh-so-confident tone?

A flicker of a smile crossed Paul's face. As if he had some plan of his own and everything was going according to it. Which is what the other man suspected to be the case.

That was the trigger.

He lunged across the old mahogany desk and grabbed Paul

by the front of his shirt. The movement was so sudden there was no time for the other to react and he was taken by surprise. Particularly so by the sinewy strength that saw Paul dragged across the desk and pushed up against the wall.

Paul did not have a fighter's instincts. He was a desk criminal, a delegator. He spluttered, his mouth working as he felt the hand crushing his windpipe, tighter and tighter. He didn't know how to defend himself or counter attack.

Genuine fear clouded his eyes and the older man could smell a loss of bladder control.

In a way, it surprised him. Someone as apparently hard as Paul should have been able to retain composure under pressure. But he was also emotional, too emotional, so apparently all he could do was react.

The older man leaned in close to the reddening face opposite him.

'Why are you unable to take this seriously?' he hissed.

There was no let-up in the pressure of the fingers on the throat.

'Perhaps you just don't care? Perhaps you have an agenda of your own you are not being entirely honest about?'

A flicker of something crossed Paul's face. Was it a cringe? The choking mouth tried to work itself into words, as if Paul believed he could talk himself out of what was happening to him, whether by threat or persuasion.

As he watched this gurning, the older man recognised his advantage. And, with surprise, he realised just how afraid he was of losing it. He had the distinct impression it would be the equivalent of removing his shoe from the head of a venomous snake when he let go.

He leaned in again, his voice low, threatening, his other hand itching to reach for the paper knife he kept in his desk drawer. But he couldn't, he knew that. It was another complication they simply didn't need.

'*Anything* could disrupt this, Paul,' he continued, talking to delay the moment he would no longer hold this man's life in his hands. 'It is delicate; balanced on a knife-edge. Decades of blood and sweat have been dedicated to establishing this degree of control, to maintaining it, to growing it. People have died for this. Do you understand how many lives and how many deaths you disrespect with this recklessness of yours?'

He stared into the bulging eyes opposite. Paul appeared to be trying to nod. He realised the young man was about to pass out and, instinctively, released his grasp.

He felt the power seep from his skin.

Paul recoiled out of the grabbing zone, filled his lungs and staggered sideways, knocking from the large desk a round whisky glass, which spun and then smashed against the door.

That would no doubt attract the attention of the staff.

The older man straightened his tie and took his seat. He sat and waited for Paul to do the same. He did not experience the usual rush of power. He felt nervous. It was as if he had just crossed a line he could not step back over. And nothing more had been uncovered about Paul. He felt exposed and an unaccustomed chill of terror caused the skin on the back of his hands to pucker.

When he realised what was required of him, Paul tried to sit in the chair, missed as he lost his balance and tried once again. This time, he made it.

The older man realised the voice he could hear talking was his own. Why was he continuing to speak, he wondered – to maintain the upper hand, to enforce his position? Perhaps if he simply carried on talking he would be safe.

That was doubtful. The deed was done.

'There can be no more failure, no more misjudgement. Do you understand that?'

He knew he was trying to establish his authority. It felt like the act of a desperate man. And yet, on the surface, he was in control.

'Well,' he said angrily, 'do you?'

A painful nod. No eye contact. Apparent submission.

Perhaps this was all that was required to enforce the hierarchy, hoped the older man, his heartbeat thudding hard against the inside of his chest.

He sat back in his chair; some of the terror subsided. He had seen genuine fear on the other man's face.

Hadn't he?

Eva could hear a chorus of birds. The light around her began to filter through her eyelids, which felt stuck together. She tried to open her eyes but, for some reason, the muscles in her eyelids wouldn't respond. She lay still and continued to listen but there were no sounds other than the birds. Which in itself was strange. A rush of fear swept over her when she realised she didn't know where she was or how she arrived there. As conscious feeling began to flow through her body, she ached. Horribly. All over. Certain points on her limbs burned as if the skin had been pierced. She started to run her palms over her arms and, sure enough, felt welts where the skin had been cut and blood had crusted over the holes underneath.

Dimly, she made out the beeping of a heart monitor and registered various wires once again attached to her. She moved her torso slightly and felt a pull at her chest and at points in her arms. She registered how afraid this made her feel but she seemed unable to motivate herself to do anything about it.

She heard footsteps enter the room and lay still.

'She's awake.'

'How can you tell?'

'Look at her heartbeat.'

'Wh…'

'Shhh.'

There was a silence of a couple of minutes, then the first person spoke again. A woman.

'Eva, how are you doing?'

Adrenaline was starting to melt through the hangover from the cocktail of drugs in Eva's system. She was beginning to realise how uncomfortable she felt in a room with two people she didn't know, and she couldn't see.

'I can't open my eyes,' she said, her voice husky, a croak of a sound.

'Yes...' came the response.

'Should we unglue them?'

'Shhhh...'

Glue? Adrenaline spiked through Eva's system. *Glue.*

My eyelids have been glued together, thought Eva, trying to make sense of this new piece of knowledge. She lay still. She wanted to scream, to pull at her eyes to open them, or to demand – or even plead – that someone help her, but she didn't. She felt paralysed by the information she didn't have about her situation. But she was not sure how much longer she could remain calm.

A matter of minutes.

Movement began to happen in the room around her and she felt someone at the right hand side of her bed. The presence felt large, not a woman, and the smell was of cigarettes and something earthy, slightly damp. As the person breathed on her, she could smell what was last eaten. Anchovies.

She recoiled. Apparently, the lack of sight was making her sense of smell particularly acute.

Water was dripped on her eyes and she jumped as the first drop hit her eyelids.

'Just relax. It's surgical glue, that's all.'

'Why are my eyes glued shut?' She was trying really hard to be polite, to be reasonable, not to lose control.

But someone had glued her eyes shut. And she had no idea where she was.

There was no response. Just the feel of a cotton ball wiping at the lash line of her right eye. Eva jumped at the touch and shivered involuntarily. Vulnerable came nowhere near describing how she felt at that moment.

After several minutes of dabbing with the cotton wool ball, the person moved away and Eva was told to try and open her right eye. She played along, being the docile patient, keen not to anger whoever was helping her, at least until she knew more.

She opened her eyelids gingerly, not wanting to damage herself. She was given another soaked cotton wool ball and told to carefully clean away the glue whilst the person attended to her other eye. Finally, she was able to fully open her right eye. She wasn't prepared for what she saw.

TWENTY THREE

'SHE'S NO LONGER in Berlin.'

Irene swallowed. 'Ok. Where is she?'

'France.'

'How the hell did that happen?'

She tried to reign in the emotion in her voice. She was too close to the edge.

'In the back of a lorry. She has been unconscious for days – they packed her up like a piece of furniture and moved her.'

'Still in the bed?'

'Still in the bed.'

She almost felt as if she might laugh at that. Was she completely losing control?

'And what about him?'

'Dead. We think.'

'Body?'

'Of course not.'

'Was it definitely Leon she saw in the house?'

She willed him to say yes.

'We have no way of verifying that.'

Irene shook her head. This was becoming more and more precarious. She had known that once Leon realised she had lied that he would not stop. However, she could not have anticipated just how effective he would be, or how persistent. It was almost as if something or someone else was driving him.

'Do you have any idea whether she is awake?'

'No. I can't get close enough. They are located near a small village at the base of the Pyrenees, very close to the border with Spain.'

'Name?'

'Ceret.'

'What can we do?'

'Right now, very little. I'm assuming that, if they haven't killed her yet, there's a reason.'

She listened to the silence on the other end of the phone for several seconds.

'Is there anything else?'

'No.'

The connection was cut.

'Valerie?'

Eva was staring, with her one open eye, at a dead woman.

Green eyes gazed straight back at her.

'Valerie?' she asked again, in the same tone and intonation.

The woman opposite exchanged a look with the other person in the room.

Alarm registered in Eva's brain. A judgement had just been made. But what about?

She stared again at the face opposite, so very familiar

It looked like a woman who had been her brother Jackson's girlfriend at the time he disappeared. A woman who she – Eva – had shot dead in a Paris apartment, not so long ago.

She felt the room spin and shut her one open eye. There was no way Valerie could have survived that bullet. Absolutely no way.

Unless she was not human. Eva's nerve endings flared; she felt a sliver of fear ripple across her skin. What was Valerie, if she was not human? Eva could not dismiss the thought with cold, adult logic. For some reason her brain refused to quiet its panic. Valerie remained a terrifying 'what if' in her mind.

And also in the room.

Eva tried to remember the moment of apparent death, back in Paris.

After Valerie had fallen, Eva had run, there had been no time to do anything else, no time to check whether she had actually died.

But, surely, there was no way Valerie had survived.

Leon had been there – they had fought and Valerie had, shortly before, thrown him through a glass table. He was injured so there had been some urgency to escape. No one had checked Valerie for a pulse.

Eva remembered the whispered conversation she had heard from another room before the shooting – which had revealed that Leon and Valerie had a history of working together. Leon was a mercenary. Up until then, Eva had believed her brother's former girlfriend to be a receptionist and superficial party girl. But, as it turned out, she was neither. Surprisingly, she appeared to be a mercenary just like Leon. And, clearly, also an impressively skilled actress.

Which meant she could easily have faked death.

As the adhesive on her left eye dissolved slowly, Eva felt an overwhelming anxiety rising up through layers of drug sedation. If that woman at the end of her bed was Valerie, she was in real danger.

A feeling of intense discomfort overtook her. How long had she been unconscious in this room? How long had she been vulnerable? What had happened to her in that time?

She could barely breathe at the thought of what might have taken place.

But why was she still alive?

She opened both her eyes.

From across the room, a pair of bright green irises burned into her own.

Eva couldn't move. She was pinned to the bed by the strength of the Valerie look-alike's unearthly stare. The woman was standing like a stone statue. And yet she had nothing behind her eyes; they seemed empty of anything – anger, malice, fear – there was no clue there. Nevertheless, she didn't look away.

In fact, she didn't even blink.

There was something bloodless about the action – perhaps even cruel. It was calculated, that much was obvious, but it was also almost scientific, as if it was a test.

Straight, auburn hair hung in a bob on either side of her face. Her cheekbones were sharp and eyebrows defined. Her skin was smooth, almost airbrushed, in appearance. She was frighteningly beautiful.

But there was something about the woman, whoever she was, that set Eva's nerves tingling. Something wasn't right with the way her face was put together, or perhaps it was that stare – intense, unwavering, predatory. As if she knew what was about to happen next.

Someone else was moving around the room, which Eva noticed appeared to be encased in a form of zipped-up plastic.

She broke the stare of the stranger and tried to pull from her eyelashes the clods of glue threatening to stick her eyelids back together. All the while, she could feel the woman's eyes drilling into the top of her head.

She looked up again. The eyes met hers. A wave of fear rose and fell through Eva's body. It just wasn't normal.

'Stop staring at me,' she blurted out, slightly slurring her words.

Whoever else was in the room immediately stopped moving.

The woman opposite continued to stare.

'I said,' Eva began to shout, '*stop staring at me.*'

Her voice faded away instantly, the last vowel hanging in the air.

Eva watched as a slow smile spread across the face of the woman opposite. The mouth began to curl at the corners, the cheek bones bunched, red lips pulled back to reveal sharp white teeth. Razor-sharp white teeth.

The woman continued to smile at Eva who, as she tried to move, realised she was tethered loosely to the bed. The woman was beginning to look demonic. Her face was distorting, taking on a devilish shape.

Eva scrambled for several minutes to free herself but she couldn't.

She instantly forgot that she was tied to the bed; she felt as if that stare held her in thrall, like a tractor beam.

Then they were both still.

Neither broke eye contact.

Eva felt the muscles in her jaw slacken. Her mouth was hanging open but there was little she could do.

She couldn't tear her gaze from the face opposite.

She felt as if it was growing in size. She thought she saw a drop of saliva fall from the woman's mouth. She licked her lips.

The green eyes gleamed.

Suddenly, the woman opposite took a step towards the bed.

Eva began to scream.

TWENTY FOUR

EVA WAS MESMERISED by the images on the laptop screens. She was aware she must be drugged as her thoughts were coming in confused bursts and she was talking to herself. The twirling computer-generated graphs and tables on the screens at the foot of her bed kept attracting her gaze. Each time she looked, the computer had added another line, dot or measure in colours that she didn't like. She vaguely noticed that her skull hurt when she moved her head to follow the movement, as if something had been drilled into it.

Eva was alone now in the zipped-up room which, in her moments of clarity, resembled a disease isolation tent. However, no one had been wearing facemasks so she could not be infectious.

But was she even sick?

Eva had lost much of her recent memory but she could not recall a point at which she had felt injury or illness worthy of this kind of confinement. So, why was she in this bed? A spark of anxiety lit her brain but faded again.

She just couldn't think clearly.

At the back of her mind was a drumming, tight feeling, like a voice shouting behind a shut door, but she couldn't really hear it properly so she continued to stare at the screen. And then she fell asleep.

At one point, she awoke to a velvety darkness, broken only by a large shaft of light that seemed to be shining directly onto her legs. She turned her head and realised that behind the zipped plastic there was a window and that this must be open as she could hear what sounded like the crunch of gravel outside.

Then a figure had appeared on the other side of the plastic tenting, a figure with auburn hair. The figure had stopped and leaned in to the other side of the material so that all Eva could see was the oval of a pale, eyeless face staring in through the thick white plastic. She had shut her eyes tight and tried not to cry.

Between the fear, the spikes of almost supernatural horror and the muddy confusion in her mind, Eva could work nothing out. Whenever she tried to process her thoughts they simply got stuck in a viscose, honey-like cloud and then she forgot what she was thinking about.

At some point during one of the hours that she could hear the birds singing Eva opened her eyes to see that the plastic tent had been removed. She felt much less groggy and, as the wires that had also been attached to her had gone, she thought that perhaps she might like to get out of bed. She sat forward and pulled the covers back. The effort of trying to move her legs was intense, they seemed almost completely useless. Once again she felt a strong desire to just retreat into her drugged mind and she almost pulled her legs back under the sheet but this time something stopped her. She felt the skin on her legs prickle. Leg hair, she thought, looking down at her bare calves. She tried to calculate how long that might indicate it had been since she'd had a shower. She couldn't.

For several seconds, an urge to panic threatened. She took deep breaths and the fog descended just enough to quieten the anxiety response.

Looking around, she realised she had forgotten what she had been about to do. Then, a voice chimed in her mind 'get out of the bed.'

Right.

As she slipped over the edge, Eva realised her forearms were stinging and noticed two plasters stretching along the flesh of the insides. She looked down at them for several minutes but was unwilling to lift them up and look underneath; whatever was inside felt absolutely raw. Perhaps that could wait.

She stood up, shakily, and took a step. Then sat down quickly on the bed. She had been in that bed for some time, clearly, as her legs felt as if they had forgotten the natural human action of walking. A second wave of fear gripped her. *What has happened to me?* This time it was not misted over so quickly by the drug cloud.

Made determined by the fearful thoughts, she forced herself to get up and then stood on her toes, bent her knees and began moving her body around as if warming up for exercise. Gradually she began to feel more like she was inside her own skin.

She walked over to the window. The scene outside was remote, hilly and quite beautiful. Mist-shrouded mountains were all around, it was warm and not damp enough to be English. But there was nothing about the scene that gave her any lasting pleasure. All she felt was a sense of rapidly growing unease.

Irene gazed out of the window as the car sped through the open countryside; the sun was rising. They had taken a flight from Berlin to Barcelona Girona, arriving early and collecting the car left for them at the airport. They had already passed the Spanish border and were now heading at speed towards the tiny Pyrenees town of Céret, where Eva – whatever state she might be in – was located.

Irene was anxious, very anxious. This had to happen. And yet she felt a tiny nagging doubt over Eva and her own role in the girl's fate.

On a personal level, for Irene, Eva represented the second time in her life where emotions had clouded judgement. The first had been Eva's father.

Since Evan Scott there had been many times when Irene had

looked back to that point and wondered what had overtaken her. She was living in a war zone, her world was chaos, and a love affair was a warm and wonderful place to escape to. Somehow it felt real, solid, when everything else was fleeting. But in a way her heart had tricked her because it was not real. If it had been real love then the two of them would have stayed together – got married, had children, remained together for decades. Then, although the situation was admittedly not perfect, any rational human could see that it was just life, that there was no need to do anything other than accept, forgive and move on. Because it would have been something real.

But that was not the case. Evan had returned to his family.

As she took in the breathtaking beauty of the French countryside Irene realised that was the point at which she had changed. After that, emotional isolation appealed. She simply shut her feelings away, no longer fought with herself over the ethics of right and wrong. Life became a series of goals, doing what she needed to do to move from one to the next and get what she wanted. And she felt nothing. Lines that had once seemed solid were crossed – the more of them she crossed, the less the crossing mattered.

Which is why she was where she was now. It was the inevitable final step along a path she knew she had always been on. Self-destruction disguised as ambition and success. She was no longer walking in the light.

Irene realised her assistant was looking at her in the mirror and wondered, for a second, whether she had given anything away. It was unlikely.

The metallic voice of the satnav directed them off the major motorway and they began to drive along smaller, more residential avenues. Céret was a picturesque town, with traditional steep cobbled streets, as well as some new-build houses – one of which they pulled into just as the sun began to climb in the sky.

They unloaded several suitcases; just another of the numerous ex-pat couples in the area – albeit with a slight age difference. Then they crunched over the gravel of the two-storey building which would be their home until… well, until it was done.

'You're awake.'

Eva was walking down the stairs of what appeared to be a grand château, with an opulently decorated set of doors opening onto expansive lawns.

The comment came from a small man in what looked like a butler's suit who had emerged from a door as Eva creaked her way down the stairs.

How ridiculous, she thought, looking at his crisply pressed shirt.

'I'm sorry, I don't know who you are.'

She still felt relaxed, as if no action was required. Something told her that, in some way, she was sedated still. Otherwise, she would surely be in panic mode. Fight or flight.

'Would you like a drink – some coffee perhaps?'

She registered that the man had not tried to provide identification.

'I would love some coffee,' she said, as she realised she really would.

'Go and sit outside and I will bring it to you.'

Eva did as she was told, drifted through the front doors of the château, onto a large stone area overlooking broad, green lawns dotted with whirring sprinklers, a tennis court visible in the near distance. Her bare feet felt cold on the stone and she was instantly aware she had very little on.

She found a table and chairs and sat on the wood, which was warmer than the stone, lifted up her feet and placed them on a chair opposite.

The man returned, looking vaguely displeased, so she took her feet down.

He had with him a tray, but he didn't carry it as if it was natural, in fact he almost let the silver coffee pot slide off.

Eva recoiled, realising she wasn't entirely sure what she would have done if the pot had left the tray. Would the natural reaction have been to try and catch it? She didn't know.

With the coffee in front of her, the man began to depart.

'Where am I?' she suddenly thought to ask at his retreating back. He turned as he walked and looked at her, but he didn't reply.

A smudge of anger clouded Eva's mind. And then disappeared.

She sat back in the chair, uneasily, and took several sips of the hot coffee. And then she downed the entire cup. She poured another cup and downed that too. And then a third.

She sat still, very still. She looked around at the scenery and realised this pretty place was vibrating with unease.

And that's when the clouds began to lift. Stimulated by the caffeine, her mind began to turn once again – fast. She stood up.

I'm in danger.

She wondered whether she had any possessions with her, perhaps a phone, but they would surely be upstairs. And besides, she thought as she looked around, this was too good an opportunity to miss. The land around was open, there was no one here. She should just go.

Draining the last drops of the coffee, she began to walk, first across the stone and then the wet grass. Then she began to run. No one stopped her, there were no panicked shouts, nothing happened.

The muscles in her legs complained but her heart was beating healthily and the blood pumping through her veins felt good.

Perhaps it was too early for anyone to notice, she thought, and began to pick up her pace. When she reached what looked like the edge of the property, there was a small stream running clear over pebbles with concrete banks on either side. She could jump it, easily.

She took a couple of steps back.

Her right arm began to throb.

She started a run up.

Both arms felt as if they were pulsating.

Eva continued to move. And then, suddenly, her body jerked forward and back; she howled and fell to the floor.

Joseph Smith watched as Eva lay on the wet grass, writhing.

She was clearly in agony although, from his position, he could not hear her – which was a shame.

He took a sip of the watery coffee he had made for himself before spitting it out in disgust. He missed the thick, dark coffee of his homeland.

He put down his binoculars, stood up and walked over to the sink of the small cottage he was occupying in the grounds of the extensive château.

The château in which he was not allowed to set foot.

He had wondered if his exclusion was simply because he'd had contact with Eva, whether she would recognise him, or whether it was something else.

Joseph, over the years, had worked with gangs and groups of all shapes and sizes – he was not particularly fussy about those for whom he killed, as long as someone had deep pockets to pay for it. In that time, he had noticed one thing – that racism (if you could call it that) went all ways. The human condition was so evident when it came to this fundamental issue of trust – you trust someone who is like you. You instinctively don't trust what you don't understand. No matter how advanced the human race became this would never change. No matter how civilsed we consider ourselves, he thought, it all boils down to the fact that we trust people who look like us – we assume that they *are* like us. And even if we make an effort to overcome those doubts it's still not the same as implicit trust.

Such implicit trust had often worked in his favour, which is why he took the time to think about it.

Yet others like him – whether from the same country, or of similar skin colour – would choose to trust him over another with a different heritage or a white face. That weakness was one of the easiest ways to gain an advantage. For he trusted no one – at all.

Joseph stopped. He realised he had become distracted. A surge of anger travelled through his body and he felt like banging his head against the wall.

He stood for several seconds until his pulse-rate began to normalise.

Abandoning the idea of making more coffee, he returned to the table. He looked through the binoculars.

Eva was no longer there.

He wondered why she had been so underdressed out on the lawn. He briefly considered what was being done to her, and why. But unless it affected his interests he didn't really care.

He put his hand in the pocket of his trousers and pulled out a key. A tiny metal key – the one he had stolen from the genetics scientist.

He turned it over and over in his hands, watching as it caught the light. It was small, but solid, hollow at one end and curved into a small circle at the other. And it was light, much lighter than it looked.

He tested its resistance by squeezing it between a powerful thumb and middle finger but it did not give.

He looked at it close up but there did not seem to be a single mark on it. There was apparently no indication as to what lock this key would fit. And then he saw it – lettering. It was only visible when the sunlight caught the edge of the key and only after he had pressed his thumb onto the metal.

Heat activated?

Must be.

Joseph looked at the blank key. He pressed his thumb hard on the metal, before turning it quickly to the light.

Three letters appeared, '...tas'.

The word he had seen before had been longer.

He tried again, attempting this time to place his thumb slightly further to the left, where the rest of the letters had appeared.

He turned the key to the sun, '...itas'.

He was becoming frustrated now, he wanted to see the word. He laid the key against his palm and pressed hard on the side on which he had seen the letters for several seconds.

Then, he quickly turned the key back towards the sunlight and there was the word.

'Veritas'.

TWENTY FIVE

IRENE LOOKED AROUND the room at the mass of electronic equipment. She missed the time when a covert operation would have required cunning and courage rather than tech. Which meant she was getting old. However, these devices were useful. Or, at least, the data they provided was. They had so far collated enough information from thermal imaging, satellite pictures and visual and audio surveillance provided by local eyes on the ground to establish Eva was not in the village itself but somewhere within a two or three mile radius.

Given Eva's reckless streak, as well as her apparent Houdini-like ability to escape the metaphorical (or physical) chains and water tank, Irene was surprised she had not freed herself. There was a dogged persistence about the girl, something her brother possessed also and, unless she was already dead or incapacitated, she probably had a good chance of engineering her own freedom.

Which could be a problem for Irene. It was essential that Eva continued to trust her – even if only because there was no one else. Irene had presented herself as the best of a bad bunch, Eva's only face from the past – friendly or not. Never mind that Irene had been involved in setting up events that had been designed to skew Eva's perception of reality, to doubt her ability to cope.

Leon's arrival had been a worry, particularly as he might appeal to Eva more than Irene did, especially given their history.

She had relied on the chemicals in Eva's blood stream doing their destabilising work and hoped that Leon's appearances could be used to further force Eva to question what was real and what was not, rather than to present him as an alternative to Irene. He was not an alternative. He could not be. She did not know what was driving him now but she doubted whether it was Eva's best interests he had at heart.

Irene sat forward in her chair and widened her eyes, forcing her eyelids open.

There was a low hum in the room, emitted by the equipment and, after several days without sleep, she was being lulled into the threat of a doze by it. She stood up, straightened her tailored trousers and picked up the large yellow pottery mug she had found in the kitchen of the house. When she reached the coffee pot, she flicked the switch and waited for the liquid to filter through before pouring herself a large measure and drinking it straight, without milk or sugar.

It was now dark outside and they would be forced to move soon. The information had been gathered, the operation had been hastily planned, soon they would have the exact details and the additional personnel would arrive. Once that happened, they couldn't stay there any longer as their presence would be noted by some curious farmer or nosy local resident. Irene wasn't sure she liked the French.

He ducked down behind a large hedge, from where he could see the bright lights of the château but where he would not cast a shadow from the moon behind. It was a harvest moon, large and yellow, and it was lighting up the entire, enormous lawn between the spot where he crouched and the house beyond, as if the area were floodlit. He had been watching since lunchtime and knew she was in a room at the front. But he had received no other information. And that worried him. Everything could change so quickly in this game. The set-up, in particular, confused him. It was not what he had been led to expect. He suspected there must be underground tunnels and exits as some people went into the house and never emerged and others appeared from nowhere. He could only hope she was still in there – in a position he could reach her quickly. Or, if she was moved, he would have to react straight away.

Instinctively, in the dark, he crouched down and checked the small arsenal of weapons strapped to him. He knew he could use all of them if he had to, he was entirely confident of his ability to win a physical fight in most situations. And he would have no hesitation defending his prize through violence.

He checked his watch again, low lit and kept under the palm of his other hand. Not long to go. In an hour, he would be on the move.

An explosion of light and noise marked the moment in which Eva became conscious again of her surroundings. Her eyes flew open, she inhaled an enormous gasp of air and tried to sit up, before her brain processed that she was confined by her wrists.

And then came the realisation she was moving. Not her body but the surface to which she was pinned.

Above her, the night sky, velvety and black, studded with pinpricks of light.

She gazed at it for several seconds.

She was outside.

And she was fastened to a moving object.

She pulled her wrists upwards but the binding prevented any movement. She felt sharp stabs of pain in her forearms as she tried to flex the muscles. Turning her head right and left, she tried to work out what was going on but her vision kept blurring, making the back of her eyeballs hurt.

After several seconds with her eyes shut, she tried again to free herself but was tied fast. She lay motionless, eyes still shut, then she turned her head sideways, opened her eyes and fought to focus. She could see the lawns of the huge building in which she had been confined. Slowly tipping her head backwards, she could see two men behind her, facing away and powering forward, their hands pulling whatever she was strapped to. A gurney, it rattled like a gurney. Eva raised her head slightly, looking at her toes, and saw two more figures in black, one looked female. Both stared straight ahead and said nothing. Neither of them looked at her. She noticed her ankles were unbound. Eva's heart was palpitating madly, she could hear a low hum in her ears; it soon became apparent that it was her own voice, a muted scream. *What is going on?*

She lay back down, allowed herself to be carried along while waves of alarm washed through her confused brain. Was this even real? All she knew was that there had been pain. She had been hurt. Recently. But that was all she had. The lack of information was almost as terrifying as the unexplained actions of those around her. She had no control over her body and no understanding as to why that was happening.

As the gurney made its jolting way across the huge lawn, Eva gradually became aware of a roaring sound. She tipped her head backwards, painfully stretching her neck, and saw the source of the noise. A helicopter. It looked like an emergency medical helicopter – was she dying? But she was hooked up to nothing and no one was paying particular attention to her other than to move the gurney across the grass. If she was dying, nobody cared.

She struggled again with the strapping and one of the figures at her feet glanced down at her.

'Where are you taking me?' she shouted, over the noise of the helicopter blades starting to turn.

His eyes registered nothing and he quickly looked ahead.

'HEY! I said where are you taking me?' She heard the tremble in her voice as she shouted. This time no one reacted. She started to struggle more on the gurney. Pain burned again in her forearms and the back of her skull. Why? What was that pain?

Eva suddenly felt a rush of anger. Raw, burning,

uncontrollable rage. The gurney began to pick up speed. She couldn't stand this situation any longer; she wouldn't be treated like this anymore. She kicked out at one of the figures at her feet. The kick was so weak it didn't even merit a swerve. But Eva could use the freedom in her unsecured legs. Turning on her side, she swung her right leg across her body and levelled a kick to the head of one of her escorts. This time she kicked as hard as she could. And she had the element of surprise. As soon as her foot made contact, the man swerved and stumbled, letting go of the edge of the gurney. The others kept the gurney moving forward as the man peeled away. They picked up speed again.

Eva shifted her weight, tried the same move on the woman on the other side but she batted away her legs. A sense of urgency overcame her as they moved closer and closer to the noise of the helicopter, whose whining blades were beginning to spin faster and faster. She couldn't get in that helicopter. She wouldn't get in that helicopter. She wanted her autonomy back.

Violently, she began twisting and turning her body, attempting to destabilise the gurney enough to stop forward momentum. The trolley began to rock precariously. She heard one of the men swear in French and suddenly the gurney was tipping to one side. She felt hands trying – and failing – to set her upright. The gurney hit the floor. Eva was face down on the ground, her wrists still attached to the gurney at her back. For several seconds there was a silence in which she had a sense that the men were backing away. Why? Then Eva could hear shouting. The helicopter blades sounded as if they were slowing down.

She jumped violently as she heard the sound of automatic gunfire and lay still on her front. The shots were coming from behind her, the other side of the gurney. Hunching up against it she tugged again at the wrist ties but they held her fast.

An uncontrolled flow of thoughts overtook her mind. Was this a recue? An assassination? Pains ripped through her forearms each time she pulled at the straps but she had to get free.

She flattened the soles of her feet against the mattress of the gurney behind her. She pushed with her feet, tensed her arms and pulled them towards her. The straps were thin fabric. They did not look made for the gurney. Surely they would not hold.

Finally they snapped, first one and then the other. The pain in her forearms almost caused her to black out. She caught her breath, rolled onto her stomach and jumped her legs up into a crouch. It was quiet all around, eerily so. The blades of the helicopter were coming to a stop, the slowing whine almost a concession of failure. The lights on the machine had gone off, plunging the very back of the lawn into near darkness but there were bodies, she could see them in the light of the moon. She had grown used to recognising the lumpen form of a slain human being.

She breathed hard. Her breaths were rasping. Looking around, she tried to see anyone or anything moving around in the darkness. She considered running but the thought made her forearms throb even harder.

Eva turned so that her back was against the gurney and suddenly a face loomed out at her from the darkness. A face she thought she had seen consumed by fire not that long ago.

Jackson.

Irene sat in the car, listening to the gunshots from two miles away, echoing over the radios. Someone else was executing their plan – and doing it fairly efficiently by the sound of it. Someone else had waited until the chopper arrived, until Eva was wheeled out on the gurney, and then had – apparently – killed everyone on that lawn to reach Eva.

But who?

And why?

The second of these questions troubled Irene but the first

was curious too. It would be a hard job to do single-handed so either there was a team of people carrying out the shooting, or one very competent individual. She could think of only a few who had both the skill and the potential interest to carry out the job and she didn't want to contemplate the involvement of any of them at that moment.

The question of who had ordered the removal was troubling – she did not know of other interested parties. Eva was only valuable to her for a very specific reason, connected to knowledge that had not been widely shared. Either this was a random happening or it was someone attempting to capitalise on Eva's value to others.

She turned to her assistant, who was listening to the ongoing chatter on the radio from the men she had concealed on the site.

They appeared to be panicking, or at least stunned into inaction. The plan was defunct and apparently they did not know how to respond.

Irene was not used to this. It would not have happened when she was inside the system.

She snatched the radio from the hand of her assistant.

'Listen, you fuckwits,' she hissed, 'don't lose that girl. DO NOT LOSE HER – do you understand me?'

A shocked silence, and then, 'Understood.'

'And keep us informed when you are on the move. We will follow.'

They had loaded up a new car with the equipment they needed, leaving the rest behind for the clean-up team to take home. Now they had speed, technology and muscle on their side. But that was about it.

Eva stared into the face of her long dead brother as he lay on his front opposite her on the grass.

It couldn't be…

'Breathe, Eva,' he said quietly, holding her gaze. Her mind hurt, it was too much to process after what had just happened. He kept his eyes locked on hers for several seconds more before turning over her forearms to look at the plasters. He held her arm up to the light and ripped off the sticky fabric.

She gasped and tried to pull her arm away but he was stronger. The dim light revealed a mass of stitches and swollen skin where the plaster had been. It hurt like hell.

'What are you doing?' she said, breathlessly.

'You can't leave here with these,' he said, pointing to her arms. 'But we have to move soon as they will come from the house.'

'With what? I don't understand. Are you really Jackson?'

He looked at her in the moonlight. 'Yes,' he said and then he produced a large scalpel.

TWENTY SIX

EVA WOULD REMEMBER, for many years, the agony of the moment the man with her brother's face plunged the scalpel into her right forearm. It was a pain like nothing she had felt before. More shocking and raw than anything she had ever experienced. The ripping apart of semi-healed flesh, the tearing of skin, the instant flood of warm, sticky blood.

As to what happened after, she would never know. She blacked out almost immediately.

He worked quickly on the unconscious woman, aware of the danger they were both in. At the same time, he queried the decision to take her with him alive. But those were the instructions he had been given and he was not the kind of person who questioned authority. He was reliable for that very reason, which was why he was here. This – right now – had to be believable, credible. Especially for her.

He had removed the two devices that would have prevented her from leaving the château grounds. The wounds on her forearms were not large but they were open and that made them vulnerable. They would hurt a great deal as they healed under the bandages he would eventually apply. He was concerned that this was not a sterile environment, but that had not been his call. As he felt the blood drip from her lifeless limbs he knew there was no way they could stay there any longer.

It was time to go.

When she was clean of the devices, he heaved her over his shoulder and began to run. He was surprised, and not surprised, that there was no one to intercept them. He had almost fallen over one of the bodies of the men who had been pushing Eva's gurney but had righted himself and kept moving forward. Eva was slim but heavier than she looked, which indicated the muscle mass of a committed exerciser. It made her difficult to carry. Nevertheless, he had to take her back before she awoke because she would be distressed, injured and frightened. And that would make her a liability.

The noise inside the château was audible from the outside. With her team in silent pursuit of Eva, Irene had taken the opportunity to move closer to the location in which Eva had been held. It was not difficult to do as the grounds were extensive and open, which made Irene wonder how on earth they had prevented Eva from making her escape, particularly given how relentlessly she would have been trying to achieve it.

From her position across from a small river at the edge of the grounds, Irene used night vision goggles to observe the figures running around the edges of the grand building. Although she couldn't see with any kind of accuracy, from the conclusions she drew as to the pattern of their movements and the speed with which they were going about them, these people appeared to be packing up, loading equipment into transport; there was a lot of shouting. Oddly enough, it seemed strangely ordered. There was very little panic. Which was unexpected, given the person who was the object of all that effort was now gone. She switched to binoculars, which she could use to see the lit-up areas of the château. She watched a man with a Mediterranean tan at the centre of it all as he stood smoking a cigar under the light of the hallway, quietly giving orders to the individuals approaching him every couple of minutes. There was also a younger man, who seemed to have some authority but stood slightly aside, very still, almost as if he were stalking the movements of the older man.

Irene was about to put away the binoculars when she stopped. There was a woman approaching the cigar-smoking figure now – striding through the well lit entrance to the château and out towards the man, with a purposeful gait. Irene adjusted the binoculars. She recognised the woman, surely. Perhaps not from an encounter in real life but certainly from photos. But who…?

Irene lowered the binoculars, then quickly raised them again.

This was not possible. That woman was dead, she had seen the report herself. Hadn't she?

She focused once again on the figure, now standing whispering in the ear of the standing man. As she readjusted the binoculars for focus, the glass cleared. Her heart double beat. It seemed as if the woman was looking straight at her.

Then, as her own vision adjusted to the distance, she realised the woman was not at all who she had thought. She was just a very clever imitation.

Eva was almost used to waking up in rooms she didn't recognise. But this was the first time she had woken up in such pain. The skin on the inside of her forearms felt raw and burned, as if someone was holding a hot iron to them. The desire to scream was overwhelming. But once again, she was strapped to a bed and it was that which gave her pause for thought.

For the first time she had memories of what had happened to her prior to waking up. Some, at least. Although there was no recall of being deposited into this bed. Or tied up.

But some memory was better than none. The small amount of context she had gave her the foundation for a sense of normality. Even though she was in desperate pain, she felt some clarity. She realised that she had not felt that since before Berlin.

I am real.

Strength started to flow in her veins – real, capable strength.

For several minutes, she focused her thoughts on the two areas of her arms that were burning so intensely. She encouraged her body to feel calm, to begin to numb the pain; it was hardly morphine but at that moment mental strength was all she had.

Once the feeling in her arms had ebbed to a low burn and her breathing slowed, she began to take in her surroundings.

They were nondescript.

Nothing told her anything about where she was.

The room was simple – a bedroom – with cream walls and a window through which she could see only sky. She was attempting to push herself up on the bed when the door opened and there stood a tall man with unruly brown hair and deep brown eyes.

Eva stared at him until the atmosphere in the room became uncomfortable.

Finally, he walked over to the bed and set a tray down on a small table next to it. The tray contained a gloopy orange liquid in a whisky glass, an apple and a bowl of couscous dotted with multicoloured blobs. It did not look appetising.

Eva noticed the man did not untie her hands.

He stared at her for several seconds, as if waiting for her to speak first and, when she didn't, he began to talk.

'First of all, I'm sorry.'

He made eye contact, brown eyes, moist. Eva stayed silent.

He seemed nervous.

'I know you have had to deal with so much on your own and some of it has been my fault... as a result of my actions.'

Still, there was no response.

He gazed at her and then looked away.

'Untie my wrists.'

Those deep brown eyes met Eva's as she spoke. Suspicion was written all over his face.

The two stared each other down, as they might have done during one of their childhood spats. She remembered a game to see who could hold eye contact the longest but, now, it didn't seem like much fun. For once, Eva won. As soon as he looked away, she repeated herself.

'Untie my wrists.'

'I'm not sure that I should.'

'If you don't, I'm going to assume there's a reason you want to keep me chained up like a prisoner.'

'You're not chained.'

Eva didn't respond. He was splitting hairs. That was not like him.

Silence.

'Jackson.' She said his name almost testingly and looked directly into his eyes to work out whether they revealed the right response. They were not the open eyes – windows to the soul – she had been used to in her brother. She had always been able to read him like a book. These eyes were guarded, perhaps afraid – it was clear he wasn't who he had been when they were last in the same room together.

I knew it, she thought to herself with a tiny surge of triumph, I knew he was still alive.

'Eva, I'm concerned about what you will do if I untie you.'

'Why?'

'You're obviously annoyed. And I completely understand that. You must be so fed up with being manhandled by people you don't know.'

She looked at him. He seemed to almost bow his head under her gaze. She just couldn't figure him out.

'Look,' he continued 'it's important that you stay immobile – for now.'

'Why?' She was sticking to monosyllabic responses. Her mouth was dry as a bone and she was wrestling internally with the situation. The face in front of her was her brother's, there was no doubt about that. However, the mannerisms, the turn of phrase, the wariness were not like the man she had known. He could be… he could be what? she questioned herself, a fake?

Of course, this had to be Jackson – how could she doubt the physical evidence in front of her? That face was his face. Down to the last stubble hair. That kind of detail could not be faked. However, the question was what kind of person was he now and what did it mean for her?

'You need to remain immobile because I don't want you to hurt yourself,' he said, indicating her arms. 'I don't have any pain relief for you and those will take some time to heal.'

'I don't understand why you cut me.'

'It's a long story.'

'I'm sure you can shorten it.'

He blinked.

'What was in my arms that you cut out?'

'You wouldn't understand, even if I told you.'

Eva's anger ticked up a notch.

'Try me.'

He met her gaze evenly, made her wait several seconds before he spoke. 'Subcutaneous tracker implants. Inserted under your skin to allow a degree of control over your movements. You are linked up wirelessly and if you try to go beyond certain defined physical boundaries – dictated by an electromagnetic field – your internal organs are shocked.'

Jesus, thought Eva to herself, how the hell do I end up in these situations? She looked back at the man who was, essentially, the answer to that question.

'They shock you unconscious,' added Jackson, helpfully.

'But these scars are not small,' said Eva, indicating her arms, 'I would have thought this would be something like a microchip?'

'It's not the most advanced form of the technology. But they are slim and long, rather than short and thick, and they weren't inserted deeply enough to damage tendons or muscles, so you should have no trouble using your arms when the scars heal.'

'So, the scars are superficial?'

'Yes. The most superficial cuts are always the ones which hurt the most.'

'Ok, untie me then.'

Gotcha, she thought.

Once again, Jackson eyed her suspiciously, obviously realising he had walked into a trap and would need fresh justification to keep her tied to the bed.

She stared back at him. Something inside her had changed course, something had snapped – perhaps the link between the decisions she was considering and the fear of their consequences. It didn't seem to matter what she did, she still ended up at the mercy of someone who seemed to wield greater power. So why be cautious anymore – where had that taken her? Irene describing her as 'reckless' could prove to be quite prophetic.

But she didn't care, she was fed up with being a victim.

'Do it,' she said, more forcefully.

'Ok, fine,' Jackson said, eventually.

He walked across the room, closed and locked the bedroom door. It was an action that made Eva's heart palpitate. He took the key from the antiquated keyhole, put it in his pocket, walked back across the room and began to untie her from the bed.

When he had removed the plastic ties, Eva rubbed the skin around her wrists and looked at the scars, now covered once again with bandages.

Jackson took a step back and opened his mouth to speak.

Eva pushed herself up slightly on the bed, raised her hand and slapped his face with all her strength.

TWENTY SEVEN

IT FELT STRANGE to Eva to be sitting in a car alongside her brother after all these years, almost unbelievable in fact. She had so much to ask him, she didn't know where to start. A part of her still couldn't process being in the same space with him. She had thought about it so much, she had almost created a memory from it. Although she had never anticipated this sense of detachment – it was almost as if she was sharing a car with a complete stranger. Which, in a way, perhaps, she was. He didn't feel, smell or respond like Jackson. If it wasn't for the fact he looked and sounded identical to her brother, she wouldn't be sitting in the car with him at all.

Although there was an incredible amount of ground to cover – where he had been for the last couple of years, the truth about his relationships with Valerie and Leon, why she seemed to be drawn constantly into his vapour trail – right at this moment there were more pressing matters. Although initially she had understood that they were to stay put and wait for the scars to heal, apparently now they needed to be on the move – fast.

After a short conversation in the bedroom at the house where he had taken her, he had clingfilmed her wounds and given her time to shower, presenting her with clothes to replace the hospital scrubs she had inhabited for far too long. The shower had made Eva lightheaded but being clean felt good and she was surprised to find the light burgundy-coloured jumper and black jeans fitted almost perfectly. As soon as she was dressed, she had hunted for her bag, her phone – before remembering she no longer had either. She'd sat down on the edge of the bed and looked around her at the plain room. She might be conscious, clean and mobile but she was still entirely in someone else's hands – and at their mercy.

In theory, she was at the mercy of her brother, risen from the dead. However, Eva did not believe in miracles and nothing Jackson had done over the past decade had been for the benefit of anyone other than himself.

Why appear now?

Eva had needed him so much over the past couple of years. Why choose that very moment to come for her? Then, there was the question of how the hell he had known where she was. At the back of her mind, Eva also couldn't ignore the suspicion she felt for his motives. Leon, she knew, was a mercenary. Valerie, it seemed, had been one also. They were people who cared little for bonds, whether they were blood or friendship. If these were the people Jackson had chosen to be his closest friends, what did that say about him and how little he valued those who loved him?

Eva wanted so much to believe this was the start of something new, an era of not feeling so alone, of not constantly finding herself filled with questions about the past. But she knew naïve impulsiveness was always a mistake.

Eva looked across the car at the profile familiar for so many years. She wanted to reach out and touch his face, to make sure it was him, but she didn't dare. He seemed to be terrified of physical contact.

After she had slapped him he had turned to the wall, his heads in his hands.

It was odd behaviour.

Eva had not remarked on it. But the memory had stuck in her mind, nevertheless.

She gazed at the road ahead, an endless strip of tarmac speared through the centre with a broken chalk white line.

She wondered whether there would ever be a point when she felt secure or was able to trust even someone who was her own flesh and blood.

It did not seem likely.

Before they had left the house, they had eaten a lunch of bread and ham. Eva had consumed her food at breakneck speed, as if, at any moment, someone might attempt to take the food away from her. At first, her stomach had protested. She tried to remember the last time she had eaten anything solid but could not.

Jackson had explained they needed to start driving but that was all he said. He had not responded to questioning. In fact he had completely clammed up. Like a sullen child.

This had both troubled and annoyed her. That irritation had only grown when he had spent almost the entire confrontation continuously touching his face. What was it they said about people who touched their faces when they spoke? Eva was sure it indicated lying.

They had left the house, a farmhouse positioned on its own in a huge field of artichokes, and driven off in a dark blue Fiat with scratches down one side.

That was several hours ago. The sun had set. The countryside had gradually fallen into black. With darkness, had come the anxiety of reduced perception. The car began to feel like more of a confined space. Eva became more and more nervous about her companion, their destination and her lack of either money or ability to communicate with anyone in the outside world. But she was too afraid to strike out on her own and, besides, this was her brother...

However, as something at the back of her mind kept repeating, she still didn't know where they were going.

She was also hungry once again. No, starving. But, as the day had drawn on, they had seen very little other than empty roads, closed shops and restaurants.

'We'll stop here,' Jackson said, suddenly interrupting Eva as she was about to speak. 'I know the man who owns this restaurant, there is a private room where we can eat undisturbed.'

Eva nodded and unfastened her seatbelt as the car came to a halt. She had not even noticed they were driving through a built-up area. She was starting to feel incredibly distracted by her arms – they were still stinging like crazy but she'd had enough of feeling drugged and so refused pain medication when Jackson eventually offered to buy some. It had not helped the condition of her arms to slap Jackson as she had. But it had made her feel much better.

The siblings left the car, slamming their doors at the same time, and walking towards the restaurant, which had rustic stone walls and a small wooden door. It was late and the restaurant would be closing soon.

Jackson was a good five inches taller than Eva. He was broad shouldered, straight backed and there was no doubting the strength that lay beneath his blue anorak. Eva was slim, light footed and shorter, but there was an unmistakable similarity between the two, a quiet power that made them an intimidating pair.

Jackson pushed open the door of the restaurant and held it for Eva to walk through. She hesitated, just for a second, and he noted the lack of trust.

Inside, the restaurant was as rustic as the outside. Kitsch wasn't even the word.

Tables laid with checked red and white paper cloths, pink paper napkins and squat French wine glasses were positioned around the room.

Jackson left Eva standing at the door and crossed the room to speak to a man behind the bar.

Eva found herself under the unwavering gaze of two elderly women, who looked slightly the worse for wear. They were sitting on the same side of the table, cradling the stems of wine glasses. Neither spoke.

It was a relief when Jackson said her name and led her through to a room behind the bar. Although nothing more than a stockroom, containing furniture, there was somewhere comfortable to sit and it was at least warm.

'We just need something to eat, Jacques. And I'll take a brandy and a packet of Marlboro.'

'Me too,' said Eva, feeling a spike of warmth at the sibling similarity in taste. Their father always proffered brandy in situations like this.

She took a seat at an unsteady table and looked at the cobwebs around the top of the musty room. On one side, it was piled high with cases of beer, which seemed odd given that she had noticed several taps at the bar. The other side of the room was given over to piles of old newspapers, some toys and a huge heap of clothes. This reminded Eva, again, that she had absolutely nothing with her – no clothes, no phone, no money. In fact, not since Berlin could she remember having access to her personal possessions, including the phone that everyone – including Leon – had seemed so interested in stealing from her. With a start, she realised her father and friends must be worried sick about her. They would not have heard from her for – how long? She had no idea. The thought created guilt which plucked at her insides. But that would have to wait for now.

When 'Jacques' left the room, Jackson pulled out an old model phone and typed something into the keypad, before turning to face her.

'I stopped because I sensed you had a lot of questions.'

'One or two.'

'Such as, where have I been all these years?'

'That was one of them, yes.'

Eva gazed at the features of the face she knew so well. A shadow passed over them.

'I'm sorry, Eva, but I can't tell you.'

'That's not a great start.'

The brandies and cigarettes arrived and Eva immediately reached for the packet.

'I didn't know you smoked,' said her brother, admonishingly.

'I imagine there's quite a lot you don't know about me now.'

'Maybe not as much as you think.'

Eva stopped with the cigarette in her mouth and a lit match in her hand. 'What does that mean?'

'I haven't been entirely off the chart for the past year.'

'And...'

'I have been keeping an eye on you.'

'On my movements?

'Yes, and on you.'

'In what way?'

'What happened with Leon?'

Eva lit the suspended cigarette, took a drag, choked, exhaled and then took another drag, taking her time to disguise her surprise at the question.

'Come off it, Jack,' she said, blowing smoke into his face as she spoke, 'you're telling me you know everything I've done over the past couple of years and that's the only question you've got?'

She watched as he also lit a cigarette, picked up an ashtray from the floor and put it between them on the table.

'He's a dangerous man.'

'No shit.'

Jackson gave her a look.

'Did you sleep with him?'

Eva exhaled with frustration. 'No. I'm not doing this. After all this time, everything that has happened, you're not going to do the big brother thing with me, ok?'

She watched Jackson's jaw clamp shut.

'He just has this effect on women, Eva. I need to know whether he has that same hold over you.'

It was a weak line of enquiry. Eva answered, she realised, from vanity.

'I think it's safe to say he doesn't. Of course, there's the fact he tried to drive me off a cliff too – kind of a passion killer.'

Eva was happy to maintain a humorous edge to her conversation with Jackson. It felt like a buffer, grasping at normality in what was a completely abnormal situation. Otherwise, it might all feel a little too much. She was very much aware her body was vibrating with anxiety, her eyes were a little too wide, her voice a pitch higher. She feared everything from the destination of this journey to the fact that Jackson knew the owner of this remote restaurant.

'Are you talking about the effect he had on Valerie?' asked Eva, as she saw a strange look come into her brother's eyes. Leon was an easy topic for him, Valerie evidently not so much. At the mention of the woman's name, immediately Jackson's face, which had started to appear as she remembered it, was closed off again.

'What do you mean?'

'Leon told me she slept with him. I don't think he thought you knew.'

'Of course I knew.' Jackson sounded angry. Maybe a bit too angry.

'It was all her you know, she set up the whole thing.'

'*I know*,' he said, standing up and pushing the chair back so forcefully it skidded across the floor and fell over. He walked to the corner and smoked several breaths in succession. Then he walked calmly back to her. He was not like Leon, Jackson had far more self control.

He picked up the chair and sat down again.

'Why don't we talk about you?'

'I don't think we've talked about you, yet. Have you had any contact with Valerie?'

'She's dead, Eva. You killed her.'

Eva withered slightly on the end of the accusatory stare. 'She would have killed me if I hadn't.'

'It doesn't matter any more. I don't know why you're asking.'

He shook his head and stubbed out the cigarette. Although he was still reserved, he seemed far more emotional than when she had known him in 'real life'. That familiar controlled façade was there but, every now and again, the door swung open to reveal the tumult inside. Although his eyes gave nothing away, somehow she had never felt so able to read Jackson as she did now; it was odd.

'It might have been all the drugs they were pumping into me but I'm pretty sure I saw her at that château.'

Slowly, Jackson raised his eyes and looked at her.

'Valerie,' he said in a dead sounding voice. 'You saw Valerie?'

Eva nodded. 'I'm almost one hundred per cent sure.'

'Almost?'

'Almost.'

She waited for him to say something else but he didn't.

'Whilst we're on the subject of the château, why was I there and how did you come to find me?'

It was the burning question she had been dying to ask but, for some reason, she had felt it might be the one question Jackson would refuse to answer.

Jacques suddenly entered the room with a bang of the door and pushed two plates of a thick looking stew onto the table, each one garnished with an enormous piece of bread.

The smell rose into Eva's nostrils and her stomach ached with hunger. Other than half a pig's worth of ham, she couldn't even remember the last time she had eaten proper food.

As soon as Jacques turned his back, she set upon the dish with gusto, unaware of the looks from her brother, who was slowly spooning the rich dark liquid into his mouth.

The stew tasted incredible, filled with beans, meat, onions, carrots and the sharp taste of fennel. Eva cleared her plate in five minutes flat, pushed it away and looked over at Jackson's. He laughed and pushed it across the table to her and she finished it too. After that, she lit another cigarette.

She felt fat and content.

'Where were we?'

Jackson shook his head. 'I just don't know how much I could or should tell you right now, that's the problem, Eva. It could put you in a position of real danger.'

She laughed at him and drained the brandy glass. She felt slightly tipsy.

'You don't want to put me in danger?'

'No,' he insisted.

'That's hilarious.'

'It's not funny.'

'You really don't have to tell me that.'

'It could be even worse than this.'

'I doubt it.'

'Seriously.'

'Just tell me.'

TWENTY EIGHT

'A JOKE. THIS must be a joke.'

The staccato sentence echoed from the microphone in the side of the laptop. It melted away into a sinister silence. The man with the Mediterranean tan sat looking at the screen. He had a bullet hole in his head.

From behind the chair in which the corpse sat – sat? could a corpse sit? – Paul stood still. He was, himself, in a state of shock as this was not something he had planned to do. He was nervous. He knew he had essentially made a mistake – perhaps a serious mistake – and he wished he had more control over his temper. This hadn't been part of the plan.

He looked at the three faces on the screen in front of him and knew they were watching him, waiting for a reaction. That was why he was hiding behind the dead man's chair. Like a shy child behind its father.

He doubted these three men cared personally about the loss but he knew they would care very much about any impact it might have on their carefully laid plans. They were no doubt assessing him right now, wondering whether he could fill the enormous shoes he had caused to be vacated by silencing the pompous old man for good.

Which, of course, he regretted now. But this was the one action that simply could not be undone.

As he waited, for either a response from the screen or for some kind of inspiration to strike, Paul tried to be positive. On the upside, the other man could have revealed him at any time and that threat was now gone. On the downside, he had very little knowledge of the people for whom the pair had been working – he had not been given any information when he was parachuted in, although it was clear those supplying the parachute certainly knew plenty about them. The older man had been a shield, an additional layer of defence that he no longer had.

The silence in the room – and across the internet connection – was beginning to feel oppressive.

Finally, he took a step forward so he was next to the chair in which the dead man sat, rather than behind it. He tipped the screen of the laptop so they could see his face.

'I will handle this.'

The answer was instant, angry. 'How? You have absolutely no idea what you need to handle.'

'I can do this, honestly, just tell me what needs to be done.' There was a part of Paul that just wanted these men to have faith in him. It was a part that surprised him. Why was he always searching for approval?

'There is a great deal about this situation that you aren't aware of. We have three teams working without any knowledge of each other and it was up to him...' there was a pause while everyone regarded the silent, dead man, 'to ensure that all worked separately, but together.'

'I can *do this*.' Paul realised he may as well have finished the sentence with 'Dad'.

He shook the thought from his head. 'Honestly, I have been observing him, I can step up.'

'It is not ideal.' The comment was between the talking heads.

The faces turned once again to Paul. 'You have placed yourself at the head of an operation that is several decades in the making and now in the final, critical stages. We know very little about you and, so far, almost everything you have brought to the table – the technology that was the only reason we allowed you in at a low level – has brought additional issues.'

'It was teething problems,' he repeated, trotting out the same excuse once again, 'it's innovative technology, that's how it...'

'*Regardless*,' said one of the faces on the screen, interrupting mid-sentence. The word sounded as if it was spoken through gritted teeth. 'We don't have knowledge of you, we certainly don't trust you and we currently see very little value in you.'

Paul lowered his eyes and looked at the floor.

'But you have put us in a position where we have no choice – at least at present – but to operate with you. Which I imagine was your intention.'

Paul looked up and stared straight into the webcam embedded in the slim frame of the laptop. That was not the case but it was preferable to appear a cold, calculating killer with an agenda than to reveal he simply could not control his temper.

'You will step up then. Whether this part of the project stands or falls now comes down to your actions, as it did his.' The eyes on the screen moved momentarily in the direction of the corpse.

'Your task is to establish control over the teams in play, keep them separate – they must believe they are working alone, in isolation, for this to succeed. Ensure that your technology works, no more *innovative* teething problems. The rest you will have no role in.'

'I understand.'

'If you fail...'

Paul was beginning to regret accepting the offer that had brought him here.

Now, one of the other men spoke. 'I suppose you had better hope there isn't another "Brutus" waiting in the wings to dispatch you, too.'

Nobody laughed.

A beeping sound started at regular intervals on the other end of the connection.

One of the men looked down and moved something on the table in front of him.

'You have two hours to confirm to us that you have taken control. After that, you're relieved of responsibility for everything.'

'You mean leave?'

'No.'

The screen went blank.

Eva was still waiting for Jackson to continue speaking, watching the smoke from yet another cigarette curl around the strong contours of his face and wind its way into his windswept hair. She was beginning to feel the unrealistic events of the past week coming into sharp focus in her mind – too sharp, almost agonising; she desperately needed answers. It was becoming clear she was emerging from whatever combination of shock and drugs had kept her suspended in a blind, emotionless fog. Physically, she felt as if she had a bad hangover – she was a little shaky on her feet, there was a headache that came and went periodically and she felt constantly either starving hungry or incredibly nauseous. And then there were the mental effects; the gaps in her knowledge were now becoming frightening. Extremely frightening.

An awareness of someone physically tampering with her body but no other memory to rely on. She had clearly been held in some sort of medical stasis but, for what reason, she could not fathom. There was nothing on her body to indicate what had happened – nothing she could see. Whatever it was had left no scar, other than the two on her arms, apparently unrelated. Either whoever it was had finished with her once the 'treatment' was at an end or they had left something inside her.

Eva had never found ignorance to be bliss. A lack of knowledge left her anxious. As her mind returned to speed, it became clear she was ignorant of everything since the explosion in Berlin. Where to even start trying to piece it together?

Well, she had started trying with Jackson.

When Jackson failed, again, to provide an answer to a straightforward question, she stood up impatiently, lit another cigarette and walked to the pile of clothes in the room. She felt the layers on the top for damp but they were dry and almost warm. She picked up a large sweater and held it against her. She needed to re-establish contact with the world again. She needed clothes, a phone, money, credit cards. Right now, she was completely at Jackson's mercy. He might be her brother but she hadn't seen him for so long and had no idea of the person he had become.

Besides, she did not like to be 'kept', guided or looked after. She craved the independence provided by a phone, bank card and her own possessions.

When she turned around he was watching her. She stopped where she was and inhaled the cigarette. The light in his eyes was odd. It was strange but it made her skin crawl, slightly. It was almost lascivious. She stared at him, trying to understand why he was looking at her with apparent desire; the look on his face flickered to the much more defensive expression of earlier that day.

He looked away, leant forward and stubbed out his cigarette. 'We should go.'

She nodded silently and walked out of the room with the jumper still in her hands. It was absolutely paramount she obtain money and a phone, she thought to herself, as she walked back through the bar and towards the car. Even more so given the discomfort she had felt minutes earlier.

There was something wrong with this Jackson. Instinctively, she felt she couldn't trust him, regardless of any blood ties. There was too much unexplained – and that look he had given her in the restaurant. It had made her skin crawl. It wasn't right. Instinct was all she had to go on and her instinct told her to find an opportunity to obtain the tools to escape.

That moment came several hours later. With directions to stay on a single motorway, Eva had taken over the driving whilst Jackson slept. He had seemed exhausted and, after the soporific effects of the brandy, had appeared only too pleased to let Eva take over for a while. The trust he had shown had appeased her alarm and suspicion of him – momentarily, at least. Although, at the back of her mind, she was aware that this could have been exactly what it was calculated to do.

As he slept, he snored. Loudly.

Eva had turned on the radio to block out the noise and he hadn't even flinched, so deeply asleep was he.

At one point she leaned forward to change the radio station and, as she did so, spotted a black wallet falling half way from his pocket onto the seat below. She sat back and then looked again, glancing between the wallet, the road and his sleeping features. Briefly it had seemed as if his eyes were open and he was looking straight at her. But the next light they had passed under had shown his eyes shut fast.

Finally, she slowed the car down to around 50km an hour and, in one swift movement, reached over and grabbed the wallet. She sat with it in her lap for several seconds, glancing repeatedly at the sleeping man next to her, but his head was now facing the window on the other side and she had no way of telling whether or not he was awake.

Fumbling slightly, she wedged her right knee against the wheel, held the other side with her left hand and began using her right hand to try and liberate the wallet of its contents. The first thing to fall out was a thick wad of euros.

She glanced up at the road and then quickly over at Jackson. Her heart was beating fast.

The notes were large currency – 200 and 500 Euros – and

she took a quarter of a centimetre's worth of money and shoved it into her jeans.

Another glance at Jackson.

No reaction.

Next she began trying – one-handed – to pull the rest of the contents from his wallet. Perhaps unsurprisingly, there was very little in there. A credit card in a name she couldn't quite read in the darkness of the car, but which certainly wasn't his, several incomprehensible business cards, an identity card in what was presumably the same name as the credit card. She put everything back into the wallet – slowly, painstakingly, with one leg and one arm still wedging the steering wheel between them – and then, as she was lifting the wallet to put it back against Jackson's hip, another card fell out. It tumbled down below the handbrake but she had been sure she recognised it.

She took another look at the sleeping man next to her, then gently rested the wallet against him. She looked back at the road ahead; empty. She took her eyes off the road ahead and reached down for the card.

Immediately, she sensed movement next to her and quickly wrapped her left hand around the card on the floor. Then she was wrenched upright by strong hands.

As she sat up, her face was bathed in bright lights flooding the car. Her heart was in her throat. She was on the wrong side of the road!

Her hands flew to the steering wheel and she shoved it back to the right, taking them out of the path of a van steaming towards them at high speed, its horn on full blare.

Eva struggled to steady the car and felt Jackson's hand next to hers on the wheel. Her heart was beating so fast she thought it might explode. Her arms throbbed.

Fuck, she thought to herself.

Did he see her reach for the card? How had she not seen the van coming? Where had it come from?

But there were only seconds to think because the other vehicle had screeched to a halt, executed a swift turn in the road and was now behind them, bearing down at high speed, honking its horn and flashing its lights.

She looked over at Jackson, who was reaching across into the back seat for a large bag that lay in the footwell.

He turned to her. 'Drive,' he said firmly. 'If you want to live, *drive.*'

Eva pressed her foot to the floor and the car shot forwards.

The van behind picked up even more speed and the lights were switched up to high beam; she almost couldn't see for the glare in her mirror. She turned it away so it was not reflecting into her eyes and took the car up another gear. It was a good car, fast, and they were now going well over 130km an hour. Eva felt a slight gust of wind push the car from its course. At this speed, the forward trajectory felt fragile. But it was clear whoever was in the van behind was more of a danger than her driving. Or so she hoped.

Jackson wound down the window to his right. He had been assembling a large gun and seemed to be trying to lodge this on the descended window of the moving car.

Suddenly, there was a thud from behind and a screeching sound and the car was thrown forward as the van shunted them at high speed. Eva screamed inside her head as the steering wheel seemed to go from underneath her fingers and then she gripped the leather as tightly as she could, forcing it to stay in the same place.

There was another loud crash from behind and Eva struggled with the wheel once again.

Still Jackson fumbled with the gun, now apparently trying to load it.

The van behind was gearing up for another shunt. Eva was not entirely sure how much longer she could keep the car on the road.

What is he doing, she thought to herself, against the whining noise of the engine, her hair flicking in snapping movements around her face as the wind coming through the open window whipped it around.

She glanced over at Jackson.

He seemed to be waiting for something. He was staring hard at the vehicle behind them, as if trying to make out the passengers.

Then he looked up into the sky.

The van once again drew closer. Eva rallied the car and pushed it further up the speed dial. She felt the effect on their car as the back bumper was grazed by the larger vehicle coming at them at full speed.

Still Jackson did nothing.

Was he afraid?

Was he hesitating?

What was he waiting for?

Eva tried to focus hard on the road ahead. But another headache was developing. Her vision was starting to swim, there was a blurring around the edges. The car was shaking now, they were going too fast, and at such speed that Eva could feel every single bump in the road.

Again, the edges of her vision went soft.

She glanced pointedly at Jackson, willing him to meet her gaze so she could communicate with him, perhaps so he would provide an explanation for his slowness. But he seemed to have frozen completely.

Then he was touching his face again – that same odd movement he had gone through back at the house after she had slapped him. Touching various points on his face as though he was trying to make sure the skin was still on.

She looked back at the road, realised she had drifted again, and righted the car.

She glanced in the wing mirror and realised the van was

once again readying to shunt. They were going too fast now to cope with the pressure if it took her off guard. This could be it.

She turned to Jackson and screamed *'Just fire the fucking gun!'*

TWENTY NINE

As IF KICKED from behind, Jackson suddenly sprang into action and began firing the automatic weapon. Once again, it changed the balance of the car on the road.

Eva used all her strength to keep it on its path. She could feel the vehicle was reaching the edge of its tolerance for the forces pressing in on all sides and a stray rock or a momentary lapse in concentration could send them careering off the road. She stared straight ahead and the steering wheel vibrated under her hands, her foot pressed painfully hard on the accelerator.

She felt the car reaching to the right.

She pulled it back to the centre of the road. Her arms – already weak from the recent 'surgery' – began to shake ominously.

It didn't help that Jackson was firing his gun, creating an additional destabilising influence, and introducing yet another force pushing the struggling car intermittently to the right. But at least he was trying to warn the other vehicle off now. And it seemed to be working.

The van behind them was no longer trying to shunt into their back bumper but the lights were still shining full into the mirror. It was maintaining speed. Despite the sporadic gunfire from Jackson, the vehicle was clearly not going anywhere.

Eva glanced over at him. He did not seem particularly focused on the task in hand.

In fact, was he even aiming at them? She couldn't hear any impact from the bullets, no metal hitting metal, no smashing glass. Ok, it was a moving target but a very close one, surely some shots should be hitting home?

Despite the rushing wind through Jackson's open window, she thought she might at least be able to hear a couple of hits. She glanced quickly at Jackson.

He had stopped firing the gun.

He looked at her.

His face changed.

Eva stared.

The flicker happened again.

Eva's grip loosened on the steering wheel. The man's features were distorting horribly. His face seemed to be melting, right in front of her eyes.

She blinked and looked harder and then, remembering the road, pulled her eyes back to the front. She stared hard at the road ahead as she heard Jackson put down the large weapon. Nothing wavered and nothing changed in the scene in front of her. Not the road, the inside of the car or her hands on the steering wheel.

Her thoughts were out of control.

Had she really seen that? It had been as if his face moved, shifted shape and changed altogether, as if a mask had been lifted.

Irene had kept her head low as the bullets whizzed past the side of the vehicle. They had to push that car off the road. They had to reach Eva, Irene needed this.

'Stay as close as you can!' she yelled at the back of the driver's head.

'He's shooting at us, it's too dangerous,' was the response.

'That's an order!'

She was fed up with such insubordination in such a pressured situation. She could not help feeling they would have naturally accepted the authority of a man, without query. Life was full of that kind of everyday sexism, dismissed as paranoia or laughed off.

The bullets from the car in front had stopped. All they could hear was the whistling of the wind past the open windows as the van kept pace with the car in front.

She glanced down at the lit screen of the phone in her hand and continued trying to type the message. She knew they had very little time to get to the airfield, to deliver Eva into the hands of those who could give Irene what she wanted. There was no way the car in front would be allowed to escape. She still didn't even know how the two people in the car had managed to leave the château without being caught. She had the sense that this well ordered organisation was in some chaos, that there were forces working at odds within it. Or perhaps this was all intentional. Either way, it was unnerving. If ACORN didn't get what they wanted then neither would Irene. She had betrayed people left, right and centre for this and she could never go back.

She finished typing their coordinates into the lit screen, sent them immediately and turned to face the windscreen.

The bright lights of their van were shining into the car in front and she could clearly see Eva at the wheel. It was obvious she was struggling to keep control of the car. Irene watched as Eva apparently seemed to lose concentration, staring at the man in the seat next to her, before looking back at the road. She saw her glance again as the man continued to fiddle with some sort of weapon – he was sitting sideways on, so Irene could see his profile.

She did not recognise him.

The next time Eva glanced at Jackson, he raised a small hand gun. The muzzle was directed at her. She inhaled a quick, sharp breath and then her eyes wandered to his face, which had begun to morph again. His features seemed to be blurring like a TV picture receiving interference.

'*What are you doing?*' she shouted at him, looking him

directly in the eye whilst trying to ignore the shifting shapes of his features, and pretend she hadn't seen anything.

But she could see he knew she had.

When he didn't reply, she tried again to reason with him. 'Please, I need to drive or we're going to crash. Do you want to die?'

When there was no response, Eva turned her face back towards the road, her heart smashing against the inside of her ribs. She righted the car and continued to drive, with the gun still pointed at the side of her head. She was barely breathing. The road in front seemed to rise up towards the car as she fought to maintain the fast pace at which she was driving, while also attempting to process what was happening .

All at once there was a crack, a shattering of glass and a sticky thud as the windscreen in front of the passenger seat was coated in thick red blood. Eva looked at the figure of Jackson collapsing into the seat next to her, glanced back through the shattered rear window and could have sworn she saw Irene Hunt. Then she lost control of the car.

Paul was watching the scenario play out on a screen, filmed from 10,000 feet above. He'd felt some admiration for Eva's driving under those conditions, handling a car at that speed and under that pressure. And then, suddenly, a shot was fired from the vehicle behind – unexpected. For several seconds, nothing happened before the car lurched to the right and departed the road, careening into a field and turning first onto its hood and then back onto its tyres.

The drone feed showed the other vehicle come to a screeching halt.

Paul checked a figure on his screen and sent another instruction. He had half an eye on the screen and half on the movements of the extensive and colourful ownership portfolio he had inherited from his dead boss. It was literally a goldmine and to those involved it represented decades of intricate work, strategising and risky bargains. To him, it was simply a springboard, a means to an end. There was only one reason he had accepted the offer to become involved in this in the first place and that was access to Leon. He was still waiting for that next opportunity to get to him. Nevertheless what he was doing gave him a thrill. If anyone knew this portfolio existed...

Paul was now feeling relieved to have removed the other man, despite the pressure he had felt during the earlier meeting. Just as Jackson had said he would, he'd found the detail of this all quite fascinating – now that he could see the whole picture. It was an ingenious notion, essentially 'invading' a country without anyone noticing, establishing control not with physical might but with purchasing power and ownership. The free market undermining itself. And he was enjoying being the 'general', leading the digital charge. He'd arrived just in time for the best bit.

Looking at the laptop, he stroked its smooth metal. What he imagined this represented was control – ultimate, long term, silent control – and, while he didn't benefit from it personally, he appreciated its ironies and its impeccable construction. Such a thoroughly modern coup.

He knew little about the mechanics but blind eyes must have been turned and backhanders accepted at so many stages to avoid a suspicious mind somewhere connecting the dots. He assumed none of those who had 'just this once' compromised on their ethics would have realised how much their apparently insignificant action would have contributed to this incredibly powerful whole. Its very existence was unprecedented. And he had access to all this only thanks to Veritas. The system he himself had developed. No, he corrected himself – borrowed. Briefly, he realised he was beginning to believe his own deception. He shook his head. Veritas, he continued – a key based on truth – the only key that could not be faked, forged or recreated. It was the kind of security a project like this required.

Except it had been misused. It had been tested on one subject who had ended up dead as a result and the other... he glanced again at the drone feed... the other was the focus of all this effort. With the inventor of Veritas gone it could not be set up with another test subject. Thanks to Jackson, Eva was the key.

Eva wiped blood from her eye.

She yanked the key from the car's ignition.

Smoke was rising all around, she had to get out.

But what had just happened?

She looked down at the body of the man who had been sitting next to her, now twisted and sprawled backwards over her lap.

She used the tips of her fingers to turn the half blown apart head towards her. The face was not Jackson's. It was not anyone she recognised.

But it had been...

An impulse to escape rose fast and strong but she was trapped by her seatbelt and by the weight of the body pressing down on her. She tried to move, and when she realised she couldn't, she screamed. And screamed.

She beat out at the body with her fists and kicked at the pedals on the floor and didn't even notice when the passenger door was opened. She only stopped when she felt the sharp sting of a slap on her cheek.

Her vision popped into sharp focus. She looked up into Irene's soft grey eyes.

'Jesus, Eva, get a hold of yourself.'

Eva was breathing heavily, still hyperventilating. 'Fuck. You,' she said, loudly. She raised her hand to hit back, but stopped.

There was no reaction from Irene.

She undid her seatbelt and kicked the door further open, ignoring the fact Irene had to jump back. Then, with super human effort, she heaved the body from her and pushed it away. Irene's presence was motivation to get free. As the body slumped stiffly over towards the other side of the car Eva looked down at smeared blood on her clothes and grazes all over her face and hands. She used the side of the car to haul herself out of the seat, dropping to her knees before pushing herself up to standing; then she limped around the front of the car, wrenched open the passenger door and began hauling out the body, pulling it out onto the ground, ignoring the sickening crunches as the skull hit the car's bodywork.

When it landed on the floor, she fell on it, ripping the clothes away and righting the head, which was lolling sickeningly to one side.

'Give me a torch,' she shouted to Irene.

When the other woman didn't respond, she yelled again until, finally, Irene's driver cautiously approached her with an industrial sized light.

Eva held the light over the body in front of her.

'It's not him,' she mumbled. 'It's not him.' And then louder. *'It's not him!'*

Irene and the driver exchanged glances.

Eva was now frantically scrabbling over the pockets on the body, apparently looking for something. She then progressed to the car itself.

When she found nothing, she returned to the body on the floor. As the frustration welled up inside, the confusion and the disappointment, all she felt was rage. She kicked out at the prone body, an almost unintentional kick which could do no damage. And then she kicked again – harder. And again.

The sickening sound of her foot connecting with the body was all she could hear. But she could not stop.

The gaps between each kick shortened; the strength behind each one was harder.

She was exhaling loudly every time she kicked him, this man who had pretended to be her brother; who she had almost believed.

How could he have looked like him?

What was happening?

Irene watched as Eva kicked out again and again. She was exhaling, grunting, almost screaming and each time she did more damage to the corpse. But apparently she could not stop. With a howl which made Irene's blood run cold, Eva gave in entirely to the rage and the attack became frenzied.

Irene stood at a distance.

There had been no warning or explanation. Although she had been told to expect a personality change as a result of the drugs, this was unlike anything she had seen from Eva before. Irene was almost afraid to go near her.

But they could not stay here.

Irene walked back to the driver. They exchanged a look and she noted he clearly did not want to be tasked with bringing Eva back under control.

Irene was not surprised.

'Clean up here. I'll deal with her.'

THIRTY

ONCE AGAIN EVA found herself staring at Irene as the two sat side by side in the front of the van Irene was driving along the motorway in the dark. She had a strong profile, delicate nose but hard cheekbones, and there was a slight sag in the skin under her chin. Despite this, Irene's face displayed no weakness, not even side on. It was an impressive degree of control and if it wasn't for the suspicion Eva felt towards someone so adept at disguise and untruth, she may well have had great respect for her.

She looked away, leaned her head against the headrest and shut her eyes.

They had left the driver behind at the site of the car crash, along with a selection of clean up tools, and – Eva had noted – a small arsenal of weapons. Eva could not help noticing the wary way he regarded her when she finally stopped attacking the corpse by the car.

Her brother. And yet not.

She still could not make sense of what had happened. He had looked, even sounded, like Jackson. And yet there had been a moment in the car when his face had changed – physically changed from one person to someone completely different. But how was that possible? It wasn't.

Eva remembered the red-haired woman in the château she had mistaken for Jackson's ex-girlfriend, Valerie. Why was she hallucinating these people? Was this connected to recent events and, if so, how much? Most of all she wanted to know why, *why* was this all happening.

She thought back to the conversations she'd had with

'Jackson' during the last 24 hours but they were difficult to remember. Had she instinctively known he was not her brother? The only moment she could recall her suspicions was in the back room of the restaurant when she had caught him looking at her – appraisingly, appreciative. It had been confusing at the time but, clearly, her own sibling would never have regarded her like that.

So, who was that man and why – and how – had he done what he had?

She had a thousand questions but she was also exhausted.

'What did you mean back there, Eva, when you said "it's not him?"'

'What?'

Eva was surprised to realise she had been about to fall asleep.

'You said "it wasn't him". And then you attacked him. What did he do to you while he held you captive?'

'Captive?'

That face flashed again in front of Eva's eyes – rough skin, heavy jowels and light, watery blue eyes, not at all her once much loved sibling.

Should she tell Irene?

'I don't understand what happened back in Berlin,' she said, changing the subject.

'In what way?'

'Do you know who these people are – do you know about the château?'

'We did track you there, yes, but I'd like to make clear it took us a while to find you.' Irene glanced at Eva's covered forearms. 'If we had known where you were, we would have removed you immediately.'

'Why didn't you know?'

Irene seemed to hesitate. 'Someone made a mistake.'

'I thought the house in Berlin was meant to be safe?'

'Mistakes happen.'

It was an unsatisfactory answer but neither knew how much one owed the other or where the boundaries of their commitment lay. There was no contract, no agreed terms.

An awkward silence fell, as Irene crunched the van's gears.

'Do you know what has happened to me over the past week?'

'No. Tell me.'

'I can't.'

'I don't understand.'

Eva turned to Irene in the darkness of the van. 'I can't tell you because I don't know. I have no memories.' She paused before she spoke again. 'Ninety per cent of me doesn't even care. And ten per cent... well that part feels... crazy... like back there,' she said, indicating with her hand the direction behind them where her attack on the corpse had taken place. 'It's the strangest thing.'

Irene looked over at her briefly, then back at the road.

'How do you feel now?'

'Confused, uncomfortable,' Eva said, pointing to her forearms, 'but calm. Occasionally afraid of all the missing time and what it might mean. But not as much as I feel I should be. That's not how I would normally react.'

'No.'

After several minutes of silence, Eva started to speak again. 'Do you think they could have done something to me – permanently altered something inside?'

'I really don't know, Eva,' Irene lied.

'Why was I even there?'

'Again, I'm sorry but I just don't know.'

'Do you know *anything*?'

Irene ignored the aggression.

'I can tell you the man you were with works for an illegal cartel, financial terrorists.'

'Financial terrorists.' Eva almost laughed out loud.

'Yes.'

'That sounds like tabloid scaremongering.'

'It's not a laughing matter.'

'What does it mean?'

'A group using violence, intimidation and manipulation for the pursuit of economic aims, rather than those that are purely political.'

Irene waited for Eva's reaction as she described the real ACORN. She had no idea who that man actually worked for but it would be interesting to see Eva's reaction to what she was about to say.

'I don't think I understand.'

'They don't want to kill people to make a political point. They have no particular manifesto. They are focused purely on achieving aims to provide them with economic power and influence. It's much more subtle.'

'Why call them terrorists, aren't they just criminals?'

'They are organised in the same way as, say, Al Qaida or IS, they have cells all over the world. Their network is not large but it's almost impossible to expose the people who are involved because they are so well protected and well trained; some are even part of the establishment. Many are simply temporarily attached,' she said. 'Either they make a bargain for cash, for favours, or because they are being blackmailed.'

Irene stopped talking. She realised she couldn't help giving Eva this information. Yes, the context was a lie in that she did not have the degree of separation from ACORN she implied, but still it was information that could change things for Eva. Whether it would clarify or confuse depended on how much they had broken Eva. What Irene couldn't work out was whether she just enjoyed toying with the younger woman or if she was trying to surreptitiously confess to soothe her guilt for what was about to happen.

'Simply because of the number of unknowns they are a bigger threat than your average criminal.'

'But, no suicide bombers?'

'No. Their work is far more delicate than death.'

'What is it they're trying to achieve – I can't imagine what would tie all this together?'

'We don't know.'

Irene hoped the lie would work. She had no idea who Eva had spent the last 24 hours with but attributing his actions to ACORN's might help Eva to believe that Irene was still her only ally. Eva would not know Irene's connection to them until it was too late.

Eva was quiet for several seconds before she replied. 'You don't know or you won't tell me?'

Silence. Irene knew if she went too far, provided too much, Eva would be suspicious. She had to continue the same pattern with her.

'So what's the link with me?'

'Again, we don't know.'

'Right.'

'But the likelihood is this has somehow originated from Jackson.' Irene needed to know whether anything had been said to Eva about her brother.

Eva felt her body begin to tense.

'From Jackson?'

'Yes.'

'Why would there be a link to Jackson from these people?'

'It's difficult to understand at the moment, for us too, but it seems he may have become involved with them in Paris. In what context, we don't know.'

'Do you think he ever switched sides?'

'To be honest, Eva, anything is possible.'

Eva stared at the road ahead and wondered whether she should tell Irene what she had seen – the man's face changing from one identity to another.

'They are incredibly well resourced,' continued the older

woman, 'with more wealth and connections at their fingertips than you could possibly imagine. They could have offered Jackson anything – more money than he could ever spend or even a complete change of identity.'

'A change of identity, how?'

'We know science is one of their most coveted weapons. They have the most innovative and advanced science on the planet at their fingertips. All the philanthropic advances of mankind are available, at a price, to the highest bidder.'

Eva couldn't help but pick up on the jaded note in Irene's voice.

'One of their developmental areas has been improving the way they provide security to members of their organisation – through disguise. They could completely change his face and body, erase the Jackson you knew.'

'Could they do it the other way around?'

'What do you mean?'

'Could they make someone else look like him?'

'I don't really know, Eva, but I imagine it would be possible. Although it would presumably be very difficult if the face was going to be exposed to anyone who really knew him.'

Eva was silent.

'Why do you ask? Did you see him?'

Eva looked at Irene in response to the direct question. Did Irene know what might have happened?

'I… I am not sure.'

'Are you sure it wasn't actually him?'

'One hundred per cent.'

'Where did you see him? At the château?'

Eva took a deep breath. 'Irene, I thought the man driving the car I was in was Jackson.'

This time it was Irene's turn to stay silent.

'He looked just like him.'

Eva felt Irene glance over at her.

'At least, he did – earlier. By the time you arrived, it clearly wasn't him.'

'I'm not sure I understand, Eva. Are you saying you thought that man was Jackson, or aren't you?'

'He looked like him, Irene. For a day he looked so like Jackson I believed it was him. But his face changed.'

'Changed, how?'

'Kind of morphed. Like a TV losing signal.'

'And then what happened?'

'He didn't look like Jackson anymore.'

'I don't think I understand.'

'Neither do I, I'm just telling you what happened.' Eva exhaled to try and release the anger. 'I suppose the other possibility is I've lost the plot and am going mad.'

'It's always a possibility.'

'Do you think so?'

'It's always possible.'

'No, I mean do you think somehow they could have altered his face to make him look like Jackson, just temporarily? You said yourself they have huge resources at their disposal and employ many scientists.'

'Anything is possible.'

'Possible', that word again. Irene had said it three times in a matter of seconds. Which had irritated Eva beyond belief. They continued to drive in silence. Eva unconsciously lifted her hand to her head, which ached with the weight of all the questions.

She shut her eyes.

Instantly, she saw in her mind the card falling from the wallet of the now dead faux Jackson in the car.

It was a design she had seen before and a word had rung a bell – Veritas. But at that moment she could do nothing other than register it as another potential connection. Something to try and work out when her head was less heavy.

As the motion of the driving and the warmth of the car gradually took over, Eva fell asleep.

VERITAS. Both men looked at the word as it appeared, disappeared and reappeared on the tiny metal key.

Paul enjoyed the way the other man seemed almost reverent of what he held in his hands. And so he should be. It was one of the greatest pieces of innovation the world had seen recently. Except the world had not seen it, as it remained a secret.

Did he feel guilty he had not developed the technology himself, that he had stolen it?

Of course not. Besides, he almost felt as if he *had* developed it himself now.

In the same way he felt no guilt for having profited from the face mapping technology – although that had proven far less effective in the various encounters in which it had been used so far.

It too, had been stolen – by the man who now sat in the seat opposite.

Joseph Smith fascinated Paul. He had done from the moment he had met him. He was the kind of man Paul felt he understood completely. Smith never formed attachments, never trusted anyone, would always be available to the highest bidder and was driven reliably by profit, whether financially or power motivated.

Paul realised the other man was looking at him. 'What is it for?'

'It's a key.'

'But there is no lock, is there?'

'Not physically, no.'

'So, what does it do?'

Paul had been given strict instructions not to share the nature of the invention with Smith. Those who had engaged Smith knew nothing of the experience he and Paul had of working together or Smith wouldn't be here. Smith was one of the 'teams' Paul had been told to keep separate from the others, and he presumed that also meant from himself. From experience, Paul knew Smith often felt belittled, talked down to or patronised by those who engaged his services. He saw being honest as a way of forming a bond with Smith, just in case he needed him.

It was possible he was making a mistake. And, in many ways, it went against much of what Paul knew about Smith. But he did it anyway.

'It unlocks a system.'

'What kind of system?'

'A financial system.'

Smith looked puzzled. Paul wondered whether that was genuine. For a split second, he tried to work out just how much of this Smith already knew.

'How can it unlock a financial system?'

Paul applied pressure to two points on the tiny metal key and it began to open itself. He withdrew a small needle-like implement.

'The key is in the blood.'

Now, Smith really did look confused. 'Whose blood?'

'Whoever is nominated to be the key. Via the blood you can access their DNA. In your DNA, Joseph, you have a code which is completely unique – there is no one in the world who has the same genetic code as you.'

Smith nodded. He picked up the key Paul had placed on the table between them. 'But how does this use your DNA?'

Paul took the needle from him. 'This can be used to take a blood sample from whoever is "the key". It will analyse that blood sample and produce a version of the genetic code in a format that can be communicated to a receptor embedded in a very specifically designed laptop.' He patted the laptop on the side of the table next to him, now closed.

'It is impossible to replicate the key because of the unique nature of DNA. And it's impossible to fake it because it only works with the blood of a single person.'

'Surely, you can just take a blood sample by force?'

Paul shook his head. 'No. When you are placed in a stressful situation, 99.9 per cent of the time your body will respond by releasing a stress hormone into the blood stream, such as cortisol or epinephrine. Where there is a trace of these hormones in the blood sample drawn using this key, the genetic code becomes corrupted and the sequence transmitted is fake. The same is true if there are sleep hormones present, sedation – anything unusual and it won't work.'

'So, you can't use this key unless blood is willingly given?'

'Exactly. The sample should be provided at a time of optimal relaxation, for example just before going to sleep.'

'So, how will you obtain the sample from Eva Scott?'

Paul stopped short. How did Smith know a sample would be required from Eva Scott?

The two men stared at one another. Joseph Smith had drawn this conclusion himself but, until he saw the fear in Paul's eyes, he had not been 100 per cent convinced he was right. He now felt angry with himself – if he had worked out earlier how essential the woman was going to be, he could have used her as a bargaining tool.

He watched as Paul considered his options in terms of a response. In the end, he seemed to decide he had few.

'She was never intended to be the key. It was supposed to be someone else. However, the technology was developed with her brother – he wanted to give it to her as a gift. That is why she is the prototype.'

'Does she know?'

'Unlikely. She was accidentally sent a confirmation code via her phone when the key was activated but I doubt she would have been able to make sense of it.'

'So, how do you propose to make her unlock your key?'

Paul hesitated. Was telling this man really wise? It wasn't but Paul was entirely isolated from those further up the chain now. He craved an ally. Every inch of his brain told him Joseph Smith could be no one's ally. But nevertheless...

'There is another type of technology we have developed.'

'Also stolen?'

Was that judgement? That was laughable from a murderer. 'Also stolen,' agreed Paul, after some hesitation.

'What does it do, block the stress hormones?'

'No, it engenders trust. Trust makes human beings feel calm.'

'How?'

'It can be used to recreate a person.'

'I don't understand.'

Paul leaned forward. He loved this technology, he couldn't help but be enthusiastic about it, despite the fact that it had repeatedly failed.

'It is a combination of drugs and conditioning that change the brain's response to certain situations to make it more accepting of some things and less so of others. After weeks of drug prep, there are implants. It's a long process, so not an ideal piece of technology for an unwilling subject, as they must be detained physically and monitored. But it can be done – if you really need it to be. However, the implants only last for a specific period of time.'

'And then what happens?'

'We don't know. There's a possibility the implants can leak.'

'Leading to death?'

'Possibly.'

'How does it work?'

'The technology can make someone believe they are speaking to a person they know. The person who is to be the "actor" wears "mapping points" attached to certain facial contours.

The combination of the chemical alteration to the brain, the mapping points, and the cranial implants create a convincing recreation of the face you want them to see. It means you can control a specific element of a person's perception of reality. With control, you don't need violence.'

'Is it believable?'

'The visual effect is usually enough to convince the person seeing the face that it is speaking with the same voice, even that it has the same skin colour. However, you have to pick someone of similar height and build or it is not as effective, and the recipient may also notice where behaviours are not the same, or if certain responses are different.'

'Does it work?'

Paul thought back. It had worked temporarily almost every time it had been used – the drugs had been administered gradually to Eva way back in London, by a man posing as her boyfriend, by a couple in Berlin and then in high volumes during her stay at the château, when the implants had been installed. However, the flaw, they now knew, seemed to be longevity.

'It will work long enough for our purposes.'

'To convince Eva Scott she is interacting with her brother?'

'Yes – the person she trusts the most. She will provide him with the blood sample for analysis.'

'But he is dead. I saw him die.'

'No one really knows if he died, you know that, Joseph.'

Joseph scowled. He felt responsible for the lack of closure on that job – even now he couldn't quite bring himself to admit he might have failed.

'He cannot be alive. There was virtually nothing left of him.'

'He is – was – a resourceful man.'

'But he cannot be alive,' Smith repeated, robotically.

Paul just looked at him and smiled. 'It doesn't matter. He is not here.'

THIRTY ONE

EVA AWOKE MINUTES later. She stared at the road ahead of her. She was struggling to feel... anything. That wasn't like her at all. She had often had to work hard to gain control over her feelings, to make sure they didn't disable her in certain situations – or overwhelm her when she was alone. During all the events in Paris, with Leon and the relentless spectre of Jackson, that emotional wave had returned. She never allowed it to overwhelm her but she had been aware of its presence.

But now? Rather than grappling with emotional frequencies there seemed to be nothing there at all. When she thought about what might have happened to her over the past week, there should be extreme fear, intense apprehension about the future, but there was just a vague sense of confused unease. It wasn't pleasant because it wasn't normal. There was no triumph in being free from emotional baggage, instead she felt something had been stolen from her, as if she wasn't judging situations correctly because she felt nothing. Like she'd been broken somehow.

'You're deep in thought.'

The sun was beginning to rise over the broad, open countryside as they drove along the road, flanked by the dark shapes of the Pyrenees on either side. The light was pastel pink, orange and shades of purple. It was aesthetically beautiful but Eva did not feel its warmth.

'I don't know what to think, Irene. Again, I'm in a situation completely out of my control, apparently – again – because of Jackson.'

No reply.

'But this time,' continued Eva, 'It appears impossible for me to get perspective on what's happened. And I've lost a week. Maybe more.'

Irene inhaled and exhaled steadily. 'If I may say so, Eva, there's very little we can do about this right now and over thinking it – as you're doing – is going to drive you mad. Why don't you just go back to sleep?'

Eva looked across the cab of the van. Go to sleep? Irene met her gaze.

'You look exhausted. If you can't sleep, just watch the sunrise. You couldn't see these colours if you were colour blind.'

It was an odd comment. Eva didn't reply but turned around in her seat, folded her arms and stared out of the window in front of her, watching as the colours of the sunrise changed before her eyes. I couldn't see this if I was colour blind, she repeated to herself. What I would be seeing would be entirely different.

She knew very little about sight, about what made the brain comprehend what the eyes were seeing. But she had often wondered how people could see the same thing so differently. She felt as if biology was only predictable up to a point – until you reached the mind. She knew about 'retinal cones' though, which transmitted a perception of light and colour to the optic nerve – she had researched it once for an article, and the physical idea of 'retinal cones' had stuck in her mind. Like ice-cream cones. Colour blindness, she mused, must either be caused by a problem with the retinal cones or with the brain itself.

What, she thought to herself, if someone had tampered with her retinal cones to make her see Jackson?

Or – worse – with her brain. Was it possible for a hallucinogenic substance to have been administered to make her believe she was in the company of her long dead brother? It was such a specific perception, surely achieving it would be impossible? But Irene herself had talked of the way science could be used to alter what nature had given. Perhaps that could be done via perception, as well as reality.

Eva tried to make sense of the moment at which 'Jackson' had rescued her. It had all happened so quickly she had very little memory of it. As she thought about it she realised that, other than the four people pushing her gurney, the 'rescue' had met with little resistance. The adrenaline fuelled situation had ensured she didn't question anything at the time and the pain inflicted by the knife blade plunged into her arms had made her black out, blocking out at least an hour afterwards and causing her to become hazy on the minutes before he had appeared too. Maybe that was intentional.

She glanced over at Irene and wondered whether she should mention the idea she'd had. But she had a sneaking suspicion the response would be once again, 'it's possible'.

Irene kept her eyes on the road as she sensed Eva going through the motions of her thoughts. Why had she mentioned colour blindness and perception? It was almost as if she wanted Eva to work out what was going on. It was incredibly unprofessional. Irene didn't know whether she had been motivated by something in particular or whether she was simply too tired, but she was behaving recklessly.

She had no idea how much the 'it's a possibility' lines were being believed, or whether she had unintentionally given away more than she realised. Eva was as smart as her brother – all her actions would lead them to believe so – in which case it was entirely possible she could determine what had happened to her at the château, particularly after that colour blind comment. Irene knew the science ACORN used was spectacularly advanced. She knew vaguely that, for some reason, it was necessary that Eva believe herself to be in the company of Jackson, but she did not know why. Her role was one of chaperone. She merely had to deliver Eva safely and not ask questions that would require her to be eliminated. She'd never had much interest in science and it made less sense to her than cold, hard, political logic but something like this – this could change the course of many things, it had serious context and was fascinating. She glanced at Eva and noticed she was asleep again.

Perhaps now would be a good time to make the call.

Barely moving her hands, she flicked the switch on the mobile wedged between her thighs and the seat. She heard the ring tone begin in her earpiece. A voice answered and she said a single word:

'Go.'

Paul watched the small green dot travelling across the screen in front of him; a road map of the south east of France showed the dot travelling towards the French Riviera. Which was, coincidentally, where he now sat watching the sun come up from a vast private villa overlooking azure blue seas. He was beginning to enjoy his new position as the figurative spearhead of this fascinating plan to cripple a country with its own economy. And he loved his role as double agent.

Eva Scott's DNA was his only focus. Obtaining it and using it. That had been the job of the idiot who had managed to die in the car crash. He had even been given the face of the one person in the world they knew Eva would trust implicitly, so broken had she apparently been by the disappearance of her brother. But he had failed and so Plan B had been set in motion – another try. This had exposed Paul to discovery – and more abuse from the 'elders' – but he had dealt with it and, in a way, it had all worked out for the best. She was on her way to where she should be, apparently by a fortuitous turn of events that required precisely zero effort from him, even if she was not directly within Paul's control. Once she reached the transport, he would be released and all he needed to do then was to collect on the revenge side of the bargain and then disappear before ACORN found out that he had in fact been working for a third party all the time.

Irene skidded the truck to a halt in an unofficial layby off the motorway. She ran around the front of the van, her shoes slipping on the loose gravel, almost sliding sideways. She wrenched open Eva's door and pulled herself up to where Eva was jerking backwards and forwards, her mouth open, her eyes agog.

Irene reached over the shuddering girl, undid her seatbelt and pulled her out, balancing her weight and lowering her fitting body to the floor.

She laid her out flat, checked her tongue wasn't falling down her throat, and moved her into the recovery position.

She ran back to the other side of the van and pulled a small medical box from underneath the driver's seat. She yanked it open and began tossing items onto the floor, until she found the vial she was looking for. Her breath was rasping, her heart pounding in her throat.

She glanced across the van, through the open passenger door, and saw Eva had rolled onto her back and started to vomit. She was choking, spewing liquid with an oddly bluish tinge up into the air and back into her mouth again. Her eyes were open but she was not conscious.

'Shit,' muttered Irene and scrabbled in the box until she found a syringe. She ran back around the front of the van, pushed Eva back onto one side and began scooping the vomit out of her mouth with her hands.

When her mouth was clear, Eva continued to jerk on the floor, shivering and jumping with glazed eyes. She vomited again but, this time, it spilled onto the ground as Irene held her on her side.

Irene pulled the wrapping off the syringe, prepped it

and plunged it into the top of the vial she had selected. She steadily pushed the plunger down and then slowly pulled up just a few centimetres of liquid. She withdrew the syringe from the vial, quickly tapped the side and positioned it over Eva's arm.

She hesitated for a second and then stuck the metal point into Eva's skin and pushed the plunger all the way down, slowly and steadily.

She could see the instant effect as the liquid entered Eva's blood stream. She froze mid shudder. Her eyes widened even further and she seemed to rise slightly off the ground. Irene took a step back, wondering if she had used the wrong vial, or the wrong dosage.

Then there was a long, low moan from the spot on the floor where Eva lay and the girl collapsed onto her back, her face staring up at the sky.

She lay there for several seconds, her eyes without expression, and then she blinked.

'How long exactly do we have before the implants could fail?'

'It's difficult to say but I would estimate another 24 hours.'

'And after that, the technology won't work?'

'After that, we would need to ensure she receives a high enough dosage to reach the same saturation point as before, perhaps replace the implants, which would be difficult without further confinement.'

There was a dissatisfied silence from the three faces on the screen.

This irritated Paul immeasurably. He didn't even care about this any more; once Eva was on the plane he would be gone – why did he have to put up with this scathing interrogation? He was fed up with judgement from their bloated faces, with their laughable ski tans. They didn't realise how lucky they were he had come along when he did. He had forgotten, once again, that his was not the genius behind the technology – and that he hadn't 'come along' but been planted there. But he did manage to remember that, unless he played his part to perfection, he could end up with nothing.

'Are the drugs damaging her?'

One of the talking heads began again. 'I mean, is there a danger of losing her at any point?'

Paul bit his tongue. Should he really explain the imminent danger of the implants? They had only been tested once before and the test subject had escaped, so no controlled conclusion could be drawn. He reminded himself this really wasn't his responsibility.

'No, we won't lose her before the launch date.'

'You're certain about that?'

'She may become ill, for sure, but she won't die. To be honest, the more incapacitated she is the better.'

'Doesn't she have to consent to give the blood sample before the technology will work?'

Paul felt like grabbing these people and shaking them. Consent indeed…

'No, she doesn't have to consent as in sign anything.'

'But you said…'

'It's the state of her blood which is important. She must be consenting enough not to be afraid, stressed or angry.'

'And, if she feels any of those emotions at the time the sample is given, it won't work.' This was another of 'the heads' now – he seemed a little more switched on, despite being by far the greyest-haired and most lined of them all. Perhaps he was the one.

'Yes,' Paul said, 'and she's less likely to feel them if she's… fuzzy headed,' he concluded, unable to find a more scientific term.

There was a pause on the other end of the line before the same man spoke again. 'You know best, Paul.' This was the first time any of them had used his name – he hadn't even been aware they knew it.

'The timing,' continued the man, 'is crucial here.'

'I'm aware of that.'

'There's just a slight concern over the reliability of the mapping – even with the implants will it be enough to convince her she is really seeing who she thinks she is seeing?'

Paul decided not to mention the fact Eva had already been exposed to a reveal and they had no idea why it had failed. He wondered whether the men in front of him were aware this had happened. Surely, they must be, he concluded. They seemed to know every other development, no matter how small.

'She has been convinced, so far,' he responded, aware he sounded less than sure himself.

'Does it matter she has already seen one "Jackson" who turned out not to be the real thing?'

So, they did know.

Paul hesitated.

The men on the other end of the webcam seemed to sense it straight away. The two turned to each other and began whispering in such an unguarded way that, for the first time, Paul wondered about the fallibility of the project. He could just about make out what they were saying and it sounded like panic. They were blaming each other for trusting technology which was turning out to be so unreliable. It was clear the desire for security – to stop anyone else accessing their carefully laid plans – had now become a wall keeping even them out, too.

All the best laid plans, he thought to himself, smugly.

Outside the door, Joseph Smith listened with interest.

He was thoughtful.

There could be considerable advantage for him here, in fact perhaps this was the opportunity he had been waiting for.

Although he was not privy to exactly what the prize was – what 'financial system' Eva's blood unlocked – he knew it was big. In a way, he didn't need to know what it was to understand that these men valued it greatly. Which meant others would, too.

The men on whom he was eavesdropping had worked for decades to create a situation to provide them with incredible power, beyond anything ever achieved before if what Paul had said was correct. And then, apparently, they had foolishly tied it all to technology they did not understand. That they could not predict.

Why did people trust technology so implicitly, he wondered, as he heard the whispered panic continue.

It was surely the first rule of life that you only trusted what you understood. What many people would have described as a leap of faith, Joseph saw as recklessness. He did not take leaps of faith, he did not throw caution to the wind. He slowly listened, watched and waited until he was absolutely sure a situation would work to his advantage, that a person was exactly what he thought they were – only then did he take any action.

The only time in recent memory that he had stepped outside this pattern of behaviour was with the woman in Berlin, who had managed to cut his face as he attacked her. He had not thought that through, because he had allowed his ideas to supersede his reality. An emotion-driven response that, inevitably, had resulted in failure.

And that had been enough of a warning shot to send reckless impulses right back where they belonged – buried.

He looked at the tiny key in his hand and turned it over a couple of times. He pressed his finger into the cold metal and waited for the word VERITAS to appear when the heat activated it. For some reason, this fascinated him. He loved the idea that the word was revealed only to the person who knew it was there. Or who knew where to look.

Paul had not seen him quietly take the key and pocket it.

Paul was clever – academically so – but a pompous and

narcissistic man who paid very little attention to detail. Something had happened to him, he had lost people or some situation had befallen him, and now he believed the world owed him. Joseph Smith enjoyed working with him because he was easy to manipulate. Men full of bitterness were often weak like him.

These men believed in their own superiority and assumed others would too, which was what made them such an easy target for Smith.

So often power or wealth bred complacency and lack of awareness. There was nothing to keep you sharp like poverty, want and desperate need.

Smith walked away from the doorway. He had heard enough.

He made his way through the corridors of the opulent villa and into the darker rooms of the basement below. Here, there was far more activity than the sunny grounds above belied.

He entered a large room, where three men were standing against a wall, each one having their photo taken.

They were all tall, of almost identical height. Each one was broad shouldered, had unruly, brown, curly hair and dark brown eyes.

No one looked twice Joseph Smith as he made his way around the laboratory. No one even noticed him.

THIRTY TWO

IT WAS NEARING midday when Irene slowed the van and turned onto a straight road that seemed to lead right into the peaks of the Maures Mountains. The area was thick with lush green trees and fields, and more greenery carpeted the slopes of the surrounding peaks, which reflected the bright blue of the sky around them.

Eva had been still for the last hour of the journey. She felt uncomfortable in her own skin, almost unbearably so.

Irene had told her about the fit. Eva had heard her speaking but just stared at her, numbly. She remembered nothing. That terrified her. She seemed to have become a danger to herself – her body was no longer her own.

Irene apparently had no opinion on this but had calmly relayed the facts. Eva had taken this unflusteredness as a sign that Irene knew more than she was letting on, even that she had expected it.

Eva felt desperate. How could she help herself.

'Where are we?' Eva's voice was dead. She was exhausted and she had realised, over the past hour, she was starting to feel emotion again – this time a fear which was in danger of ballooning into terror. She urgently needed answers, someone to explain the events of recent days – and what was happening to her now. Not knowing felt as if it might tip her over the edge of sanity.

Irene continued to drive, without replying, but the answer had become clear. A private airfield.

'La Môle airport,' Irene said finally, almost unnecessarily.

'Am I going home?'

'Yes, we need to return you to London to run proper tests to establish exactly what's happened to you,' lied Irene.

Eva turned suddenly. There were tears in her eyes. 'Please, Irene,' she begged, 'please just tell me what's going on. I can't not know anymore.'

Irene looked taken aback. Eva's emotionless reactions of the past 24 hours were in complete contrast to the way she was behaving now. The idea had been to destabilise her mind, with drugs, faces, attacks and events – to make her ready to trust as directed. But Irene wondered whether the girl was actually going to keep it together. Perhaps they had damaged her beyond repair.

'I don't know anything, Eva.'

Eva's eyes narrowed, she tensed in her seat.

'You're *lying*.'

Another switch in emotion. This time Eva looked as if she was about to lose control. Irene drew back. Her fingers flexed as she thought of the weapon she might have to reach for in the glove compartment. She stared at Eva, who was breathing heavily, sweating. It was as if that fit had been the trigger for something inside her, like some kind of explosive primed to self-destruct.

She steadied the car on the road and took her eyes off Eva, wondering what she would see when she turned back towards the passenger seat. Ahead of them was the tarmac of the airport and the terminal building. It was quiet, just as she had expected it to be. Their plane would be standing waiting, ready fuelled in the section of the airport reserved for the most V of VIPs and where no one would see them move between the van and plane.

The van would be disposed of.

Irene continued past the terminal building. A quick glance at Eva indicated she had fallen asleep, again. It was terribly odd behaviour and made Irene feel incredibly uncomfortable.

Ahead, she saw the tiny Challenger 600 which would fly them the short trip. She drove right up to the plane – no point taking any chances – and killed the engine.

She waited for the crew of two to emerge but nothing happened.

She gently shoved Eva awake. When she opened her eyes, the girl seemed almost normal again.

Irene sat still in her seat in the van for several seconds and looked around the silent airfield. She reached forward, opened the glove compartment and took out a small handgun.

She heard Eva inhale as if about to speak, and raised a hand to silence her.

It was a warm spring day on the tarmac of La Môle. The south of France was beginning to come to life, the summer season just around the corner. It was sunny, picturesque and quiet. Too quiet.

Irene slowly opened the van door.

Eva watched Irene move out of the van with a sense of great trepidation. Inside her mind, emotions were rushing, jumping and leapfrogging over each other. She had gone from being entirely emotionless to lacking any control over the feelings that seemed to come from nowhere. Several minutes ago, she had wanted to kill Irene, *really* kill her. Now, she felt utterly terrified at the thought of losing her. A small amount of fear in this situation might be normal – Irene was obviously wary – but Eva felt she was about to be overwhelmed.

What was happening to her?

Irene indicated for her to step out from the other side of the van and she did so slowly, leaving the door open behind her so as to make no noise. Eva was surprised no one emerged from the aircraft to greet them.

Irene waited as Eva walked, on wobbly legs, around the front of the van, leaning on the bonnet for support. Looking at Irene,

Eva momentarily thought the older woman might hold out her hand. Realising she must look pathetic, she forced herself to straighten up; she came to a halt alongside Irene, who gave her a long and slightly searching look.

Eva met her gaze evenly, unsure of why she was being so appraised.

They began to walk towards the plane together, in step with each other.

When they were only a metre or so away, Eva saw a shadow fall across the open door of the small aircraft. She stopped. Irene did not.

Irene raised the gun. A sound exploded like a whip crack and Irene was on the ground. Eva stood for several seconds and then went to Irene. She had been shot in the shoulder and was clearly struggling to contain the pain.

'Move, Eva,' she hissed.

Eva turned and went to stand but stumbled as she realised someone was standing right behind her.

It was Leon.

As the small plane flew up and over mainland France, Eva studied Leon. He had secured her into the seat opposite him and now sat looking at her.

He was almost too big for the seat because of the broadness of his shoulders and the muscle definition of his arms.

Irene was behind them. He had not treated her gunshot wound and Irene had not complained but now sat, silently, in the seat behind. Eva could hear her laboured breathing.

That had been a surprise. Irene had not really reacted to being shot by Leon, almost as if she expected it. But there was a definite hostility. Eva could remember little bad blood between Leon and Irene. Although Leon's affiliations were subject to change at the opening of a chequebook, she knew.

She had felt paralysed on that hot runway and watched in

shock as he roughly hustled Irene towards the plane. There was a short exchange between them but Eva could not hear what was said.

Why she didn't run away at that point she didn't know.

Then Leon had come back for her.

Still she hadn't moved.

Even after everything that had happened between them in Berlin, how he had tried to steal her phone, the physical threats... She had just allowed him to lead her towards the plane and fasten her – incapacitate her – in the seat.

There was some sort of implicit trust in him. As if he might be on her side. She desperately needed someone to be on her side.

Eva finished her train of thought and looked up.

He was staring at her.

It was unnerving.

'She needs a doctor, Leon.'

He continued to stare at her with steely eyes but said nothing.

'Leon?'

He didn't reply. She began to feel angry.

'Can you hear me?'

He slowly nodded his head.

'Well?'

'Well, what?'

'I said she needs a doctor. You've shot her. You obviously don't want to kill her or you would have just left her on the tarmac.'

'It was best she wasn't found.'

As usual, Leon wasted few words.

Eva watched his chest rise and fall, almost as if he was sighing. She wondered how he really felt about all this, what his role actually was – and for whom. Her mind played around with who he might have been if he had not been drawn into this world of violence and deception.

She stopped herself. She was romanticising him. She was imbuing him with qualities she had no idea whether or not he possessed – such as a desire to be a good man. Perhaps this would always have been his road.

Nevertheless, Eva felt excitement as his eyes once again came to meet hers.

'I don't understand you,' she said, attempting to verbally block the connection she could feel.

'No' was all he said in reply.

Eva sat and stared at him.

Her head was a mess.

She looked away. She shut her eyes. Several minutes passed.

With a rushing sensation, Eva began to feel her emotions changing once again. She opened her eyes; she felt nothing now. It could be anyone sitting opposite her.

A boldness overtook her.

'Why do you do this?' she asked him. 'I mean, what kind of life do you have and what really makes all this,' she gestured expansively with her hands, 'more worthwhile than people and friendships and real genuine relationships?'

She leaned forward towards him. She couldn't help noticing how his eyes travelled down her neck.

When he met her gaze again, she could see his pupils were engorged.

He looked away.

'These ties hurt,' she said, softly.

He continued to ignore her.

'Take them off?'

He sat silent.

'Please undo the ties, Leon,' she asked, beguilingly, and, finally, he looked at her. She smiled, 'There isn't exactly anywhere I can go, is there?'

A muscle twitched above his eye.

'Besides,' Eva continued, quite obviously eyeing the muscles in his arms, 'you're *so* much stronger than me, anyway.'

Jesus, she thought to herself, as she heard the words come out of her mouth, will he really fall for this?

But he did. And several minutes later, she was sitting opposite him, unsecured. She realised the fake Jackson might have been wrong and it was not Leon who had held the power over her but, perhaps, it was the other way around. She glanced at her body, thin now – really thin – and dressed in jeans and a sweater customised with someone else's blood. She was hardly in seductress mode.

Nevertheless…

She stood up, locking her eyes with his. She heard Irene inhale sharply in the seat behind.

'Sit down,' Leon said flatly.

'Oh come on, I'm not going to hurt you.'

'I said sit down.'

She hesitated. The two stared at each other. Eva felt her skin start to tingle.

'Make me.'

There was silence in the plane; all Eva could hear was the sound of her heartbeat in her ears. She watched Leon, waiting to see what he would do, assuming he would stay put, but he took her by surprise. Suddenly, he was in front of her, right up against her, his two huge hands wrapped around her shoulders. He shook her slightly. She looked up at him. Their faces were close.

Leon's eyes seemed to glaze over for several seconds as he stared at her – just as they had done in the park in Berlin – and then they cleared. He pushed her down into the seat and silently began to fasten her back in.

THIRTY THREE

HE HAD OBSERVED the interaction from the front of the plane. It was fascinating the way she had manipulated him – and it had almost worked.

Was there something more he didn't know about?

When he stepped out into the main body of the plane, he could see the shock on Eva's face. But there was something else there too, something suspicious, perhaps even knowing. As if she had been there before.

He stood in front of her, at 10,000 feet, unsure of what to say after all this time and slightly puzzled by her reaction.

He had expected her to perhaps explode with anger, or maybe even with excitement in the best-case scenario, but the silent staring and the stillness were unexpected and unnerving.

He didn't know why he had chosen this moment specifically to reveal himself, it had just felt as if it might be the right time. Although, from the way Leon was looking at him, perhaps he should have waited for the signal, as they had discussed.

He took a step towards Eva. She visibly backed away.

Eva was struggling to make sense of the face in front of her. Jackson – again.

She blinked several times and checked her heart rate to make sure she wasn't having another fit, but her pulse was strong and healthy, albeit slightly raised. Despite that, she felt she couldn't trust her eyes. They had let her down once, already.

'Who are you?' she said, finally.

He frowned. 'You know who I am.'

She shook her head.

'It's me,' he said again, taking another step across the plane towards her, 'it's Jackson. Your brother.'

'How do I know that?'

He laughed, irritation insuppressible. 'Well, can't you see it?'

She didn't reply but he noticed another tiny shake of her head.

She saw him frown again. He did actually look genuinely perturbed by her reaction. But that meant nothing.

'Where have you been?'

'What?'

'All this time, where have you been?'

'It's a long story, I don't think I can tell you all of it.'

The answer was too similar to that of the first Jackson. She shifted uncomfortably in her seat.

'Well, what do you want?'

'Eva, I don't understand. I thought you might be pleased to see me.'

She fought to control her emotions, which were picking up unnatural speed once again, swirling in an ever-increasing storm of violence.

'Pleased to see you,' she murmured, '*Pleased. To. See. You.*'

It was immediately obvious that he regretted the flippant choice of words. History – even history that dated back to Paris – had proven to Eva that he was a liar. Of course she would not welcome his appearance.

With a start, Eva realised she had just thought of this man as if he really was her brother. She stared at him.

'Can we at least untie her?' the man asked Leon, after several minutes of silence. That's what she had wanted minutes before. Perhaps he could establish trust by giving it to her.

Leon was looking at Eva again, his eyes dark and liquid. The heaviness of his brow almost completely overshadowed the expression on his face and Eva realised she couldn't read him at all.

She noticed he had sneaked a glance at Jackson, too, as if he also couldn't quite believe his eyes. That confused her.

Finally, Leon nodded but didn't move.

Jackson walked over to Eva and loosened her bonds. The space was tiny; they were forced to be close. Eva felt the uncertain terrain of the situation. So many unknowns.

She tried to swallow and realised her mouth was completely dry. Nervously, she flicked her hair from her face. It was almost impossible to establish whether the people around her were friend or foe, both from the way they had behaved and from the circumstances in which they had appeared. It was all so conflicting. And now, here was another Jackson, one Leon seemed to accept. Leon and Jackson had been friends and he would know the real one. Or would he? She hadn't. Perhaps Leon was being duped, too. Or maybe he was, once again, duping her.

She closed her eyes and took some deep breaths. It was too much. It was all too much.

Behind closed eyelids, she heard the clink of a glass of water being placed on the small table by the window to her right. She looked up into Leon's eyes but they were still expressionless and cold. He hesitated in front of her, momentarily. Their eyes locked.

Then he walked away from her and began taking medical equipment from a large box positioned on a table on the opposite side of the plane. Everyone was watching him but he didn't seem to notice. Because of the size of the space, he was forced to stoop everywhere he moved.

When he apparently had what he needed, he took it and walked past her without meeting her eye. She heard him instructing Irene in the seat behind to take off her shirt.

Jackson spoke, distracting her.

'Eva, I just want to say that I'm sorry.'

She looked at him. It was a pointless thing to say given what she had been through.

Nevertheless, she nodded, still wondering how to establish whether this face was real or liable to change at any second. Not being able to trust her judgement was making the situation difficult and she felt out of control, as if the ground was rushing up to meet her.

Which was unnerving in a plane.

'I know this must be difficult for you, that everything in Paris must have been so hard. I'm so, so sorry.'

She stared at him, the emotions inside continuing to duck and whirl.

'If I could have done anything differently, I would,' he continued.

She had the feeling that he would just carry on talking if she didn't reply to him. The verbal diarrhoea of a guilty conscience?

'Jackson,' she said slowly, 'if you really are Jackson, that is.'

He frowned again.

'We could talk about this but I really wouldn't know where to start.'

A silent nod.

Eva just didn't have the stomach for the conversation.

She heard a gasp from behind and turned in her seat to see Irene flat out over the chairs behind, with Leon suturing her shoulder.

There was blood; it made the bile rise in her gut.

She turned unsteadily.

Jackson was watching her.

He looked as if he was about to make more apologies. What she needed was to know who he really was – the rest, she really didn't care about, right now. But establishing anything was going to be difficult given how off-key her perception was.

'How do I know you're my brother?'

'I don't understand, why would I not be?' he replied, indicating his face.

She considered not talking about what had happened before. If he was another fake, of course he already knew about it and she would feel foolish. But if he wasn't… 'This isn't the first time I've come across you this week.'

'What?'

'It's not the first time I've seen your face – if I didn't seem shocked, it's because I have already had the "reunion moment" with you. But with someone else.'

'I don't understand.'

She watched his face to see whether that was true.

He sat back in his seat and broke eye contact for several seconds before he spoke.

'Did you see anyone else you thought you knew? Or anything strange which seemed to be the boundaries of reality blurring?'

'Yes…'

'What exactly did you see?'

'I saw Valerie.'

The name produced an almost physical reaction in him. Of what type, Eva couldn't be sure.

Did it make her feel more convinced of his identity? Perhaps.

'Where did you see her?' His voice was aggressive, gravelly.

'At the château where they held me.'

'Not possible.'

'I thought I saw her too.' This, from Irene, behind them. No one stopped her speaking. 'It wasn't her, Eva,' concluded Irene, a lightly patronising note in her voice. 'Just a very good *lookalike*.'

Had she intentionally emphasised that word? Eva realised she could no longer read between the conversational lines.

'Eva,' Jackson turned and focused intensely on her, 'I don't know how much you know about what has happened but these people,' Eva could have sworn he nodded in Irene's direction, 'have access to the best science money can buy.'

'Irene has told me this.'

He frowned and stopped. He appeared to reassess and then continue.

'They have a piece of technology allowing them to manipulate the brain by injecting it with a combination of drugs and inserting tiny cranial implants. This can be designed specifically to communicate with a template marked on the face.'

'Marked with what?'

'Mapping points. They can use this to make you think you're seeing someone you're not.'

As soon as Joseph Smith heard that sentence, he knew it was time to move. He set the autopilot to guide them into Geneva airspace and then took off the captain's hat he had stolen from the man he had shot in the airfield in France. He felt the co-pilot glance across at him, so he smiled. The other man had not spoken a word when his colleague had been replaced and Smith had quickly realised that those who agreed to make these flights understood that the less they knew the safer they would be. Although not in this instance. Silently, he removed the small knife that he kept in his pocket. He began small talk with the man about his family whilst slipping the sheath from the knife with the hand that held it.

The sheath dropped almost soundlessly to the floor of the cabin as he activated the flick blade but the other man seemed to hear one or the other of the two motions. A silence passed between them and Joseph Smith waited to see if the co-pilot would take any action. In the seconds that followed the colour drained from the other man's face; he understood what was about to happen. How did people know that, thought Smith to himself; it was not the first time he had seen the recognition of impending death. He waited to see whether the man would beg. When he didn't, Smith took hold of his chin and cut deep through his jugular. The man did not protest. It was the quickest and most humane way Smith could kill him. Had the man begged for his life, Smith might have chosen a far less swift method.

He watched the life ebb out of the co-pilot's eyes and knew that, in those last seconds, whoever he really was, and whatever he had done in his life, his thoughts would have turned to his family. Or perhaps to everything he had done. Even all the things he had not done. Death was the greatest of levellers. Joseph Smith had never been close enough to death to appreciate what happened in the last minutes before the body ceased to support the brain. He had seen it oh so many times and occasionally he had been tempted to stop, to question his victim and ask what it was like. But he never did. It was not a process you could easily halt, even temporarily.

When the man was dead, Joseph turned his seat so he was facing the opposite window. He opened a small locker in the cabin and changed out of the pilot's clothes before equipping himself with the weapons he had brought with him – the small knife, a larger knife and two guns. Then he placed the mapping points at the correct parts of his face and activated the sensors.

Finally, he stood and walked out of the cockpit, silently closing the door behind him. He stood for several seconds in the area between the cockpit and the curtained off cabin. Then he pulled back the cabin curtain, standing in the doorway, waiting for the passengers to notice him.

Eva looked up at the doorway. The sentence she had been speaking to her brother was not finished. Her voice simply trailed away. For there, standing in the doorway, was a man with the same face as the person sitting opposite her.

Behind her, she heard Leon swear and then there was

stillness. Eva wanted to turn but she couldn't tear her gaze from the identical faces in front of her. Two Jacksons, exactly the same in every respect.

She looked from the face of the man in front of her to the face of the man who stood at the door. There was no way to tell them apart. Neither looked more menacing, neither held a weapon. They were even wearing almost the same clothes.

She watched as they regarded each other. As the man sitting opposite turned to face the man in the doorway, both jumped slightly, an almost identical reaction.

Slowly, she stood up.

'What's going on?' Her voice was unsteady, wavering. Her knees were shaking. She leaned, so that the backs of her calves were pushing against the solid material of the seat.

The plane juddered, as if there was no one at the controls, and Eva immediately lost her balance and sat back down.

'Eva.' The man at the door spoke. Jackson's voice. No, it couldn't b... Her head hurt. Eva was nauseous. This could not be happening.

She looked across at the man with whom she had been talking several seconds ago. He was still staring at the man in the doorway. She could only see the side of his face, which gave away nothing.

Finally, he turned to her. 'What's wrong, Eva?' he asked, glancing behind her as he spoke. He seemed far more unsure of himself than he had several seconds ago. She did not answer him.

It was not possible there could be two of him. Her mind might be struggling, but that at least she did know. For a brief moment, she almost felt like laughing. The situation was so ridiculous it was almost comic. But there was a sense of foreboding behind these two faces. One or both of them was pretending to look like her brother and there could be no good reason for that.

She turned and looked at the seated Jackson. Minutes ago, he had been telling her about drugs and implants able to manipulate the brain to make someone believe they were seeing a face which wasn't there. That was exactly what was happening here. That's all, she told herself – it's just science. You are not going mad.

But she felt her heart flutter as she looked at the two identical faces and she wondered whether she could still trust her instincts, her brain.

Then the man by the door moved towards her. Immediately, Eva was on her feet again. She looked around for a weapon but there was only the glass of water on the table in front of her.

'Eva,' the man said, as he took another step towards her. 'Eva, I am your brother.'

'Don't come any closer to me.'

He stopped moving.

Now the seated man spoke too. 'What do you see, Eva?' He was not angry, was he even surprised?

Eva tried to work out whether it was a typical Jackson reaction. But they had been apart for too long.

The standing man took another step towards Eva and she stared at him hard. 'Stop.'

'Eva, this man is black,' said the seated Jackson.

She looked at him. 'What?'

'He has black skin. His voice is nothing like mine. I don't understand how...' his voice tailed away and then returned. 'The face mapping,' he said slowly. 'Eva, this is the face mapping we were talking about.'

Either he was an incredibly convincing actor or his reactions were consistent with being as surprised as she was. But he seemed to know an awful lot about that technology – too much not to be involved in this on some level. Besides, she didn't even know why he was here, what he wanted with her. Why hadn't she asked him when she had the chance?

Eva stared at him, coldly.

Silence descended on the cabin.

Eva looked again from one to the other. She knew the technology required 'mapping points'. If she could feel their faces, she could see who was the imposter and who was real.

'Am I the only person who can see two Jacksons?' she asked out loud.

'Yes,' Irene responded, her voice dull.

'Leon?'

No response.

Now Eva turned to the area of the plane where Leon had been patching up Irene. But it was Leon, not Irene, who was horizontal in the seat.

'Leon?' she took a step towards him. She realised Irene had a gun.

'What are you doing, Irene?'

'Tie her up,' Irene said to one or both of the Jacksons.

Eva started to panic.

There was no one in this small space she could trust.

So far, no one had moved. Whoever responded to Irene had to be the fake Jackson, which presumably was why neither had yet given themselves away.

With a growing sense of panic, Eva realised how powerless she was. In fact, she had been helpless for weeks – from the moment she had arrived in Berlin. At every stage, someone had been pulling the strings. And she could do nothing. Her heart began to beat faster as she turned to Irene. Somehow, she felt this woman was responsible, whether that was logical or not. She'd been pretending to be Eva's ally but she was not. Perhaps she never had been.

'I *trusted* you, Irene.'

The two women stared at each other. Eva realised she was

willing Irene to shoot her. She felt appalled, with herself, with Irene, with this entire situation. A red mist of rage began to descend.

Then she sprang at Irene over the back of the seat, just a metre from where Eva stood. The gun fired, sending a bullet into the wall between cabin and cockpit.

There was a struggle, gravity had pushed Eva on top of Irene, where she was pinning the older woman to the floor. She repeatedly smashed her closed fist onto Irene's wrist, trying to force the release of the gun, but Irene would not let it go.

They grappled.

Irene did not have the space to aim the gun and so hit out with her fists. Eva responded with the back of her hand.

Then Irene landed a punch that made Eva see stars. Eva made a grab for the nearest seat as her vision darkened, dragged herself to a crouch and turned back to Irene, lunging at her as the other woman tried to stand.

Irene staggered, one hand shot out and she grasped Eva's throat, fingers quickly closing around her windpipe but she lost her balance, dragging them both to the floor again.

On her back, Irene held Eva's throat in her left fist, her arm rigid. She began trying to aim the gun she still held in her right hand at Eva. Then both of them had fingers around the gun.

'We need her alive, Irene.' Jackson's voice from behind them both. But which one?

Eva screamed as frustration overwhelmed her, the noise muffled by the vice around her throat. She felt another surge of white hot rage and ripped the gun from Irene's grasp by sheer brute force. The surprise Eva felt at her own strength registered in Irene's eyes, too. Eva smacked the gun, with all her strength, against the side of Irene's head. The woman was still, her hand dropping to the floor, fully releasing Eva's neck.

Eva rose and turned slowly to the two men behind her, with the gun in her hand. Both still looked like Jackson. Neither had moved. But one had spoken. And that one she had to kill.

THIRTY FOUR

PAUL WAS DIZZY, elated. He felt a sense of excitement, as if what was about to happen was all his work. It was nothing less than an entire country they were taking by stealth; a bloodless coup. He had finally been given the full picture of what was about to take place and it was fascinating. It was unprecedented.

The thing about countries like the UK was that they were inherently undermined by their profit motive, which won over human interest every time – even when it came to the decisions of an elected government.

Of course this was the oldest of conspiracy theories. And that was what made this so perfect. As if there was some kind of double jeopardy rule with conspiracy theory – the more times it was aired the more unbelievable it became. The more it appeared like the plot of a book or a film, the more it seemed like fiction.

In his experience, the truth was always stranger than fiction.

He scrolled through the list of electronic instruments at his fingertips, those that gave him such complete control – him. He realised, of course, that he was just the caretaker but he also felt privileged to have been so trusted, even at this late stage. Even the old man hadn't been given this high level information. Had he? It left Paul with rather a conundrum. It was at this point that the plan had been for him to parachute out but Paul wondered whether this might be a good career move for him. It surely shouldn't matter to Jackson either way.

He might like this life of high end crime, it seemed to suit him. What troubled him was what might happen next.

He knew, within the technology that Jackson had instructed

him to obtain, that there was a failsafe, a way to undermine the system when it was in use.

The thing about holding someone or something to ransom was that whatever you were using to do it potentially made you just as vulnerable to being held to ransom yourself. He was surprised no one at ACORN had checked for such vulnerability. Or considered he might have an ulterior motive, or be in the pay of someone else.

And then he stopped. His fingers froze.

Had they?

He blinked.

Perhaps they had.

How would he know?

Paul removed his hand from the keyboard as it dawned on him that, in this situation, whilst he sat here pondering his ability to undermine those who had paid so much for his stolen technology, perhaps the same could be done to him. Maybe right now. By the same people he was targetting.

With a start, he realised he wasn't sure where reality lay anymore; he wasn't certain of anything.

Eva stared at the two men in front of her and knew reality was not something she had any appreciation of at that moment. This was going to come down to instinct. An instinct that felt precarious, at best. Neither of the men had shown any reaction to her confrontation with Irene.

Her gaze moved from one to the other and she quickly made a decision as to which she should shoot. Her finger began to press on the trigger of the weapon. And then she stopped. Could she trust her instinct? After so much had been done to alter the chemicals in her brain, did she really – actually – know she was making the right decision?

Reality. Truth. Weren't they an entirely subjective thing in any situation?

There is no truth, only points of view…

Her finger moved away from the trigger. Philosophy breeding inaction.

The arm holding the gun dropped slightly.

Then there was a sudden movement and, instinctively, she turned and shot in the direction from which it came.

The bullet pierced the shell of the plane and the entire structure began to shake and swerve. Oxygen masks fell from above the seats.

Eva stumbled.

She opened her eyes wide as she saw Leon, clutching the top of his shoulder, blood pouring through his hands. That was wrong. Had she shot him? Had someone else shot him?

He was staring at her. No one else moved.

The plane lurched.

Suddenly, everyone fell to the side.

Eva, wrong footed, stumbled, hit her head on the top of the seat to her right. She managed to keep the arm holding the gun aimed in front of her. She squinted. Her vision was beginning to blur again. She felt her heartbeat flutter, a missed beat, another. She was about to have a second fit, she could feel it.

And then her vision cleared.

With horror, she saw clearly the two men in front of her. The first face she recognised was that of Joseph Smith.

Instantly, Joseph realised something had happened when Eva hit her head on the seat.

He calculated his options. He had only one.

He began to move towards her at speed. She was only two paces away. But she was faster.

She shot him, first through the leg and then the chest.

As he fell, he activated the device he had been given to understand would destroy the key. Not out of necessity, just out of malice. Finally, he had some sort of power over her. He watched Eva react instantly as the trigger in his hand released a stream of chemicals into her bloodstream from the delivery mechanism under her skin. For several seconds, nothing happened. In the time that elapsed, he felt as if the space around him was suddenly silent, there was no one there except the two of them.

He opened his mouth to speak to her when he realised she was just standing staring at him. Or was she – was that his imagination? He knew his life-blood was ebbing away, his heart was beating at a weaker rate. She had shot him, first disabling him, and finally the potentially fatal wound. But she would not win, he would not allow it.

Once again, he made contact with her eyes but they were glazed. As his head hit the floor he saw her body begin to move, almost as if she was dancing.

In front of his hand, Paul's screen began to flash red. The words 'key compromised' jumped out at him.

He sat still for several seconds, not realising what was happening.

Key compromised? He fumbled quickly with his phone, calling up the basic instruction manual he had pieced together from the research he had stolen, a crib sheet for being convincing.

Key compromised – the key was about to be destroyed. It was a final protection, built in to allow someone to permanently deny access: death. But to activate that series the physical key would have been required and he had the only copy.

He sprang to life.

He began pressing the pockets frantically on his suit, trying to feel for the shape of the tiny key. He couldn't believe he could not immediately bring to mind its location.

After several seconds, he realised he did not have it.

It was gone.

And there, he thought, is the only flaw in this piece of technology – there is just one key. Although he knew the flaw was not in the technology but the human being who had allowed it to be taken.

He sat for several seconds, fists clenched in front of him and stared at the flashing words on the screen of the laptop.

Key compromised.

She was failing. And it was unlikely he could stop it, which meant that he was compromised.

There was only one person who could have taken the VERITAS key from him, Joseph Smith – perhaps the only individual he had chosen to trust in quite some time.

He pressed the 'locator' key on the laptop and the system began to circle across a map of the world. The locator drilled down, country by country, and settled on a route somewhere between France and Switzerland. But it did not stay there. It was moving.

And it was not only moving forwards but seemed to be dropping in altitude, too.

'Fuck,' he muttered, under his breath, and began frenetically typing into the key pad in front of him. Consecutively, the three mobile phones on the table in front of him began to ring. Their tuneless tones rang on and on but he ignored them. Briefly, each one stopped and then instantly began again.

He was not going to be able to stay – and neither would he be able to escape. Joseph Smith had effectively erased him too.

A crew member stepped out from behind the curtain of the front section of the private plane.

'Sir.'

'Not now. I told you not to disturb me.'

'But, sir, I think this is urgent.'

'I said not *now*!' He hurled the first thing which came to his hand at the stewardess. A bone china coffee cup. It struck her on the shoulder.

Jackson watched as his sister fell. He looked briefly around the shaking cabin of the plane they were in – it felt unstable and unsteered. Autopilot. Irene was dazed, possibly unconscious, possibly dead. He didn't care particularly about her right at that moment, he didn't even know why – or how – she was there.

Leon was bleeding, not profusely but enough to disable him soon if it was not stemmed. As always, the huge man was looking to him for guidance. It seemed to be a natural instinct of his, even after all that had passed previously between them.

Then there was the man he recognised but could not name – Eva had shot him and he lay on his back, staring up at the curved, shaking ceiling of the plane. Was he dead? Jackson would have to check but he could not seem to move. His old paralysis returned, the result of his near death all those years ago, scars that would never heal. He had never been able to recall those injuries – or who had inflicted them – and so he had never had the chance for revenge. Other than on ACORN. Their betrayal of him would now extract a huge price.

He looked at the man on the floor and concluded that the other pilot – the man Jackson had paid – must be dead. He glanced at Eva. Jackson was well aware of the time pressure he was under.

And yet he could not move.

He felt Leon's eyes on him.

He almost thought he felt Eva's eyes on him.

He turned his gaze towards his distressed sister.

After all the years he had been forced not to be a part of her life, her importance to him had slowly diminished. That's why he had been able to make her his 'key'. She didn't matter. In reality, he felt little guilt for anything she had endured as a result of his actions. Because he felt nothing at all for anyone.

The part of the brain that enabled emotional reaction no longer functioned for him – not since he had almost died.

He watched as her body rocked back and forth where she stood then she, too, began to head for the floor.

He didn't move.

He knew the exact make-up of the chemicals released into her system at that point – if the composition had not changed since he had worked on the VERITAS technology.

He did not know 100 per cent what her chances of survival were but he knew that he had the tools to influence that and he knew that he must try to keep her alive. Even if it meant momentarily killing her.

Eva was on the floor now. Jackson remained still.

He glanced over at Leon, who was still staring at him.

'Can you move?'

A grim nod from the Frenchman.

'Tie her,' he said, indicating Irene, and, with considerable effort, Leon began to move from his position and head for the prone form of the older woman.

Jackson took two steps towards his sister. He touched her skin and quickly withdrew his hand. She was cold, clammy.

He steeled himself to touch her once again and then put her in the recovery position on the cabin floor as she began to vomit blue liquid.

He looked up and realised Leon was staring at Eva.

Jackson pulled a protective glove from a medical bag on one of the seats, put it on and ensured that Eva's airway was clear. He left the blue, gel-like vomit where it was. The implants were dissolving.

He took a step back, removed the glove and sat in one of the seats closest to the man Eva had shot. He appeared to be dead.

Jackson checked his pulse.

Apparently expired. Or close to at least.

He looked into the man's eyes for the customary 'lights out' effect all corpses had once the life had ebbed from them.

He hesitated. It seemed as if the man's eyes had moved. There seemed to be light behind them. But this would not be the case for much longer.

Jackson sat back in the seat and watched Eva shaking and jerking on the floor.

When she was still, he stood and reached again for the medical bag. He found a bright silver cylindrical tube and removed what looked like an epi-pen.

He walked back to Eva and waited for Leon to finish dealing with Irene.

When Leon was at his side, the two of them stared down at Eva who was now still, unmoving and apparently unbreathing.

Jackson hesitated.

He looked at Leon.

'Was there ever anything between you two, Leon?' He had been in Berlin, he had seen how ineffective Eva caused Leon to be. For the next stage that would be an interference that he could not afford.

The same hesitation was mirrored in the man opposite.

'Don't lie to me,' he said quietly.

Blue eyes glared back at him. Resentful of the prying.

'No.'

Jackson pushed the pen up against Eva's skin and drove the plunger home.

THIRTY FIVE

In a nondescript office in Whitehall, a solitary figure sat in front of a computer screen. It was late and there was no justifiable reason for the slight woman at the terminal to be there. She knew that, and she had been careful to avoid registering her presence late at night – she had not used her own entry pass, she had looked away from the security cameras and she had even taken the precaution of identifying an exit route which would involve a two-storey jump to the ground. She had brought sensible shoes for this part. Flat shoes. As she pushed off her left heel and pressed the sole of her foot to the cold floor she looked forward to them. It had been a long, long day and, with the pressure of this evening hanging over her, she had felt an almost constant stream of adrenaline. It had left her exhausted.

Although, now, she was beginning to wake up.

In front of her, a steady flow of numbers was starting to appear on the muted brightness of the screen. The last of the trades and transactions were coming through. In her mind she imagined it like a wall, one with a number of missing bricks – these trades were those missing bricks. Each completed trade or contract would fill another hole in the overall matrix, making it into an impenetrable whole. Many were private government contracts, so the only way they could be credibly monitored was from here inside the intranet, which was the reason that she had been asked to become part of this network.

She was in awe of the way this had been set up, it was not only incredibly clever but almost unassailable, too. The UK had nailed its flag to the post of commerce.

And now commerce would prove to be its Achilles heel. She had only a slight interest in the eventual outcome – the potential for anarchy excited her. But otherwise she was happy to take the money and run.

After everything was complete, she would remove the laptop so it was physically outside the government network. She didn't expect to ever return to this building but neither did she want to find her name added to Interpol's wanted lists. It had to be quiet and anonymous; like everything this organisation did.

Once the laptop was safely out of the building, she would deliver it and disappear. The first set of instructions she'd received had required her to personally ensure the laptop reached its destination but now that was someone else's responsibility. She was simply a link in a chain. A man had appeared almost at the last minute and changed the arrangements. Perhaps she should have questioned him but what could she do at this stage?

As her mind wandered, her eyes were drawn back to the lit screen. The numbers were beginning to slow. The last bricks were almost in the wall.

In a matter of minutes kolychak would be complete. Every essential service, every privatised infrastructure, every aspect of the country that could be bought or sold – from its government bonds, to shares in its biggest and best established utilities businesses – would now be majority owned by kolychak and its myriad of front companies, all hidden by clever structuring, bribes and corruption. The UK was now a puppet – controlled by those who could shut off access to essential services, infrastructure and reserves if decisions were not made in line with certain interests. Of course, these threats would never be carried out – and the fact that kolychak had even happened would never be revealed. It was genius really; the ultimate, silent, hostile takeover.

Leon shut his eyes as the plane began its descent. It was quiet inside the cabin. They had quickly dealt with the bullet which had almost depressurised the cabin. Jackson had examined Leon's shoulder wound, pronounced it superficial and retrieved the bullet from the seat where it had embedded after passing straight through the flesh. It ached. But it was a clean ache. It would heal. Irene was still, silent and bound. Joseph Smith lay on his back in the position in which he had fallen. He was dead. Leon was glad.

Jackson was flying the plane. This did not trouble Leon – it was not the first time he had seen Jackson at the controls of an aircraft and he entirely trusted the man he had known for so long. Plus, there was always the autopilot.

Eva could not be seen.

She was hidden in the container in which Jackson had placed her body.

Leon understood little of the science of what was happening to Eva but he knew it was Jackson who had placed her in the position of being this 'key'. What he had not been able to work out yet was whether this was intentional or was a decision forced upon him.

Because Leon still struggled to work out how he felt about Jackson. He had been so overwhelmed by guilt after believing himself to have been responsible for not preventing Jackson's death that he had found himself unable to refuse the other man's requests. Even though they directly compromised Eva. Guilt was more powerful than love.

Of course, he had been shocked when Jackson reappeared, first in Leon's mind in the desert fight and then after that in the flesh.

How had he survived and why had he not contacted Leon before now? With Jackson in front of him, the guilt he felt about not being there for him had been an overwhelming force and he had accepted Jackson's explanation of the intervening years without question. Leon was aware that there was a strong desire to believe Jackson, which may have caused him to dismiss suspicions he wouldn't have otherwise. And he knew Jackson may have been using the guilt to manipulate him.

Leon had been commissioned by Irene to protect Eva, but he had dropped that assignment with Jackson's arrival – and now it seemed that even Irene had her own private agenda. He had followed Jackson because he owed him. And because he could not let go of Eva.

Eva. Who knew nothing of any of it. Who never had. And yet who was always caught up in the centre of it all.

He pitied her. And he feared her.

He wondered whether Jackson knew what kind of woman Eva had become. Perhaps they were evenly matched.

He glanced once again at the inflated coffin shaped structure that contained her still body. Apparently, she was not dead, she was simply 'preserved'. They needed her alive. Her blood literally held the key.

She was the key.

But to what?

He wondered how much Irene had known. She had mentioned nothing of her ACORN connections when commissioning Leon to Eva in London, and discovering that had surprised him.

But Irene hated Eva. The fact that she had finally sold out showed just how much she had lost perspective as a result of her hatred for Eva – and all of Irene's failures she represented. Leon suspected Irene's motivation was also to betray the organisation she had worked with for so long. The organisation she, perhaps subconsciously, blamed for stealing the best years of her life. Only once had she hinted at this motivation but it had been enough – she had said 'all I want is, just once, to get home in time to pick up my kids from school – just once' and the desperation and guilt in her voice had loomed large in the room.

However, he had realised in Berlin, after Jackson reappeared, that Irene was capable of incredible deception and more than able to look after her own interests. So he had to tread carefully. Because he knew Eva would instinctively trust Irene more than she trusted him.

'You're deep in thought.'

Jackson, leaning against the doorway to the cockpit, was watching him.

Leon looked up, guarded; it was almost as if Jackson had been able to read his thoughts.

'I'm still not sure I understand what we're doing.'

Jackson's face flickered with annoyance. He had never been a patient man and Leon had always felt the stupid sidekick around him.

'We have to deliver Eva.'

'Why did they choose to make Eva the key?'

'They didn't, I did.'

So it had been intentional.

'Understand this though, Leon, I did it when the project was my own. I wanted to present this as a gift to Eva. It was to prove my identity, to show how serious I was, that I wanted to be a part of her life again – my life's achievement, hers to do with as she wanted. I would have been at her mercy.'

'But now she is at their mercy. And yours.'

Leon felt a flicker of mistrust. Was it really a plausible explanation?

Jackson looked at him, brown eyes hard.

'You know I would have changed that if I could.'

'Could we not just take her to a hospital now? Remove the implants – and whatever else is inside her? If you really want life for her surely that's the only way?'

Jackson didn't reply. He continued to look at Leon. Slowly his head tipped sideways, a questioning movement. There was something about it which set Leon's teeth on edge.

'I feel as if there is something you're not telling me about your relationship with Eva, Leon.'

Jackson's eyes seemed to burn from brown to black. He was still, staring across the small space, his head still cocked on one side.

Leon felt himself shiver.

'There's nothing to tell. Really.'

An iPhone on the table buzzed to life. Jackson's gaze didn't waver from Leon. After several seconds, he finally looked down at the phone. Leon glanced away, to remove himself from the offensive stare. He looked again. He could have sworn the dead corpse of Joseph Smith was looking right at him.

THIRTY SIX

IT WAS A DREAM. Or perhaps a memory. There had been so many occasions recently when she hadn't been able to distinguish between the two.

Eva was lying still.

She was encased in something holding her fast, completely frozen. Her first instinct was to panic and yet she couldn't seem to react. She tried to move one body part at a time but nothing responded.

Fingers, hands, feet, legs, arms, even her head refused to acknowledge the desire for flight which loomed large in her mind.

Only her eyes moved.

She lay where she was, looking up at a dark night sky.

She tried to move again but the only response came from her eyes. If anyone had cared to look, they would have seen her straining to communicate. Anything.

To anyone.

After several seconds, Eva realised she had felt like this before.

Sleep paralysis.

The sensation of waking, of being unable to move, of being locked into her body. Trapped in stillness. More than once, she had experienced this when waking suddenly in the middle of the night. Each time, she had been convinced someone was in the room with her.

Once, she had been right.

But she was not awake now so it couldn't be happening to her. This was a dream.

Surely this was a dream.

Once they were safely on the ground, he felt as though he could relax – just for a moment. There had been hiccups, but overall everything was going mostly as planned.

He looked across the private airfield in which they had landed. It was moonlit and silent, the only movement coming from small teams of people working quietly to move everything on to the next stage.

He sat in the back of a large lorry, waiting. The interior had been converted so it resembled a moving medical facility. The doors were open and a cool breeze was almost making him shiver.

Eva was strapped to a secured gurney. He could see the outline of her face through the semi-sheer inflated material which enclosed her. She was entirely still, her bodily functions paused until required again.

He briefly wondered what that must feel like, whether she was aware of anything that was happening to her.

But he didn't really care.

He understood how keenly she must have felt the loss of her own autonomy, not just the physical loss of control but the fact her life had not been her own for some time. But it had no effect on the way he felt about her – or the way that he would use her.

How frustrating to think you're making decisions for yourself only to find out someone else has been pulling the strings all along. He smiled to himself.

He understood her well enough to know it would have been agony for her. Which, in a way, was why it had been necessary. Taking away someone's autonomy was the fastest way to remove them as a threat.

And she was a threat to him, even though she may not have realised it yet.

Slowly, it began to dawn on Eva that the sky she could see was real. The cool air caressing the small area of exposed skin on her face had too much detail for a dream.

But she could not move, not to speak, not to sit up, not to find a way out of whatever she was encased in.

It felt like a coffin.

With her eyes – the only responsive part of her body – she began searching for clues as to where she was but, because she couldn't even sit, she could do no more than look up. If someone's gaze had met hers, they would have known she was awake, that she needed help, but no face came into view. She was completely helpless.

Gradually, pieces of memory began to filter into her consciousness and she knew she had been intentionally incapacitated.

Joseph Smith.

It had been something to do with him, she knew that much. But no more.

His appearance made her feel even more afraid because it meant this was no accident. It was a part of someone's next move. And, for the first time since she had attempted to rescue the man at Waterloo Station, she found herself entirely without resources.

This time she really couldn't do anything to help herself, as control of her body had been taken from her. Suddenly, urgently, she wished she had just shot herself when she had the chance. It would surely be less painful than whatever was coming next.

With no physical way to dispel the anxiety, Eva found it hard to stop her worst fears from becoming overwhelming. Was it permanent? Was she to be imprisoned like this forever?

Who had done this and why?

Everything – the word 'kolychak', the odd interconnections between people in her life, the reappearance of Jackson, or at least someone who had the ability to appear to be him – she knew there had to be some link between it all, some party pulling the strings.

But, even when she was mobile, she had never been able to discern who it was. Now all she knew was that someone wanted her in this condition, had intentionally put her in this condition.

The worst thing was that, even if she managed to make the connections, to use her still functioning brain to work out exactly what was happening all around her, she would be the only person who would ever know it.

Because she couldn't speak. Or write. Or even gesture.

She was locked in.

In the back of the lorry, Jackson began to work through the diagrams on the tablet computer, locked so only he could operate it. The grid was an ingenious creation of confusion, designed to be so believable even the smartest financial brains around the world might stop and pause if they were presented with such a convincing network of deception.

Lines represented connections between companies in different jurisdictions, there were careful notes of share purchases, of dates of acquisition of business interests so very dull until one looked at what they represented as a whole. Altogether, this picture defined the inherent weakness in contemporary society, as far as Jackson saw it. Everything was available for sale and so, over the past decade, everything that could be bought had been – or at least so the picture here indicated.

Of course, it was all lies.

But he had anonymously pitched the idea to ACORN via a third party in order to set them up for the ultimate fall. Years ago they had disposed of him as if he were nothing – after everything he had sacrificed to join them, his family, his job – and they had left him damaged. So terribly damaged. But what had started out as revenge had turned into merely a stepping-stone.

Jackson had been keen to choose something to capture the imaginations of the powerful of the world when it was revealed. Something to make people stop and think 'what if this could be done, what would happen if our country was to be compromised like this?' Perhaps it was actually possible, the fiction he had created, but he personally didn't have the breadth of knowledge or expertise to make it happen.

He had consulted the very best financial experts – in particular, a woman in California who was known for her unique expertise – and even she had been convinced by what he had sent her. But, at some point, it would become obvious this was a fake. That certain key shares had not been purchased and trades marked on this map could not possibly have taken place.

He thought briefly of the one person who could have noticed the flaws – Paul. But Paul was most likely unaware of the full extent of this brilliance and, anyway, seemed blinded by the desire for revenge. Which is why he had proven so useful. All Jackson had needed was to offer Leon up as bait.

'What are you doing?'

Leon. Jackson looked up.

'I was just checking the schedule,' he said, as he quickly depressed the off button on the tablet. There was a small chance Leon might believe him.

The two men stared at each other, Jackson from his seat inside the converted lorry, Leon from his position by the head end of Eva's coffin.

Jackson waited to see if Leon would look down at Eva.

He knew that resisting gazing down at his sister would be hard for Leon, even if it was likely that the light had gone out behind her eyes.

Still Leon stared ahead.

Was he waiting for a command, wondered Jackson, or was

there something more worrying happening here? Leon had never turned against Jackson, even when he had been fed the most questionable lies, he had resolutely stood by him. That was what happened to a man like Leon when he believed he owed you.

Jackson continued to stare at Leon. The tension became almost unbearable. And then Leon's expression changed, a very slight flicker of something that Jackson couldn't discern.

Quickly, Leon looked down at Eva. He looked up, eyes wide and glanced quickly back at Jackson. At the same time, he inhaled a sharp, shocked breath.

But Jackson could not tell whether it was a reaction to what he saw on the gurney or whether it was to the man who had emerged, stumbling, bleeding, from the shadows.

Joseph Smith.

When the sound of metal slicing flesh, exhalation of punctured lung, crunch of bone upon bone had subsided, the area around the lorry was still. The airfield was sufficiently large that no one had noticed the fight for life taking place only seconds earlier.

No mercy had been shown.

Blood oozed from lifeless flesh, spreading in slow, unhurried rivulets across the tarmac of the airfield and the metal floor of the lorry.

Two bodies lay, one unresponsive, one almost so.

They were slumped against each other, almost companionably.

To their left, the gurney with its precious cargo. Inside, Eva, her body chilled and lifeless, her mind filled with the reflection of death she had seen moments before in Leon's eyes. She was screaming at the top of her lungs, desperately crying out, terrified and trapped. But not a sound escaped her lips.

All was entirely still.

Then the darkness was disturbed by an oblong of light

appearing suddenly in the darkness, accompanied by the buzz of a vibration and a generic ring tone.

It rang on and on into the night but no one answered it.

On the lit screen, just two words.

'Jackson calling.'

To find out more about Eva Scott read
Alex Blackmore's debut novel

Lethal Profit

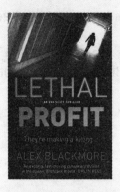

Lethal Profit

ALEX BLACKMORE

**Inspired by the ordered and logical approach of
Henning Mankell's heroes, combined with the action
of a Harlan Coben thriller and the conspiracy undertones
of a Robert Ludlum plot**

Eva Scott is caught up in a tangle of deception her brother
left behind, facing violent assault, brutal murderers and
deeply embedded corporate corruption.

At the heart of it is a dirty biotech business making
a lethal profit from compromising human health.

Behind that, an organisation with a devastating
viral blackmail tool.

Their targets? Global power, capital, manipulation,
and Eva.

£7.99
ISBN 978-1-84344-063-5
EBook available

Praise for *LETHAL PROFIT*

'This is immensely lively fare, delivered with a skill
that belies the fact that this is the author's first novel'
– *Crime Time*

'A down-and-dirty tale of survival, a la *Taken*; a hi-tech
corporate thriller; a '70s style political conspiracy; a Bond-style
spy drama. Thats a heady, intoxicating mix.'
– *Crime Thriller Fella*

'Offer me another Alex Blackmore and I will snatch
it from your hands in glee!!'
– *Shelfari*

'Alex has forged a unique tale'
– *Mystery People*

'A real page turner... one to watch!'
– *Best Crime Books to Read*

'clever and enjoyable... Recommended' - ***Eurocrime***

'This is a rollercoaster of a ride and best read in one
sitting as I could not put this book down'
– *Shelfari*

'I couldn't stop turning the pages of this fast-paced thriller.
It's an action-packed and exciting book and the
cleverly interwoven stories left me breathless.
I can't wait to see what happens next!'
– *People's Book Prize*

About Us

In addition to No Exit Press, Oldcastle Books has a number
of other imprints, including Kamera Books, Creative Essentials,
Pulp! The Classics, Pocket Essentials and High Stakes Publishing
> oldcastlebooks.co.uk

For more information about Crime Books go to > crimetime.co.uk

Check out the kamera film salon for independent, arthouse and
world cinema > kamera.co.uk

For more information, media enquiries and review copies please
contact Clare > cqoldcastle@gmail.com